D0268106

The Grace Allendale Series:

Hush Hush
Tick Tock

LIAR LIAR

Mel Sherratt is the author of fourteen crime novels, all of which have become bestsellers. For the past four years, she has been named as one of her home town of Stoke-on-Trent's top 100 influential people. She regularly appears at festivals and speaks at writing conferences throughout the UK, and pens a column for her local newspaper, the *Sentinel*, as well as feature articles for other newspapers and magazines. She lives in Stoke-on-Trent, Staffordshire, with her husband and terrier, Dexter.

MEL SHERRATT
LIAR LIAR

avon.

Published by AVON
A division of HarperCollins*Publishers* Ltd
1 London Bridge Street
London SE1 9GF

www.harpercollins.co.uk

A Paperback Original 2020

3

First published in Great Britain by HarperCollins*Publishers* 2020

Copyright © Mel Sherratt 2020

Mel Sherratt asserts the moral right to be identified as the author of this work.

A catalogue copy of this book is available from the British Library.

ISBN: 978-0-00-836806-7

Typeset in Minion by Palimpsest Book Production Ltd, Falkirk, Stirlingshire
Printed and bound in UK by CPI Group (UK) Ltd, Croydon CR0 4YY

MIX
Paper from
responsible sources
FSC
www.fsc.org   FSC® C007454

This book is produced from independently certified FSC™ paper to ensure
responsible forest management.

For more information visit: www.harpercollins.co.uk/green

For all staff in the Emergency Services who risk their
lives so that we can feel safe

MONDAY

ONE

Caleb Campbell freewheeled down Ford Green Road, taking the bend a little too sharply for the icy road conditions as he weaved his way past the evening traffic. It was nearly half past six and he was meeting Seth Forrester in less than five minutes. It wouldn't do to be late. He'd seen first-hand what Seth was capable of when he was annoyed; wouldn't like to get on the wrong side of him.

He turned left and raced along Rose Avenue, making a mental note to buy new batteries for his lights as he took a sharp right into the entrance that led to Harrison House.

It had been trying to snow for most of the day, the damp sludge soaking his jeans but at least he wouldn't be late. It wasn't cool to be pedalling like the clappers on his BMX. Caleb had been saving up for a new pushbike and couldn't wait until he had enough money for it. Almost there, it wouldn't take long now before he had the rest. He'd had to hide the stash from his older brother and his mum, for different reasons. His brother would probably tell his mum; his mum would want to know how he had managed to acquire four hundred pounds.

He'd earned the money from Seth. It was only fetching and

delivering parcels, small items, things he could carry on his bike. His friend Shaun had told him not to get involved with Seth; said he'd end up as a drug runner for him. But Caleb was cleverer than that. He would earn what he needed and then stop.

When he heard a woman cry out, he glanced up to see where the noise had come from. He skidded to a stop on the bike, unable to believe his eyes. Before he knew what was happening, there was a scream, a dull thud and a moment's silence before all hell broke loose.

Caleb froze. He knew Seth was dangerous, but this? Had he really just . . .

Realising he had seen too much, he turned back the way he'd come and pedalled away quickly. If he stayed here, he would be picked up and questioned by the police. If he became a witness, he would be persecuted, maybe threatened not to testify. And there was no way he could deliver his package now.

'I saw nothing,' he repeated over and over. 'I saw nothing. I saw nothing.'

There were cameras on the main road so he took a right out of the car park and skidded down an alleyway that led him onto another road. Across that and he was in the middle of the Bennett estate.

After a few minutes, he slowed to catch his breath. Chucking his bike to the floor, he paced up and down beside it, covering his mouth with his hand to stop the vomit that was threatening to erupt.

What the hell had happened back there?

Caleb had seen way too much. If he couldn't hold his nerve and lie through his teeth, he was a dead man walking.

Mary Stanton had lived in Harrison House for five years. Retired seven years ago now, she'd moved in shortly after her husband had died. Their two sons had left the city in their early twenties to do better things. One lived in Devon, the other Brighton. She didn't get to see them much nowadays; could remember the last time she had held her grandson, Sebastian, in her arms as if it were yesterday, but in fact it was over six months ago.

She didn't mind so much. They were busy, had their lives without her, and who would want to come back here when they had friendlier neighbourhoods, good jobs and prospects further afield?

Mary didn't get out much and didn't see many people, so the walkway outside her flat was her lifeline. When her legs weren't playing up, she could stand there for hours, leaning on the concrete railing. Even when the pain of rheumatoid arthritis got particularly bad, she could perch herself on a high stool. She loved to watch the activities of the people around her. Everyone knew her; waved at her when they went past. Sometimes she even looked after a child or two, if anyone was in dire need of a helping hand. She enjoyed that, as long as she wasn't taken for granted.

Plus she liked it at Harrison House. It was only three storeys high, not like one of the huge tower blocks in the city centre. There was a camaraderie she enjoyed, despite a lot of the tenants coming and going before she got to know them. She wouldn't say she was a busybody but she did know a lot of what went on. People liked to offload to her, share gossip too. Of course she never said anything to anyone, so she had garnered a certain trust among the regular tenants, often being seen as a confidante. Her eyes and ears were the best things she had left. At least she could be a small part of the community.

Should she go outside? After all, she would have been there under normal circumstances. People might notice she was missing. She pushed herself up to standing, then sat back down again with a thump.

She couldn't go out. Not after what she had seen. There had been a commotion to her right, people in the car park. And then across the way, something else was happening. That awful scream. Then she had seen something that would haunt her forever.

So when the police called, because she was certain they would, she would say only one thing.

'I saw nothing,' she whispered under her breath, her stomach swishing around with nausea. 'I saw nothing.'

TWO

Harrison House was an L-shaped building. There were forty-eight flats, eight on either side of each landing with a shared staircase at its middle. Entrances to every two-bedroomed home opened out onto a covered communal walkway, a three-foot concrete railing in front, the rest open to the elements. At the side was a residents' car park. A large strip of grass wrapped almost all the way around the building, then stretched to the main road.

Over the years, the block had got itself a reputation for housing troublesome tenants. It had been a hot spot for domestic violence, and there was even a murder there in 2015. But since Trent Housing Association received a grant to renovate the block, the area had slightly improved. Still, in amid the good people it had problem residents, despite trying to clean itself up.

DS Grace Allendale was doing her last call of the day. It was half past six, past her usual finishing time but she'd wanted to check a tenant out.

'Really, he must think we've fallen off a Christmas tree,' Grace said to her colleague, DC Frankie Higgins as they came out of flat 202. 'Croxton isn't just taking cannabis for medicinal purposes. We need to get on to the drugs team and see if they're scouting him out before we go into someone else's investigation with our size eleven's, but for my money he's under the radar and we've just stumbled on— What the hell is that racket?'

She could hear shouting; it seemed to be coming from the car park to their right. She was just about to go downstairs and intervene when a blood-curdling scream rang through the air. It wasn't a cry of anguish, or fear. It was one of sheer pain and it was coming from below them.

She and Frankie stepped towards the edge of the walkway and looked over the rail to where the noise had come from. To their left this time, a woman was running across the grassed area, followed closely by a man. Grace could make out a shape in the direction they were heading. The woman dropped to her knees as she got to it and screamed again.

'Oh no.' Grace raced to the end of the walkway and hurled herself down two flights of stairs, Frankie hot on her tail. She pushed open the entrance door in the communal hallway and tore across the grass towards them.

The woman had long blonde hair, a small frame and skinny arms and legs underneath her jeans and jumper. Water from the grass was seeping through her slippers. The man was medium height and build. His hands grasped fistfuls of his short, dark hair as he paced the ground, breath coming in rasps.

'My baby,' the woman cried.

'Wait!' Grace shouted, trying to get their attention.

'He's broken,' the woman sobbed. 'My little boy, he's broken.'

'Don't move him. Please be careful!' Grace drew level with them. 'What happened?'

'I don't know,' the man said. 'He just fell.'

'From which floor?'

'The first.'

'We're police officers.' Grace took out her warrant card and identified herself and Frankie. She dropped to the ground next to the infant. The boy's eyes rolled back inside his head and then he lay still. She could already hear Frankie on his phone to control.

'Male, toddler. Looks like he's fallen about five metres onto hard ground. Pulse, Grace?'

Being careful not to move him, she felt around his neck, and nodded with relief when she found it. It was weak but he was still alive.

Please don't die, little man.

By now several people had come to join them and Grace could see residents in the flats above standing looking over the rail.

'What's his name?' she asked. The woman had stood up now and was in the man's arms.

'Tyler,' the man spoke for her. 'Tyler Douglas. Why don't you do something? Don't just leave him. He'll die!'

'As police officers, we're trained first responders only. I've checked to see that his airway is clear and that he has a pulse. But I'm not medically qualified to assess injuries from a fall like this,' Grace explained. 'It may cause him more damage if I move him. The paramedics will be here soon. How old is he?'

'He's two – three next month.'

Grace took off her coat and laid it over the boy's chest to keep him warm. The mid-February temperature seemed to be dipping by the minute, puffs of cold air coming from everyone's mouths. Really, she wanted to help him more but she didn't know how.

'He isn't making any noise,' the man said. 'Shouldn't he be crying?' He paced again before turning back to them. 'Can't you do something?'

Grace stood up. 'Are you his dad?'

He nodded.

'What's your name?'

'Luke Douglas.'

Grace eyed the woman. 'And you're Tyler's mother?'

The woman nodded too, her bottom lip trembling and her body already shivering. 'Ruby Brassington.'

'What happened?' Grace asked again, glad that Frankie was with her as he told the gathering crowd to move away. In the distance, sirens could be heard getting louder by the second.

'He fell.' Luke pointed down to the lifeless figure, a trickle of blood now appearing from the toddler's left ear.

'Was he on his own on the walkway?' Grace had to be clear.

'I don't remember! It was all so quick.'

Grace turned to the woman. 'Ruby?' she urged.

The woman shook her head. Their eyes locked but she didn't seem able to focus.

'Ruby,' Grace repeated, feeling relief flood through her as the ambulance pulled up. 'Did you see what happened?'

'No, I saw nothing.'

Before Grace could ask anything else, the paramedics were running towards them. The few people who had gathered moved back to let them do their work.

It was several minutes before Grace could tear herself away from the scene unfolding in front of her. Tyler had been moved to an ambulance, its door closed. Ruby Brassington had gone to fetch her handbag so she could travel with Tyler to the hospital. Luke Douglas was talking to Frankie, looking shell-shocked as he stepped from foot to foot. Eventually, as uniformed police arrived and cordoned off the area, she beckoned Frankie over.

'Where's the father gone?' she asked as they stood to one side.

'Upstairs to get his car keys.'

She paused for a moment, taking in what was happening around them. The ambulance with its doors closed, lights flashing. The crowd of onlookers now moving away. People on the walkways above looking down at them.

'That little boy can't have got up over that concrete railing and fallen on his own.' She glanced around before continuing. 'I don't buy that they saw nothing, like Ruby said.'

'Oh, I hear you.' Frankie's face darkened.

One of the paramedics got out of the ambulance and waved for Grace's attention. A man in his late forties, she knew he would see the same thing in his dreams as she would tonight, even though neither of them had witnessed the accident. A helpless child falling to the ground. Regardless of how it had happened, it was a tragedy. It was going to be an emotional few days for the family.

Grace jogged over to him. Through the open door of the vehicle, she could see Tyler attached to monitors and strapped on a board to keep his head and neck still. It wasn't needed at the moment as he lay motionless, but who knew if he would suddenly come to life again during the twenty-minute trip to the hospital? She prayed that would be the case.

'We'll be off soon,' the paramedic told her.

'How is he? He's so quiet,' she murmured.

'Touch and go, I think.'

'Is the mother travelling in the ambulance with you?'

'Yes, she's gone to fetch her bag.'

A minute later, Grace heard the entrance door bang loudly, and turned to see Ruby running back towards them.

'I'm here, my little soldier,' she said as she got inside the ambulance. She sat down next to a uniformed officer who had been assigned to accompany them to the hospital.

'What number flat do you live in, Ruby?' Grace asked.

'114.'

'I'll head up afterwards.'

'Tell Luke to check on Lily.' Ruby didn't take her eyes from

11

Tyler's as she rested a hand on his forearm. 'He's following in the car.'

'Lily?' Grace queried.

'My daughter. She's with our neighbour, Norma. She took her in so that she wouldn't have to see . . . He needs to ask if she can stay there while we go to the hospital.'

The ambulance doors closed, the sirens switched on and Tyler Douglas was swept away in a flood of blue lights.

Grace hoped that the little boy had luck on his side.

Grace entered the communal hallway with its smell of bleach and fake flowers. There were several rows of mailboxes, three bicycles chained in a line and concrete steps leading to the first floor.

At the top, she turned and marched along the walkway. A woman with a baby in her arms stood on her doorstep. She wore a look of genuine concern.

'Is everything okay?' she asked as Grace passed by.

'Everything is fine,' she told her, cursing herself for being so self-assured. But she didn't want anyone to relay anything until she had got the gist of what had happened.

The door to Ruby and Luke's home was wide open. Grace snapped on latex gloves and rapped her knuckles on the glass before stepping inside.

Luke appeared in the living room doorway.

'I need you to step outside for a moment while I take a look around,' she told him.

'Right.' Luke went out onto the walkway. He stood with his back to where the incident had happened, preferring to look at her, she assumed, rather than see what was going on below.

From her work at Harrison House so far, Grace knew that each flat was identical in layout; a small hallway with a kitchen and bathroom to the right, two bedrooms to the left and a door leading to a living room at the far end.

The living room was decorated in floral paper with a navy-blue settee, a large TV and a cheap flat-pack sideboard. A faint smell of cheese lingered in the air and there were two mugs on a coffee table. Curtains hid a picture window covering most of the back wall.

'You can come in now,' Grace shouted.

'We always told him it was dangerous to go out alone,' Luke said as he rejoined her. 'He – he's not going to die, is he?'

'He's in the best place possible at the moment,' Grace answered. 'I need you to gather together some things for Tyler – pyjamas, underwear and a change of clothes. Ruby mentioned your daughter was with your neighbour, Norma?'

Luke nodded. 'Next door, 115. She came out as soon as she heard the commotion and took Lily for us.'

Grace pointed to the hall. 'Do the children share a bedroom?'

'The first one behind you, on the left.'

Grace pushed open the door. She looked around. It seemed a typical children's room, albeit a very basic one. There were bunkbeds, a safety rail on the top bunk and an array of toys in a pile on the floor. A small bookcase held numerous well-read children's board books, two red storage boxes crammed with toys next to it. The walls were painted white, a few crayon marks here and there. The curtains hanging either side of the window were thin but adequate.

Luke was behind her, holding a black sports bag.

'Make sure you bring along Tyler's favourite toy.' Her tone was gentle.

Luke nodded as he held in his tears, his bottom lip quivering. She knew that picking up whatever it was would bring it home to him just how serious the situation was.

'Right, a quick visit next door to see Lily and then we can head off to the hospital,' she told him.

THREE

Grace let Luke knock on the door of flat 115. A lady in a pale pink jogging suit answered it. She looked to be in her sixties, with lilac curly hair and frame-free glasses.

'Luke!' She opened the door wide. 'Come on in. How is he?'

'He's gone to the hospital.' Luke stepped inside.

Grace flashed her warrant card as she followed him. 'DS Allendale.'

'Norma Farrington. Lily is in the living room. I've put her in front of the television. Hopefully it will take her mind off things. Such a terrible thing to happen, isn't it?'

'Luke!' Lily ran into his arms.

Norma pressed a hand to Grace's wrist. 'They're good parents,' she spoke quietly. 'I can tell you that for nothing.'

Grace didn't reply. Good parents or not, something had happened to Tyler Douglas.

As she went through to the living room, the heat hit her like stepping into a sauna. Her cheeks flushed even before she'd unravelled her scarf and removed her gloves.

The flat was the same layout as the one she'd just been in but you'd be hard pressed to tell, Grace thought. It was cluttered with old furniture – two dark wooden bookcases, a sideboard and a dresser – and filled to the brim with knickknacks and photos in frames. The darkness contrasted with such a colourfully dressed woman.

The child who was now sitting on the settee was the image of her mother with long blonde hair, pale skin and the bluest, widest of eyes. Grace noticed the tear-stained face now that she was closer.

'Hi Lily. My name is Grace.' She smiled. 'Can I sit down with you?'

Lily nodded slightly, pulling her knees up to her chest. Luke sat down on the other side of her.

'I'd like to ask you a few questions about your brother, Tyler.'

'Do we have to do this right now?' Luke protested. 'I really want to go and see how Tyler is.'

'He's dead, isn't he?' Tears pricked Lily's eyes.

'No, no,' he replied, shooting Grace a cold look. 'He's gone to the hospital.'

Grace grimaced. She couldn't question the girl now. It was plain to see she was traumatised by what had happened. It could wait until they had more details about Tyler's condition.

'*Will* he be okay?' Lily's voice was low and trembling.

'We'll know more soon,' Luke replied. 'But for now, I need you to be a big girl and stay here with Norma.'

Norma sat down beside Lily and smiled. 'You can stay overnight, if you like? We can have hot chocolate and marshmallows.'

'I want to go home, really,' Lily whispered.

'I'm sure you do and you'll be able to soon,' Luke said, 'but I expect we'll be at the hospital for a long time.'

'Can I see him?'

Norma's smile dropped from her lips momentarily before appearing again.

'Once the doctors have examined him and fixed him up, he'll be under everyone's feet again in no time,' Luke soothed. 'You'll see.' He gave her a hug and said his goodbyes.

Grace went onto the walkway ahead of Luke and waited for him there. Once in the fresh air again, she let out a huge sigh. It was heartbreaking to see Lily's face. But she would always keep an open mind. For all she knew she might have something to do with what happened and her parents may be covering for her. It could even be one of them.

Luke came out moments later and they walked downstairs. There was something she wanted to know.

'I heard Lily call you by your first name back there,' she said.

'I'm not her father, although I treat her like my own daughter. I've known her since she was four. She's a great kid.'

Grace had felt a pang of agony for the child. Lily reminded her of herself as a fragile eight-year-old when she'd been living with her late father, afraid to do anything for fear of retaliation; trying to protect her mum without getting into trouble herself. Always unsure if she was saying the right thing or digging a deeper hole.

As they got to the car park, Luke took out a set of keys.

'I can give you a lift, if you like,' she offered.

'Thanks, but I'll need to get back so I'll take my car.'

She looked at her watch: quarter to eight. 'I'll follow you shortly.'

As she observed Luke driving off, she got out her phone to ring Simon. It was going to be a late one.

'I had a call from work about it,' he said once she'd told him about the accident.

'I was there by chance when it happened.' She gulped, closing her eyes and pinching the bridge of her nose to stop her tears from falling.

'Christ, Grace – are you okay?'

'Not really.' She appreciated that he was upset for her. 'I didn't see it but I was there straight afterwards. He was so quiet.'

'How is he now?'

'He was taken in an ambulance about half an hour ago. I'm heading to the Royal Stoke now.'

'Do you want me to come to you?'

She shook her head, even though he couldn't see her.

'It's news for me regardless,' he added.

Simon was the senior crime reporter for the local newspaper, *Stoke News*. Sometimes Grace resented that fact, like now when his journalistic nose was twitching for a story. Other times it had come in useful. It was such a hard line to toe, keeping the balance of professional and personal between them, but so far they had managed it well.

'I'll let you know more when I get home,' she said. 'Although I'm not sure how late I'll be.'

They spoke a bit longer and then she disconnected the call. Stomping her feet again as she could barely feel her toes, she rammed her hands in her pockets. Her gloves were useless in this weather.

While she waited to warm up, she looked around. Crime scene tape flapped around the site where Tyler Douglas had lain. More officers were arriving to investigate the fall and she'd been briefing them as and when required. An hour ago, there were lots of people around, probably coming to have a nose. All she could see now were closed doors, no one talking to the police. And what had all that noise in the car park been about earlier? Whatever it was had gone quiet when Tyler Douglas had fallen.

As Frankie came over to her, Grace pointed across towards the scene of the incident.

'Luke Douglas. Have you seen him before?'

'I haven't met either of them. I don't know what to make of it.'

'Me neither. I'll get more of a sense of them when I go to the hospital, I expect. Hard to tell anything when they're both in shock.' Her phone rang. She wrestled it out of her pocket and removed a glove. Before answering it, she checked her watch and then looked at Frankie.

'This is Allie. Why don't you finish for the evening? I'll take it from here. I'm going to the hospital to see both parents and put my mind at rest.'

'If you're sure.'

Grace waved him away and answered the call. It would be her DI's shout whether it was a police incident and worth them pursuing more, but the case would be referred to Children's Services to see if the children needed to be assigned a social worker, or even added to the at-risk register, regardless.

It was good to have Allie as her line manager now. After the last case she'd worked on had become personal, she'd had a chat with her previous DI, Nick. It had been suggested that she join the Community Intelligence Team to work with Allie for a twelve-month period. Grace had been pleased at this outcome. She had enjoyed getting to know Allie. The woman had a vast knowledge of Stoke-on-Trent and its occupants.

Grace still worked alongside her old team and when they needed any kind of involvement with the public, she headed up the meetings and house-to-house enquiries. Not being directly involved in the murder cases had been good for the past ten months and if truth be known, she hadn't been looking forward to getting back to the team. She'd enjoyed talking to people, forming relationships, and it had made her realise her skills were more suited in the community at large. She liked wheedling information out of people, coaxing out secrets and lies. Sometimes it was easy to get intel, sometimes not. It was these latter times she enjoyed the most.

PC Michael Higgins, also known as Frankie, had moved to

join Grace as a trainee DC two weeks earlier. It was change everywhere.

Since last summer, her time had been busy but more relaxed. So far, she had cleared up a sexual assault, two muggings and helped put numerous domestic violence and neighbourhood nuisance incidences to bed. She'd even visited a number of schools and chaired many Neighbourhood Watch meetings. People needed to feel safe on the streets. Here was no exception.

The previous eighteen months as Detective Sergeant on the team had certainly given her food for thought and she'd been ready for a different challenge. It had made things easier for her too, knowing she might not have to work alongside her estranged family, the Steeles. That had been awkward to say the least during her first murder investigation, and even the second case had put someone she dearly loved in danger. So it hadn't come as a surprise to anyone when she'd asked to stay on to head the Community Intelligence Team when Allie had been successful in getting Nick's job after he'd taken early retirement from the force.

Grace knew some of her colleagues would see her move as a side-step. Allie had been an acting DI doing the role, with several PCs covering the six towns. Now the positions had been changed to a DS and one DC but Grace didn't mind. She was much more comfortable with the hands-on aspects of the role, and she would still be on call to work with the Major Crimes Team when necessary.

It was a clean resolve, and Nick was happy too. His wife had been badgering him to take early retirement for a while. Now Sharon would have him all day. Grace smirked to herself, wondering how long it would be before she was moaning that she'd preferred it when he was at work. Not that Nick was one to finish completely; Grace knew that he was taking some part-time work at first.

The move had given her more time for a home life. Before, when she'd been Detective Sergeant, she'd blamed the long hours on a need to do the job, rather than a necessity to be with people because she was lonely after the death of her husband. But now she had Simon, things were working out well and it was nice to work more regular hours. He had moved in with her a few months ago, and so far, so good. Grace had even got to know his daughter, Teagan, who at seventeen knew her mind and had accepted Grace in her life. It was good.

After the call had finished, she walked towards her car. Time to visit her least favourite place.

2010

Ruby Brassington was a ball of excitement as she sat on her bed doing her make-up. Most of what she would be wearing that night was in her bag as her dad would go nuts if he saw anything more than a lick of mascara and pale lipstick.

Underneath her sweatshirt, she wore a slinky halter-neck top that showed off her cleavage in her new Wonderbra. She would change when she got to her best friend Naomi's house, and she was borrowing her shoes too – red heels that she could hardly walk in, but were well worth the pain.

It was Naomi's sixteenth birthday. She was having a party at her home. Her parents were going out and she had the run of the house until midnight.

Their friendship had always been something Ruby had treasured, especially after her mum died when she was just starting high school. It was hard on her own with her dad. She had lost her mum to talk to and the girls at school couldn't take her place. Slowly she closed herself off from them all, except Naomi – the one person who had always been there for her.

Ruby's mum had had breast cancer. She'd been diagnosed only six months before her death but it had left mental scars on Ruby, seeing her suffer so much. Since then it had been just the two of them – her and her dad. Before, when Mum was around, her dad was always there and did a very good job of looking after her. But trying to be both parents had broken him. He couldn't do either very well, choosing to spend long hours at work instead of trying. Her mum had only had a part-time job, fitted around school hours, so was always there for her. At twelve, Ruby was neither a child nor a grown-up, and she'd required supervision and guidance. Consumed by grief, her dad had shut himself off from her when she'd needed him the most.

Now she was older and more independent they got on better, but the closeness they'd had when she was a child had been lost forever. Ruby didn't mind so much. There was always food on the table, and they kept the house clean between them.

'Are you ready yet, Ruby?' A voice came up the stairs.

'Just a minute.' Her stomach flipped over as she glanced at her watch. It was nearly seven thirty. Dad was giving her a lift and even though he insisted on picking her up earlyish, if it meant she could go, then she was fine with that. She was up for a good time, no matter what.

She picked up her phone and sent a message to Naomi to say she was on her way. The handset she had was embarrassing; it didn't even have a camera on it. She couldn't wait to have a newer model for her sixteenth birthday, just three weeks away.

Naomi's house was set in its own grounds off a main road. A dilapidated Victorian detached house had been knocked down and her father had built a modern rectangular family home in its place. Most of its frontage was glass with chrome panelling. Ruby had never seen anything like it before. It was definitely a one-off.

A sweeping gravel driveway led to an area at the front where her dad swung his car around in a circle easily. She never felt envious when she visited – it was like her second home, given the amount of time she spent there – but she often wondered what it would be like to have so much money. The house had five bedrooms and four bathrooms. The garage housed several cars and there was a stable block out the back, though they had no horses now.

Her dad turned to her in the passenger seat. 'Make sure you're out front here at eleven.'

She grimaced as she had already opened the door and people might hear.

'I promise!'

He was so annoying at times. Sometimes he'd only allow her to have certain friends, people he was happy with her seeing, even though she had the house to herself a lot. She could easily slip them in and out without him knowing, yet she hardly ever did. He went through phases of being overprotective one moment to leaving her to her own devices the next. She often wished she hadn't been an only child. If she had brothers like Naomi then maybe her dad wouldn't be like that.

The music from the house became louder as she walked towards it; lights on in every room downstairs. In the hallway, which was as large as two rooms in her own home, she smiled at a few people as she made her way through the crowd.

'Ruby!' Naomi waved at her from the kitchen.

Ruby pointed to the ceiling. 'Just going to change.'

Naomi nodded before turning back to get another drink.

She nipped upstairs to Naomi's room. Every time she went into it she had to stop herself from jumping up and down on the colossal bed covered in white drapes and cushions. Naomi was a lover of lilac and it was everywhere. She had her own ensuite so Ruby could change in there and also stash her bag.

Once she'd applied full make-up, and changed her lipstick

to Vampire Red, she slipped on the heels and gave herself the once-over in the mirror.

'Looking good, Rube.' She pouted and blew herself a kiss.

Downstairs the music had changed to a more R&B vibe. After grabbing a can of lager, she wandered around until she found Naomi. She draped her arms around her friend.

'What time do you have to leave?' Naomi shouted to her.

'Eleven.' Ruby rolled her eyes. 'My dad's picking me up.'

'Ugh, well at least you're here. Let's dance!'

As Naomi pulled her to the middle of the room, Ruby felt glad to have her. As a friend Naomi was so understanding of her controlling father and often covered for her with the odd white lie so that she could stay out late.

She danced along to the music, sipping from her can and waving it in the air. It wasn't long before she felt eyes on her and turned to see someone standing on the far wall. The boy looking at her was tall, with a tight black T-shirt showing off an athletic build. Dark sultry eyes and hair shorn close to his head. A stud earring glistening in his right ear, and a gold chain around his neck were the only things she didn't particularly like. She reckoned he was no more than a few years older than her.

Ruby recognised him vaguely too. She continued to dance before chancing another look. He was still watching her – not in a leery way, she decided, but in an interested way.

'I need another drink,' she shouted to Naomi. 'Want one?'

Naomi shook her head.

When she glanced in the boy's direction again, he was gone. Disappointed, she made her way through the crowd to the kitchen. There the music was quieter, the crowd thinner, and after grabbing a can of coke this time, she decided to go out into the garden to get some air.

The night was warm, the garden lit up and inviting. She

wandered over to sit on a bench, looking back at the house. The music was blaring and it was lit up like Blackpool illuminations, but there were no neighbours nearby to complain.

It was there that he found her. She watched him walk along the path, and looked up as he stood in front of her.

'I think we had the same idea,' he said. 'Loud in there, isn't it?'

She nodded.

'Mind if I join you?'

'No.'

He sat next to her, throwing his long legs out in front of him, crossing them at the ankles.

'You're Naomi's best friend, aren't you?'

'Yeah, we've grown up together since junior school. I don't remember who you are, though.'

'I'm a few years older than you, and as you're sixteen that makes a *huge* difference.'

'I'm not sixteen for another three weeks. July fifteenth. I'm starting sixth form in September.'

'You look so grown up.'

She smiled, looking away for a moment.

'I used to hang around with George and Will.' George and Will were Naomi's older brothers. 'I'm Finn.'

'I'm Ruby.'

'Yeah, I know.'

She smiled shyly at him, wondering where the night was going.

FOUR

In the relatives' waiting room, Luke Douglas kept his head in his hands, unable to look at his partner Ruby for fear of breaking down. How had things gone so terribly wrong?

He gave an involuntary sob as he pictured his son lying on the icy ground, unable to make a sound. Usually Tyler was so vocal they were always telling him to be quiet. He was a real live wire. And now his boy, his two-year-old son, might not even see his third birthday next month. He might not even get through the night.

Luke would give anything to be telling him off right now. It had been such a shock to see him lying there. But when the police had turned up so quickly, well, he could have easily run the opposite way. This was all down to Seth Forrester, he knew it. But he couldn't say anything about him or Ruby would find out what he'd been up to.

He ran through what he'd been doing over the past few months. Who knew about it? He'd been clever to cover his tracks, or so he thought.

Getting involved with Seth had been a mistake. Like a fool, he'd ignored all the rumours about him putting people in hospital. Despite seeing how much damage Seth had done on a mate of his, Luke had still gone along with getting reeled in. There was even talk of Seth being involved in the disappearance of a few men. He worked for the Steele brothers, a known criminal family who should never be crossed. But Luke had been desperate for money.

Seth lived next door but one from him at Harrison House. He could do whatever he wanted to Luke – or Luke's family – as he lived so close. Luke had never been more aware than he was right now that he couldn't protect everyone. He needed to be at home, to keep an eye on Lily: Seth hadn't threatened her, nor Ruby, yet he wouldn't put it past him.

But he couldn't leave the hospital. Not without Tyler.

The room they'd been put into was drab, all pale creams and beiges. Luke wondered how many other families had sat in here waiting to hear good or bad news. He couldn't even think of the possibility of Tyler dying. He closed his eyes and held back his tears. He couldn't be responsible for his son's death.

He just couldn't.

Allie had told Grace that it was fine to go and see Tyler Douglas's parents. Usually, she wouldn't be investigating this type of incident but as she was first on the scene, Allie had given her instructions to speak to them and report back to her in the morning.

On the drive to the hospital, a message from control came in for her.

'Go ahead,' Grace answered.

'Just to update you, there's been an anonymous call about a commotion in the car park at Harrison House as well as the incident you're dealing with. We have nothing reported on that but we do have a witness who said they saw a man running away from the scene shortly after the little boy's accident. The caller wouldn't leave a name, nor any contact details.'

'Copy that, thanks.'

Grace wondered what, if anything, either of them could have to do with Tyler Douglas. Could the man have been someone late to be somewhere else – racing across to their car, or running for a bus? Could the commotion be kids hanging around making too much noise?

It was during regular visiting hours so the car park at the Royal Stoke was busy. Once she found a space, she headed to A&E. Before going to the parents, she asked how the little boy was. A nurse on the station went to check for her. Grace sat down while she waited, immediate memories of sitting in hospital anxious to hear about Matt flooding back to her. She didn't think about her late husband all the time any more. There were days when she hardly thought of him at all, which both saddened and pleased her as she had to move on. But it was times like these that brought her right back to a period in her life that was wracked by so much pain she sometimes wondered how she had got through it.

It had been unbearable to see him suffer. Acute myeloid leukaemia had taken him when he was thirty-five. She had been thirty-two and even now, five years later, a smell of disinfectant could bring back instant memories of loss and grief.

'DS Allendale?' A man dressed in blue scrubs, wearing round rimmed glasses, and white clogs on his feet approached her. He sat down beside her and crossed one leg over the other, turning to her slightly.

'Yes, how is he doing?' she asked, checking out the ID badge that hung around his neck to discover he was a paediatric consultant.

'Tyler's brain is swelling at the moment so we've sent him off for a CT scan. We may need to put in a peg to reduce the pressure and drop him into an induced coma, but for now we're monitoring him closely.'

Grace blew out a breath. 'Any life-changing injuries?'

'We're running tests. Physically he has a fracture to his left ankle, which we've put in a cast for now.'

'Is that it?' Grace frowned. 'He fell nearly five metres. I know he landed on grass but it would have been hard owing to the weather we've been having.'

Winter storm Nigel had been with them for two days before leaving a cold blast of air behind. Temperatures for the past few nights had dipped below zero. Grace recalled not wanting to get out of her warm bed that morning.

'You'd be surprised how many children are fine afterwards. I'm sure some of them bounce.' The man's smile was warm. 'But most children tend to break the fall themselves, catching on something else on the way that stops them landing so hard. In Tyler's case there was nothing to do this and he dropped in almost a straight line. My guess is he landed on his feet and then fell to his side where he hit his head. It's this that we're most worried about.'

Grace grimaced. 'Is he likely to have damage to his brain?'

'It's possible and we won't be clear on that for a while yet. Like I said, we'll know more in the morning.'

Grace nodded as the doctor turned to leave and then spoke again, calling him back. 'Wait a minute, you say he fell in a straight line?'

'Yes.'

'Surely he would have gone head first and landed on his hands, or flipped over onto his back?'

'I don't think he fell over. He would more than likely have landed on all fours if he'd done that. Although nothing is certain.'

Grace said her thanks and stood up as he left. Gut feeling had told her at the scene that this wasn't an accident, and now she felt even more certain. It was crucial they get to the bottom of things as soon as possible.

It was time to speak to the parents.

FIVE

Ruby Brassington sat across from Luke, her right leg jangling as it rested on her knee. The skin around her thumbnail was bleeding, she'd been biting at it so hard; the tissue in her hands balled up, wet and almost in shreds.

A sense of déjà vu came over her as she sat waiting. Things happening around her that were beyond her control. Another loved one in danger. She pushed away the images trying to settle in her mind.

She glanced across the room, to where Luke was sitting forwards in his chair, head in his hands. She wanted to talk to him, to see what story he thought they should stick to until they had time to be alone and she could deal with things the only way she knew how.

Luke was good-looking when he wasn't under duress, appearing to be a lot younger than his thirty-four years. With olive skin and dark hair, he had a look of an Italian without any of the nationality in his blood. Their son had the same dark colouring too, with brown eyes that would melt any heart.

Ruby thought about her life with him, how they'd met. She'd

been living in Sheffield then. The flat was the second one she'd moved to and much better than the first and the cheap B&B that she'd spent months at before that. She felt safer in the new flat. She'd made friends and got herself a part-time job at the newsagent while Lily started nursery classes at the local school. Both of them were enjoying life, settling in.

Luke had been doing some temporary work on the garden in the flats and had popped into the shop most mornings. After a while, they'd started chatting and then he'd asked her on a date. She'd been wary at first, telling him she had a child but he insisted they went out for a meal and took Lily with them. Lily had been sick everywhere after picking up a tummy bug, bringing a halt to everything, but Luke had been undeterred and they'd arranged to meet again.

That had been the start of their relationship. Within a few months, they were an item; within a year, they had moved in together. Two years later, Tyler came along. Everything had been fine until Ruby had got another letter. This time, she'd had to persuade Luke to leave too. Now, she feared they would have to move again. It was so much of an upheaval for the kids, for them all, every time she was in danger. She was tired of looking over her shoulder but she'd have to do it, to keep herself and her family safe.

She kept waiting for the door to open, for someone to tell them what was happening to Tyler. *Please let him be okay,* she repeated inwardly.

Ruby had never wanted any more children after Lily had been born. It had seemed too risky. Keeping one child safe was hard, but she had at least been able to become mobile as quickly as possible. Yet, when she'd been caught pregnant, there was no way she could have had a termination, and it just seemed right. But with two children it had become a problem keeping them both out of harm's way, as she'd seen today.

She found she couldn't cry. How could there be tears when she didn't feel anything but guilt? It should have been her that went over the railing that evening, not Tyler. He was a helpless little boy. He hadn't done anyone any harm.

She still couldn't believe it had happened. It was hard to take in. If she closed her eyes, she could picture it in slow motion. Him falling; her looking over the rail to see him lying there; quiet, vulnerable, crushed.

Everything caught up with her eventually. Why was she always in a mess? Because of her past she was a wreck, a useless specimen of a person, and yet she tried so hard not to be. Things had even been looking up recently – now nearing twenty-seven, at least she had a decent roof over her head rather than living hand-to-mouth as she had before she'd met Luke.

Ruby longed to be at home with Luke in the armchair and Lily and Tyler curled up on the settee with her, laughing at something on the TV. All of them together, safe. She'd rather be anywhere than here, really, waiting for news.

Her boy was a fighter. She had to believe that.

Her conscience was playing tricks with her, frowning upon her for leaving Lily with her neighbour. She needed her here; she wanted to be the one to comfort her. She had to keep an eye on her in case he came back. But she hadn't been thinking when Norma said she would look after Lily.

Or maybe she had. She hadn't wanted to cause distress to Lily if . . . if . . . No, she wouldn't think like that. Her son was *not* going to die.

Luke lifted his head and caught her eye. She wondered whether to go to him. Would it be more obvious that they were wracked with guilt if they weren't sitting together? She moved quickly to him. He gave a half-smile as he grasped her hand, tears instantly forming in her eyes.

Why had the police been so near? She wouldn't be letting

anyone know the truth, that was for certain. She was in enough trouble without that.

Grace took in the two forlorn figures sitting together and tried to keep her anger at bay. The mother couldn't be much older than mid-twenties; the father a little older. Both were well-dressed but nothing too flashy. Clean and healthy looking, which always pleased her where children were involved. They looked like any normal couple, except for the fact that their child was in grave danger right now.

Grace stepped further into the room, noticing they leapt apart as if they'd been stung. The movement felt suspicious, almost a guilty reaction, as if they didn't trust each other. Grace didn't know what to make of that just now.

She needed to know what had gone on at their flat that evening.

Ruby sat upright, waiting to hear what she had to say. Luke had his head in his hands, as if he didn't want to listen.

'How is Tyler?' Grace asked, even though she'd already spoken to the consultant.

'Still unconscious. He's gone for a scan.' Ruby shook her head. 'We won't be going home until we can take him with us, will we, Luke?'

'No.' Luke wiped at his nose with the back of his hand. 'We're waiting here until we can see him.'

Grace sat down across from the couple. Spotting them glancing at each other, she looked at them each in turn. Then she spoke into the loaded silence.

'I'm so sorry for what happened to Tyler but for now I need to ask you a few questions.'

'They shouldn't put tenants with kids in a first-floor flat,' Luke complained. 'It's their fault. I'm going to sue them.'

'Even so, Mr Douglas, how did Tyler get out onto the

walkway?' Grace asked. 'Did he unlock the front door and go out unsupervised? Or was the front door open?'

'You're blaming us already.'

'No, I'm not. I just need to understand what happened. You didn't see?'

Luke shook his head, his eyes landing everywhere but on her.

'Can you explain to me why? Where were you at the time?'

'We were in the living room. Me and Ruby were watching TV. Tyler was with his sister, in their room. The next thing we heard was a yell from Lily. We rushed into the hallway to find the front door open and Lily looking over the railings. She said Tyler got out and climbed over the rail; that she couldn't grab him in time to stop him falling.' He stood up. 'He is going to be okay, isn't he?'

Ruby began to cry and Grace felt a pang of guilt for upsetting them. But she had to press on.

'Just a few more questions, please.'

'Look, she's upset and we're both tired. Can't this wait until the morning? Our son is unconscious, and we can't think of anything else right now.'

Grace nodded. There was so much she wanted to ask and for them to answer, but they'd suffered a huge trauma.

'I'll come and see you in the morning. We have your details.'

Once the detective had left, Ruby grasped Luke's hand, wiping at her tears with the other one.

'What is wrong with you?' she asked.

'What?' Luke looked confused.

'We wanted her to think it was an accident!'

He looked sheepish. 'Did I say something I shouldn't?'

'You said way too much. If we don't stick to our story, we'll both be in for it.' She waited for him to look at her. 'You think

I don't know what's been happening with Seth Forrester? Why you've been hanging around his flat? If you've put any of us in danger, then I swear I'll be out of that door and you won't see me again.'

'I'm not! I love you, Ruby. You're my everything.'

He pulled her into his arms and she let him. Exhausted by the emotions of the night, she sobbed until there was no more left to give. Seeing Luke so upset added more guilt to her load. How could she let him think he was the one at fault?

'I'm sorry for snapping,' she said when she eventually spoke. 'I'm just worried, that's all.'

'We need to stick together,' he told her. 'It's just you and me against the world. We can get through this, and if you want we can move somewhere else. Get a house perhaps, with a garden for the kids to play in.'

'I'd like that.' Ruby smiled through her tears, noting the fact he hadn't said anything further about Seth. 'You promise me you haven't been borrowing money from anyone?'

He wouldn't look at her, which made her suspicions that he was lying even more palpable. But he replied eventually.

'I promise,' he said.

She wanted to believe him but found that she couldn't.

2010

Ruby looked towards Naomi's house for a moment. The music was soothing where she and Finn were sitting at the back of the garden. She could hear laughter from time to time. The weather was warm, a breeze across her shoulders making her shiver slightly.

'Do you want to go back inside?' Finn asked.

'No.'

They smiled at each other.

'What are your plans after sixth form?'

'I'm not sure what I want to do yet, if I'm honest. I keep changing my mind – maybe physiotherapy.'

'There's a lot of pressure at your age to think of what do for the rest of your life. You take your time.'

Shadows were falling now as the night grew darker, making Finn all the more mysterious. She glanced at him surreptitiously, wondering why he was sitting with her when he could be with any number of the girls back in the house.

'What do you do?' she wanted to know.

'Security at a nightclub. I look after the bouncers on the doors. I'm one too.' He pointed towards the house. 'It's very impressive, isn't it?'

She nodded. 'I'd like to be loaded like Naomi's mum and dad one day.'

'Me too,' Finn agreed. 'But we all have to start somewhere.'

Ruby kicked herself inwardly. She was trying to impress him and coming out with some terrible drivel. She was making him feel inadequate. There was no point in putting on a show and being false from the beginning.

Finn seemed to sense her awkwardness.

'I know this sounds cheesy, but I've not long ago picked up a new car. Do you fancy going for a drive?'

Ruby glanced at her watch. It was already quarter to ten. She shook her head, cursing inwardly.

'My dad is picking me up at eleven.'

'Ah.' He placed his hand over hers for a moment. 'How about we go out for a drive for ten minutes and then come back? That way you'll have plenty of time?'

She gnawed at her bottom lip.

'I promise I won't bite.' He held up his hands. 'Trust me, I've known Naomi's brothers since I was a child. I was bullied in junior school and when I went on to high school, my bully followed me. Luckily, I met George who had a go at him when he was picking on me one day. It ended up with George lamping him and ever since then we became friends. That's when I started to look out for myself. He gave me confidence, and I took up weightlifting too.' He smiled. 'Will is older as you know. I get on well with him as well.'

'But I'm Naomi's best mate. I haven't met you before.'

'I don't come here often, that's why. But they adore their little sister so it would be more than my life's worth to see any harm come to you. I just want to show you my car.' He pointed at the house. 'And get away from the noise.'

Ruby still wasn't sure. He was older than her. What if he wanted more than she would offer?

'Ten minutes, and I'll have you back,' he added. 'We can just go around the block.'

It was his mannerisms that did it. The cock of his head, the mischievous look in his eyes. She felt her stomach flip over as it had done earlier.

'Go on, then,' she said.

Ruby couldn't find Naomi downstairs when they went back inside the house. She was about to go upstairs when Finn took hold of her hand to stop her.

'We'll be back before anyone notices we're gone,' he said.

His smile made him trust her. Outside, there were five cars in the driveway. Finn pointed to a blue Subaru Impresa.

'That's my baby, there. Isn't she awesome?'

It took Ruby all of her might not to smirk. It was just a car.

'I know what you're thinking.' He wagged a finger at her. 'But wait until you've been for a ride in her. You'll love Scooby as much as I do.'

'Scooby?'

'Scooby-Doo – Subaru.' He winked as he pressed the key fob. Then he ran around to the passenger side, opening the door for her.

Ruby jumped inside, waiting for him to join her. That new car fresh smell – leather intermingled with some kind of air freshener – engulfed her. It was a nice motor, she had to admit.

He started the engine up, pushing his foot down on the accelerator to rev it up.

'She purrs,' he laughed. Then he popped it into first gear and drove off slowly.

Out on the open road, Ruby was surprised he didn't want to floor it.

'Are you okay?' he asked, placing a hand on her thigh for a moment. 'Having fun?'

She nodded, although relieved when he put it back on the steering wheel.

'It's a smooth ride,' she acknowledged.

'I could open her up but we don't have time. A promise is a promise.'

They were back at Naomi's house before she knew it. Almost disappointed as they drove along the driveway, she was pleased when he parked up the car and stayed in his seat.

'It's quieter in here.' He turned towards her. 'Do you want to go inside or sit with me for a while longer?'

She could stay here all night, she'd enjoyed his company so much. She wanted to know everything about him, and stare into his eyes as she told him about herself. He was so mature compared to anyone else that she knew. None of the boys from school had a car. Only Naomi's brothers had wheels and Ruby would never go out with either of them. It would be like kissing a member of her own family.

'Let's stay here,' she said, her voice breaking with nerves.

He smiled. 'I'll grab a couple of drinks. Wait here a moment.'

She nodded, already beginning to feel safe with him. She wasn't stupid and knew what men wanted from her, but there was no ulterior motive here. He was just being friendly.

And parties always brought out the worst in her. If it weren't for Finn, she would most likely have drunk too much now to fit in socially, be throwing up in the garden, crying and then definitely getting grounded for a month by her dad for misbehaving.

Finn was back in five minutes and they sat talking in his car. They chatted mainly about Naomi and her brothers, some of the times they had shared. It was quarter to eleven when she let out a huge sigh.

'I have to go soon.'

'Okay, daddy's girl.'

She glared at him but he was smiling.

'I know I wouldn't want to let you out of my sight if I were him.'

Ruby felt so calm, and suddenly knew he was going to kiss her. He smiled, tilting her chin up. He leaned over and his lips found hers, so gently she thought she'd imagined it. She closed her eyes and opened them when he moved away, to find him staring into hers. Then he kissed her properly.

It seemed to go on for ages, tender at first then more needy. He ran his hands through her hair, caressed her face with his fingertips.

'Can I see you again?' he asked when they broke apart, his voice hoarse with desire. 'I mean after your birthday, of course.'

She nodded shyly. She would find a way. And like he said, she was sixteen soon. No one could stop her then.

He stored her number in his phone and they went back into the house. Spotting Naomi with Gareth across the room through a mass of bodies that would take her ages to negotiate, she sent her a message to say she was leaving.

She was waiting on the front step when her dad pulled up to collect her.

'Had a good night?' he asked as she fastened her seatbelt.

'Yes, it was great fun.'

Ruby turned away, glad to be leaving the lights behind so that he wouldn't see her grinning.

SIX

Since Eddie and Leon Steele had taken over the running of The Casino in Trinity Street last year, it had been refurbished, bringing in a slightly better class of clientele. Shelley Machin had been let in by the doorman. He knew her from old but turned a blind eye to anything that she did because of who she was dating at the moment. He knew that grassing on Seth Forrester's woman would be a bad thing to do, even to Seth himself.

A slinky black dress accentuated her curves, and purple heels made her look taller than her five foot three. Her long black hair was straightened and shiny, red lips and a full face of make-up giving her an alluring look. Tonight this was her persona. Underneath it all she was mostly a pussycat.

A couple of hours later, she was out again, holding on to a man's hand as she dragged him out of sight around the side of the building, away from prying eyes. She'd picked him out because he'd obviously been drinking since lunchtime so was easy prey.

There wasn't a taxi at the rank yet as it was early in the evening, but neither was there a queue of people. It was the perfect place for her to do what she had to do and this way she might not even have to leave with him.

She managed to stay upright as he staggered into her.

'Sorry,' he said, grinning.

She pushed him up against the wall, kissing him long and hard as his hands roamed all over her body. She'd give him five minutes before he was too far gone to focus and she could relax a little. Men slobbering over her was the worst thing possible, but she had a job to do. His hand went up the side of her leg and she pushed it away gently.

'Not yet, fella,' she chided. 'You don't want to spoil the fun for when we get to your house.'

He laughed, then his lips were on hers again as her hand found what she was after.

A minute later, a taxi pulled in. By now the man was really unsteady on his feet and his eyes were closing, the drinks he'd consumed taking their toll. After a struggle towards the vehicle, she pushed him into the back seat. His eyes closed as soon as he sat down.

'You not getting in?' the driver asked.

'Not much point going home with him now, bloody loser.'

'He'd better not throw up in my cab,' he moaned.

She threw a note at him.

'Bye,' she waved to both of them with a grin.

Shelley had a way with men and she was using it to her advantage. She only slept with someone if absolutely necessary, for instance if she was going back to a hotel room to rob someone of their phone, wallet and laptop. Sometimes it was lucrative; other times not so much. And she didn't do it often for fear of getting a name for herself.

She knew how to spot the businessmen who were staying in town overnight at the local hotels. Only once had she been caught and taken a beating for it. Most of the time, the men were having one-night stands they didn't want their wives or partners to know about. So they said nothing, chalked it up to experience and moved on. They cancelled their bank cards, bought new phones and laptops but never realised until it was too late that often she'd given the stuff to someone else. Details were then cloned and sold on.

Out of sight around the corner, she looked inside the wallet she had stolen and grinned. The money he'd won was all there. She pushed it inside her handbag and walked into Hanley to get a taxi from another rank. She didn't want to get her face recognised too much here. She'd been lucky enough not to get caught fleecing anyone so far. Not too often was her motto, especially as she was on Steele territory. She realised the consequences she'd have to deal with if she was caught, and ran the risk of that enough at home.

Forty minutes later, she arrived at Harrison House. The police that she'd seen earlier were still around, but only the one marked car. She let herself into the flat after talking to a few neighbours.

Shelley had been going out with Seth Forrester for six months now, and spent more time there than she did with her mum and dad. Her home was so crowded that it made more sense. She wasn't planning on staying with him forever, just until she had paid her debt back to the Steeles. She planned to go to Manchester, maybe even London; anything to get out of Stoke. It hadn't done her any favours so far.

And although Seth was quite alluring in a bad boy way, she knew of his past. She didn't want to get on his wrong side, so once she had the information required, she was out of there.

It was probably wrong for her to work for Eddie Steele but she hadn't had much choice. She'd borrowed money and then couldn't repay him. She'd spent recklessly, and then he'd come after her. To wipe the slate clean, she'd been told to get friendly with Seth, who also worked for the Steele brothers, and tell them what he got up to. There was money going missing on a regular basis and they thought he was involved in taking it.

Seth was lying on the settee when she went in. He was twenty-three, lanky with short dark hair, pale skin and deep-set blue eyes. He worked hard at the gym to bulk himself up, muscular arms showing off a sleeve tattoo and several smaller works of art spread over his body. He also had a pierced ear that Shelley hated.

He didn't even glance up when she came into the room. She'd hoped he'd be in a good mood by now. Just lately she'd been worried he was taking too many drugs. Uppers and downers; he was becoming so paranoid with it all. Only last week, he'd slammed her up against the wall as he'd thought she was someone else coming into the kitchen. They were the only two people in the flat at the time.

'You're home early,' she said, looking around at the state he'd left the room in. A folded-up copy of the *Stoke News* was thrown to the floor, a dirty mug on top of a plate next to it. His boots had been kicked off and left there too.

The room wasn't much to look at – worn furniture, tired decoration, although with the obligatory large flat screen TV – but Shelley liked to keep it nice. She was forever picking up after him.

'Earth to Seth,' she said when he didn't reply.

'I'm on again at midnight.'

Once she'd tidied everything away, she leaned over to kiss him. 'Fancy going out somewhere tomorrow night, then?'

Seth shook his head. 'Doing a double shift.'

She sighed. Seth worked on the doors at Flynn's Nightclub in Marsh Street. It was where she'd met him, as she'd planned. After a night out, she had lost her friends and he'd chatted to her outside while she'd waited for a taxi. He'd asked her out and the next evening he'd taken her for a curry and then Shelley had gone home with him. Even though his flat wasn't much to look at, he had talents in the bedroom that were an added bonus. A few weeks later, they'd been an item. He was hard to be with at times, quite moody and chauvinistic but, for now, she had to put up with his wheeling and dealing and try not to complain too much.

'Did you hear about little Tyler falling over the side of the railing earlier?' She flopped down in the armchair.

'Yeah, the feds have been here for hours.'

'There'll be more if he dies. I saw a man there before the *accident* though.' She raised her eyebrows at Seth to make it clear that it was anything but.

Earlier that evening, just after Seth had gone out, Shelley had stood on the doorstep having a cigarette. She didn't like smoking in the flat, even though it was freezing outside. Hearing voices along the walkway, she'd popped her head around the side of the frame to see a man standing at Ruby Brassington's house. The atmosphere seemed tense.

Shelley had pulled her head back quickly but listened to the conversation. Was this something to do with Seth? She knew Luke had borrowed heavily and was working for him to pay it back. Not that Ruby seemed to know anything about the problem.

Shelley didn't think it was right for her not to know what was going on. Luke was up to his eyeballs in debt. She wouldn't be surprised if someone else was coming after him too. It was only a matter of time, and who knew what that would do to their family.

But she'd heard Ruby scream, and then pandemonium as everyone was looking over the railing. She'd purposely gone back inside, not wanting to get drawn into anything, but once the ambulance had arrived, she'd leaned on the railing with everyone else.

'Is the man anyone we know?' Seth asked.

'Didn't recognise him but he said something interesting. He said that he wants what's his and he wants it by Monday.'

Seth sat up then. 'Sounds like Luke owes to someone else. Well, I want my cut first. See what you can find out from Ruby, will you?'

Shelley nodded. Gossiping was her favourite pastime.

SEVEN

Frankie Higgins was beat when he got home. Emotionally and physically drained, he was in need of a night of downtime to rejuvenate and recuperate. The day had gone from normal to tragic. All he could think of was how could that boy have fallen from the walkway.

His wife Lyla was in the kitchen as he came in, the sound of water filling the kettle. She came to the door as he was removing his coat, kissed him.

'Have you eaten?' she asked, tucking her blonde bob behind her ears.

Her beautiful face was make-up free. Frankie could see their son in her the more he grew. Ben had his mother's large brown eyes, some of her mannerisms too. Definitely her optimism.

'Finding it hard to after what I've seen.' He shook his head as he filled Lyla in.

'I'll make you something. You go and shower.'

He watched her walking back across the kitchen, the bounce of her step telling him she'd had a good day. They had met at school in their early teens. Everyone said their relationship wouldn't last, that it was a first love fling, but so far they had proved them all wrong. They were married at eighteen, eight years ago now. Call him old-fashioned but he liked the fact that neither of them had slept with anyone else. It made their marriage feel extraordinary. Lyla still made him feel special too.

Upstairs, Frankie stopped at his son's door. It was ajar, a nightlight shining. Ben had only recently stopped needing the landing light on, but he still didn't want the door shut. He had kicked off his covers and was almost lying the opposite way around in his bed.

Frankie chuckled to himself for a moment. How did they do that, move so much in their sleep? He lifted him up, a dead weight in his arms, putting him around the right way. Then he covered him, tucking him in.

Listening to him breathing, Frankie's temper rose again. If anyone so much as laid a finger on his son, he knew there would be consequences. He wouldn't be able to stop himself from hurting someone.

He couldn't imagine his life without Ben. At least for now Tyler Douglas seemed to be doing okay.

'He's fine.'

Frankie turned to see Lyla was in the doorway. She was wearing her pyjamas now. He wanted to rip them off but would save those thoughts until later.

'He was good at nursery today. He's been telling everyone that his name from now on is Poo, and it has nothing to do with Winnie.'

Frankie couldn't help but laugh.

Lyla came closer and he pulled her onto his lap. They both watched as Ben slept beside them, oblivious to the love emanating towards him.

'Come downstairs.' Lyla stood up and took his hand. 'I don't want to wake him.'

'In a moment.'

She left him alone again. He bent and kissed his son's head.

'Stay safe, Poo,' he whispered and turned out the nightlight. Closing the door, he rubbed at his eyes. He prayed he could keep him safe, that no harm would come to him when he wasn't there. He wasn't sure he would ever forgive himself if anything happened.

But you can't wrap a child in cotton wool. They had given Ben the best start in life. He hoped no one would take that away from him.

Lyla had reheated him a large bowl of pasta bolognese. She sat down next to him at the breakfast bar as he ate.

'I worry about you,' she said. 'Every time you go out of that door, I pray that you'll come home at the end of your shift. I know you love what you do, but I also know there are terrible people out there, no matter who you are.'

He was about to speak when she continued.

'But I also know I don't need to worry because you can look after yourself. Promise me one thing, though. Please don't take the law into your own hands if you find out someone has harmed that little boy. *Our* son needs a father, and I need you home with me. Don't get too close.'

She knew him so well.

Frankie nodded. 'I promise,' he replied. 'Besides, I need to finish painting the hall.'

It was half past midnight when Grace finally got home from the hospital. She hadn't had such a late night for a while. Not since that last murder investigation before she changed posts the year before.

Except for the hall light, the house was in darkness when she dropped her keys on the kitchen table. Simon had gone to bed after she'd rung him again to say it would be a while before she got off her shift.

49

It was way too late to have a run on the treadmill in the conservatory, her usual stress reliever, so she crept around downstairs, made herself a quick drink and then went upstairs.

After showering, she tiptoed into the bedroom and got into bed. The covers were cold against her skin. Simon's back was towards her. She wanted to reach across to him, yet didn't feel it was fair to wake him. But he soon stirred. He switched on the lamp and turned to face her.

'How are you feeling?' he asked.

'Pretty crap, actually.'

'Want to talk about it?'

'No, but I need you awake.' She pulled him towards her, kissing him and hoping he would respond. She needed to feel him as close to her as possible, skin on skin, so she could forget the images she was seeing in her mind over and over. The body of a young boy crumpled on the floor like a sack of potatoes.

Afterwards, they lay together. 'Nice wake-up call,' he grinned. 'Feeling better?'

'Much, thanks. At least I might sleep a little now. It was such a shock to see him lying on the grass.'

'How are the parents?'

'Staying hopeful. We'll know more about his condition in the morning.'

'He's not going to die, is he?'

'It's down to him, I think. If he's strong enough to survive.'

'That poor kid. I remember when Teagan was four and fell off the climbing frame at the local playground. As a parent, you think you should have been there. It wasn't my fault as, rationally, there was no way I could have stopped her even though I was right next to her. She was having fun, but the guilt I experienced afterwards? I totally felt as if I'd let her down.'

'You hadn't. These things happen.'

'Do you think this was an accident?'

'I'm not sure.'

It was clear he wanted her to continue – he couldn't help but fish for information – but she said no more, not wanting to talk about the case.

He turned out the light and she squeezed her eyes shut tight to close out the night, and the images. But she couldn't get the tragedy off her mind. After speaking to Tyler's parents, she had come away none the wiser. Their story that Tyler had run from the house, pulled himself up the railing and fell over as he'd lost his balance didn't ring true.

Had the parents got anything to do with it? Was his eight-year-old sister to blame in any way? Children were always squabbling; something could have happened by accident.

Whatever it was, Grace knew the case was going to be sensitive – it always was when children were involved. She prayed Tyler would pull through. A suspicious death was a terrible thing to police regardless of age, but a child even more so.

Tomorrow she would update Allie and see what else they needed to do. She also realised she'd have to keep an eye on Frankie's welfare. Tyler Douglas was only a few months younger than his son Ben and she'd seen his face contorting several times during the evening, fists clenching, the veins almost popping on his temple.

Simon stirred in his sleep and Grace cuddled into him. She had to get some rest or she would be useless to anyone in the morning.

2010

Ruby was in Naomi's bad books. She'd apologised several times but to no avail. She hated falling out with her best friend but was disappointed too. Ruby wanted to chat about Finn. She and Naomi often talked about boys. It was so much of what they discussed now, after years of dolls and games.

They were in Naomi's bedroom. If she could, Ruby always went there after school. Naomi's parents were mostly at work so they had the place to themselves. And it beat going home to her empty house.

'I spent ages looking for you,' Naomi sniped. 'It was *my* birthday party.'

'Sorry, I didn't realise the time,' Ruby replied. 'And you were having fun, anyway, if I recall.' She nudged Naomi.

'I wanted to be with my best friend.'

'I came to look for you but you were busy with Gareth.'

Naomi grinned. 'At least I had something to do while you were missing.'

Ruby wanted to roll her eyes but refrained. Naomi had been all over Gareth Fitzjohn when she'd come in to say goodbye before going home. From where she was standing, she could see Naomi's eyes closed as his tongue explored her mouth and his hands went wherever she would let them. So she couldn't have been bothered about where Ruby was *that* much.

'I didn't know Finn was coming though,' Naomi added.

'I thought he was invited. He never said.'

'He wouldn't.' Naomi rested on her elbows and put her head in her hands. 'He's a freeloader. He probably only came after a drink.'

'He was in a car so he didn't have anything.'

'How do you know?'

'I told you. He took me out for a drive in it. It was awesome.' Ruby felt pride shoot through her as she realised how important this made her feel.

But Naomi wasn't as impressed as she was.

'He's bad news, Ruby.'

'How do *you* know?'

'My dad says he's always up to no good. You should stay away.'

'Well, I'm not going to.' She grinned. 'He took my phone number.'

Naomi rolled her eyes. 'Has he called?'

'Not yet but he—'

'It's a cop-out. He won't call you.'

'Why do you say that?' Ruby folded her arms. 'He seemed to like me.'

'Oh, I didn't mean it how it sounded.' Naomi seemed genuinely perturbed that she had upset Ruby. 'I just meant that men are like that. They promise you everything and then they let you down.'

'Some do,' Ruby said. 'Not all of them.'

'I guess. So,' Naomi moved to sit on her knees. 'How many times did he kiss you?'

'A few.' For some reason, Ruby didn't want to share anything with Naomi now.

'Go on. Tell me all about him.'

'Don't want to.' Ruby thought she'd punish her for a little while.

'Well, Gareth's hands were trying to get everywhere!'

'Yes, I saw you. I think everyone did.'

Naomi laughed. 'I all but had an orgasm standing up.'

Ruby laughed then.

'Did Finn try it on with you?'

She shook her head, then wondered if he should have done. 'Would it have shown that he liked me more?'

'Not really. He might have been shy. Or bothered about where he was. I reckon you'll just have to keep your fingers crossed that he does call. Else you won't be able to get in touch with him, and that will be a shame.'

'I'll find him again somewhere.' Ruby laughed this time. 'He'll be my Prince Charming. I will get my man.'

Naomi got off the bed and took her friend's hand. 'No more talk about boys. I'm starving. Let's go and make chip butties.'

Ruby followed Naomi down the stairs and into the spacious kitchen. As Naomi raided the freezer, she thought about what her friend had said. Finn might give her the runaround but she hoped he wasn't like that. He had been lovely when he'd said good night. He would call soon.

Slipping a sneaky look at her phone, she sighed. There were no messages yet.

TUESDAY

EIGHT

Grace was situated back at the same desk as she had shared within the old team layout. They were on the first floor of Bethesda Police Station, a large open-plan office with several partitioned box offices in a row in front of her. It was much better to be in the same building again, after working in Stafford Street where Allie had been based, or even out somewhere on one of the estates. It was good to be in close proximity to everyone. Besides, sitting in the main office meant she was a part of the banter or could catch up on the gossip circuit. The station was rife with it, internal and external chitter-chatter.

First up that morning was a chat with Allie, who was in Nick's old office. Grace was glad to see she, too, had an open-door policy.

Perry arrived and threw his keys down onto the desk. 'Morning. I heard about Tyler Douglas last night.' He removed his coat and placed it over the back of his chair before sitting down.

'It was terrible. I couldn't stop thinking about it. It took me ages to drop off to sleep, hence these.' Grace pointed at the bags under her eyes. 'And why I was up at stupid o'clock.'

'How's everything now?'

'I'm not sure yet but he was in a pretty bad way last night. Do you know anything about his parents? Ruby Brassington and Luke Douglas.'

Perry shook his head. 'They're not on our radar, but if I find out they had anything to do with the accident, they'll feel the wrath of me.'

Grace knew his threats were empty but she realised it must be hard for him. Like Frankie, Perry's boy, Archie, was a similar age to Tyler Douglas. It must get to them both. It got to her enough and she wasn't a parent.

'If you need any help let us know,' Perry added. 'You are okay?'

'Yes, thanks.' Grace appreciated his concern. 'Anything come in for you overnight?' Perry was acting Detective Sergeant for the Major Crimes Team at the moment.

'An assault on a fourteen-year-old. His mum called it in so I'll be off to see them soon.'

'No rest for the wicked.' Grace spotted Allie standing up in her office and headed over to her. She knocked on the door frame before going in.

'Do you have a minute?'

'Barely.' Allie pointed to the ceiling. 'I've got a meeting with the Gods.' Upstairs was where the DCI and those ranked above were based.

Grace smirked at the in-joke. 'It won't take long. It's about Tyler Douglas.'

Allie indicated for Grace to sit down on one side of the desk and then sat the opposite side herself. 'Did you get anything else after we spoke?'

'Most people didn't see anything.'

'I saw nothing.' Allie rolled her eyes. 'It's laughable that they still use that. What do you think happened?'

'I can't tell, so me and Frankie are going to try and get some sense out of the residents this morning. I'm not sure it warrants police interception unless a crime has been committed. Unless we can find a witness, we only have the parents' statements to go on.'

'Gut feeling?' Allie asked.

'Something doesn't feel right but I'm not sure if it's suspicious or not. It could be that his eight-year-old sister was involved and the parents don't want to say. Or it could be that she tried to stop Tyler from falling and couldn't. Although then, why wouldn't they tell us the truth?'

'Maybe they think she will be in trouble.'

'She will be if she's pushed him.'

'Does she look like she would?'

Grace screwed up her nose. 'Anything's possible but I didn't get that about her. More that she was scared to talk.'

'And the parents?'

'I don't think they did it either if I'm honest. But I'd like to see what I can find out for sure.'

'Okay, keep me informed,' Allie agreed. 'It won't hurt to properly interview the parents now they may be a little less emotional, and see if everything tallies with last night's account. Until an accident is or isn't ruled out, we need to know as much as possible. And there are no warning markers against either of them, or the property?'

'None at all.'

'I'll leave it with you then.'

'I'll give it my best shot.' She nodded. 'Someone *will* tell me something by the end of the day.'

Grace followed Allie out of the room and back to her own desk. The cold weather called for a cuppa. But first she'd ring the housing officer that covered Harrison House.

NINE

Caleb pulled the duvet up around his neck and turned over in bed. It was gone school time but he wasn't going in today. He'd faked a headache when his mum had come to wake him. Usually she saw through it, gave him a lashing with her tongue and sent him on his way. But today she'd taken pity on him.

It was a good job he had such a strict mum or else he and his brother would have got up to much worse than they had so far. Johnno was five years older than him, living at home but Mum wouldn't allow him to claim dole. He had to get a job or find somewhere else to stay, that was the rule.

She was a good influence on them both, but still he had secrets from her. She didn't know what he'd been doing for the past few months. But he was done with that. He wasn't sure he wanted to earn the rest of the money he needed. Because what he'd seen Seth do last night meant he'd never trust him again. And in his haste to get away, he hadn't delivered the package.

His phone went off. It was his friend, Shaun.

'You heard about Milo last night?'

'No, what happened?' Milo was another of the boys fetching and carrying for Seth.

'Thanks, but do I have to go to school? Can I have the day off, seeing as today's so important?'

'Nice try.' Dad shook his head. 'Come on, let's get you up and out and on that bus.'

The day dragged and all the way through her lessons she thought of Finn. How could she get away with seeing him? Perhaps Naomi would cover for her. After all, she'd done it on a few occasions so far.

But when she asked, Naomi flat out refused.

'He's bad news, I'm telling you.' She linked her arm through Ruby's as they made their way out of the school gates to catch the bus home. 'You mark my words, he has girls falling for him every night at the club.'

'Says who?'

'My brothers. He works at The Majestic – they see him. You don't want to break your heart over him.'

It stung Ruby to hear Naomi badmouthing Finn, especially when she didn't have any proof. Ruby never criticised Gareth, so it wasn't really fair. Especially as neither of them knew him well.

So it had shocked them both to see him waiting for her outside school in his car. He papped his horn. As they approached, the window went down.

'Need a lift, ladies?' he shouted to them.

Ruby looked at Naomi and indicated a slight nod of her head. Naomi sighed. 'Okay, then. Just this once.'

Ruby climbed into the passenger seat and Naomi got in the back behind her.

'All right, Nay?' Finn grinned at Naomi. 'Haven't seen you in a while. Things good?'

'Cool, thanks.' Naomi nodded in reply.

Ruby buckled up and Finn sped off. He drove a little faster than he had the first night she'd met him but secretly she was delighted. Her boyfriend had a car! Some of the girls who had seen her must be green with envy. This was one up on nearly everyone in year eleven.

Finn and Ruby chatted away in the front, Naomi joining in every now and again as Finn encouraged her. Ruby told him her address and asked him to park at the end of the street. If her dad saw her, she'd be in trouble. Naomi was coming home with her. It wasn't often she did, but they were going to watch a film later as her birthday treat.

They pulled in at the end of her road and Finn parked up. He turned to Ruby but before he could speak, Naomi slid along the back seat.

'I'll wait for you over on the wall,' she said quietly. 'See you, Finn.'

'I won't be a minute,' Ruby said before the door banged behind her.

'Alone at last.' Finn reached into the glove compartment and pulled out a small pink box. It was tied with a white ribbon, a large bow on its top. 'This is for you.'

'For me?' Ruby whispered.

'Well, it's your birthday.'

She took it from him and opened it up. Inside was a necklace with a tiny heart pendant. She looked at him, unsure what to say. She hadn't expected this at all. She'd been slowly getting used to the idea of never seeing Finn again. Of course she had fantasised about him turning up every day, but it hadn't happened. The longer it had gone on, the less she was inclined to talk about him to Naomi, especially as she was seeing Gareth a couple of times each weekend and twice in the week. It was okay for her. Gareth could come to Naomi's house and hang out in the room above their garage. There was always some-where she could be away from her family. Ruby's dad would never let her bring a boy into the house at her age. It wasn't even worth sneaking anyone in, in case he came home early one night from work.

'Thank you,' she said, finally finding her manners. 'But this is too much. I don't even know you.'

'Call it a sorry present too.' He chucked her under the chin. 'I've been working too hard lately. And also you were only fifteen when I met you. You were a girl. Now,' he gazed into her eyes, 'you're a woman.'

She could hear her heart beating erratically as he kissed her. Trying not to think of what would happen if any of the neighbours spotted her, she relaxed into it, enjoying the sensation of his tongue against her own.

When they stopped, he helped her to put the necklace on. Then as she turned back to him, he kissed her again.

'I haven't stopped thinking about you since we met, Ruby. I don't know how to explain it; you got under my skin. You're different from anyone else I've met. But I'm nineteen and you were only fifteen.'

'And now I'm sixteen?'

'We must find a way to make this work.' He nodded. 'Can you meet me tomorrow night?'

Ruby knew the odds were stacked against her but she was determined to find a way around it.

'Yes.' She nodded vehemently.

'I'll pick you up here at seven. I have to work at nine thirty but I can see you until nine. We can go for a coffee.'

She nodded and he kissed her a third time.

When she got out of the car, she felt lightheaded, almost floaty.

'Happy now?' Naomi smiled, once Ruby had walked over to her. 'I know I'm not much for him but he does seem into you.'

Ruby laughed. 'He does!' She showed her the necklace. 'Look what he gave me for my birthday.'

'That's lovely.' Naomi took a closer look. 'Really, it's gorgeous.'

'Thanks. Although, can I say it was from you? You know my dad won't let me keep it if he knew where it came from.'

Naomi nodded. 'Sure you can.'

'Right, let's go and get ready for the cinema. Cake first!'

As they linked arms, Ruby brimmed with happiness. This had been the best birthday ever.

TEN

Shelley was at the Royal Stoke University Hospital for ten a.m. Her takings the night before meant she could easily afford a taxi, although she wouldn't be able to go back to The Casino for a while. She had a feeling the guy she fleeced might complain to the club, even though she had been careful to pick him out. Obviously everything would have to be proved and she'd been very careful to avoid the cameras. But even so, she realised that her luck might run out. For now, she had a few hundred pounds in her purse that no one knew about.

She visited the shop inside the entrance, bought magazines for Lily and Luke, a paperback for Ruby – who she knew loved to read – and chocolates for them all. She wasn't going to get anything for Tyler until she had seen him – she didn't even know if he was conscious or not.

She located the children's ward on a nearby map and made her way through the maze of corridors to get there. She didn't know if they would see her, and wasn't even sure if she would be let in.

As people, Ruby and Luke seemed okay to her. Luke was a friend of Seth's so she saw him often, yet Ruby was a tough nut to crack. Shelley had tried to befriend her for a few months now but she preferred to keep herself to herself. Ruby wasn't *unfriendly*, just guarded.

But Shelley was after information and what better way to get it than to visit the hospital and act all concerned and neighbourly.

At the Paediatric Unit, she asked at the nurses' station for Tyler's whereabouts. A nurse was pointing out the intensive care ward as Luke came around the corner carrying two coffees.

'What are you doing here?' he gasped.

'I had to come and see how Tyler was doing.' She walked towards him.

'You shouldn't have come.'

'Look, what's happening between you and Seth can stay between us, if that's what you're worried about.'

'Yeah, like you're going to keep your mouth shut. I want you to leave.'

'It's forgotten.' Shelley shrugged. 'As long as you don't look too guilty when the three of us are together.' She pointed down the corridor. 'You're down there, aren't you?'

'I don't want you visiting.'

'Well, that's a bit tough. And I'm coming to see how Ruby and Lily are doing, not you, so don't get all arsy with me.'

'You'd better not say anything.' He marched off and she followed after him, mentally kicking herself when she realised she hadn't mentioned Tyler.

'He's okay, then?' she asked as they got to the door and she sanitised her hands using the pump on the wall.

'He's having tests at the moment.'

'The police are all over Harrison House. They're asking if anyone saw what happened.'

Luke paled. 'Have you heard if anyone did?'

She shook her head. 'It was an accident, wasn't it?'

He nodded. 'Yeah, it was.'

She followed him into the ward, trying to keep the smile from her face. He didn't know she knew he might be lying.

Ruby was sitting next to the cot-bed in bay two, holding Tyler's hand. She looked up as Shelley came into view.

'I hope you don't mind me coming.' Shelley brought tears to her eyes purposely. 'I was so shocked when I heard the news and wanted to rush straight round. Obviously I knew you'd be here for a while, so I thought I'd pop by and see if you needed anything.'

Ruby began to cry. Shelley rushed across the room and hugged her. 'It will be okay,' she soothed as she rubbed her back. Over her shoulder, she could see Tyler's still little body, his eyes closed, machines attached to him making all sorts of noises. His face was red and puffy. He looked so fragile that at first she thought she shouldn't even be here. But then she swallowed her pride. She had a job to do.

'How is he?' she asked again.

'We'll know more over the next twenty-four hours,' Ruby replied, wiping at her eyes. 'They've put him in an induced coma. For now, it's sit and wait. He's a fighter, though.'

'What has the doctor said?' Shelley pulled a chair out and sat next to her. Luke passed a coffee to Ruby and then did the same.

'He's responding but they want to keep him sedated a little longer. The doctor said he's been very lucky.'

'That's good news.' Shelley handed the bag of gifts to her. 'I brought you some things to keep you occupied. You might not need them now, but . . .' She shrugged. 'For when Tyler is home and causing riots again.'

Luke snorted. 'He's never going out on that walkway again. And we're putting in for a transfer to a house.'

Ruby said nothing, just looked at Tyler.

71

'So it was an accident then?' Shelley posed the question.

'I told you it was,' Luke sniped. 'Why are you asking again?'

'I forgot I'd already mentioned it.'

'Anyone would think that you're trying to blame us.'

'That's enough, Luke,' Ruby spoke out. 'It *was* an accident.'

'I'm sure it was,' Shelley said. 'Do you know when he'll be able to come home?'

'It depends on what happens when he comes out of the coma.' Ruby wiped a hand across her boy's brow. In the background, a nurse was tending to another patient, their machine going off loudly. A curtain was pulled around for privacy.

Shelley sighed. She wasn't going to get much from either of them.

'Where's Lily?' she asked next.

'Staying with Norma.'

'Nutty Norma from next door?'

'I had nowhere else to take her,' Ruby snapped. 'I don't have family.'

A woman at the next cot-bed looked over at them, her expression stern. Ruby mouthed sorry to her.

'Hey, relax.' Shelley put up a hand. 'I would have had her, you know that. But I was going out just as it had happened. I didn't get in until ten last night and by that time there were police everywhere.'

Ruby's eyes widened. 'Were there?'

'They were just asking around, that's all.'

'Who did they speak to?'

'I'm not sure. But you have nothing to worry about, do you?'

Luke and Ruby said no at the same time.

After a few minutes of small talk, Shelley couldn't stand any more. 'I'd best be going,' she said. 'I don't want to get in your way when the doctors come by.' She stood up. 'Do you want me to fetch Lily round to mine and look after her?'

'No, thanks.' Ruby shook her head. 'We're going to collect her later. She needs to be with us.'

'I guess.' Shelley wasn't sure, but she wasn't one to question.

Once out of the ward, she gave a sigh. That hadn't been as productive as she'd hoped. She needed to get Ruby alone, but this was definitely not the place for it. She'd try again once Tyler was home. At the very least, he was alive.

Until that man came calling again, that is.

ELEVEN

Grace sat at her desk, making a list of what she needed to do that morning. As well as going out, she had a lot of paperwork to catch up on. It was endless in this job. Everything had to be actioned, ticked off, recorded, signed off or filed away. Deep in thought, she visibly jumped when Frankie put a mug of tea down beside her.

'Ooh, ta,' she said.

Frankie's desk was directly opposite hers. He reached out the packet of ginger biscuits he always kept in his drawer and offered her one. She shook her head. Too early in the morning for her.

'How did it go with Allie?' he asked.

'We're good to go for now,' she told him. 'We need to gather as much information as we can. You and I can head up to the hospital. I want to chat to Ruby and Luke separately. Then we can go door-to-door at Harrison House.' She waved her hand in the air. 'I don't need to tell you what to do really.'

'Good to hear, Sarge,' he beamed.

Grace grinned. She had struck lucky being able to have Frankie working with her. It was imperative she had someone firstly who she could trust to get on with the job and secondly who she enjoyed spending a lot of time with. Frankie was a laugh, but he also knew when to be serious too. The perfect antidote after a late night, and always up for an oatcake breakfast.

Having DC Sam Markham on hand to help when she needed her was a godsend. Sam was meticulous in cracking cases wide open with her scrutiny and diligence. She was glad that Perry had a chance at DS too. Everything had worked out quite well. Even the Steeles were off her back now that she didn't have to work so closely to them. But she was still keeping an ear to the ground to see what they got up to.

'I also spoke on the phone to the housing officer from Trent Housing Association covering that patch. Dave Pendigran. He's investigating the incident from their end and says he'll tell us if he hears anything and vice versa. Obviously, he can only speak to the parents, and arrange a maintenance inspection. The association don't seem at fault to me, though.'

'Yeah, I guess the railing would have given way if it was faulty.'

'I just hope Tyler survived the night,' Grace said, finishing off her list. 'I tried to ring the hospital but the line was engaged. We'll be there within the half-hour, I expect if we start out now.'

Frankie drained his coffee and grabbed his jacket, shrugging it on.

Arriving at the hospital, Grace cruised the car park until she found a space. They made their way into the main building with its expansive reception area, people milling around inside. Some were on a mission, knowing exactly where they were going. Others loitered, looking lost, asking for directions from receptionists and helpers, plugging details into a computerised system. It was all done in an orderly fashion.

'How are we playing this, Sarge?' Frankie asked as they made their way across the floor towards the stairs.

'I'll speak to Ruby and you can chat with Luke. Take him for a coffee – but go easy on him for now.'

'I'm all over it, boss.' He doffed an invisible cap. 'Nice not to be weighed down either. It was ridiculous what we had to carry out on the beat.' He laughed. 'Even though it was a necessity, I feel two stone lighter without all my gear.'

'Yes, you do look a little less pudgy,' Grace teased.

Frankie was always smart out of uniform. Since he was now in plain clothes, he'd taken to wearing jeans and casual jackets, always with a crisp shirt and a tie. He was a good listener, and Grace had already seen people putting their trust in him. They told him things they might not have mentioned when he'd been in uniform, as he was a natural at making them feel at ease.

In the Paediatric Intensive Care Unit they were shown into the main reception room. There were three groups of families waiting including Ruby and Luke, who were sitting huddled together on plastic seats. They made their way over to them.

'Morning,' Grace said, taking a seat and noting the looks that were passing between them. 'How is he today?'

'He's stable,' Ruby replied. 'The nurses are tending to him at the moment. The consultant is doing his rounds and he'll be able to tell us more when we see him. But we're told the signs are good, although we don't really know what that means.'

'It sounds positive.' Grace smiled. 'I know this seems insensitive but we need to talk to you. Shall we find a side room so we can speak in private?'

'Why?' Luke asked.

'We just need you to run through what happened last night.' Grace gave a friendly smile.

'But we've told you everything,' he accused.

Grace said nothing, the tense atmosphere getting thicker by the second.

'Come on, Luke,' Frankie said. 'Let's grab a coffee.'

'Do we have to?'

'Yeah, we do.'

Luke stood up like a sulky child. Grace nodded at Frankie as he led the other man out of the room. She stood up and looked at Ruby.

'Let's find that room, shall we?'

2010

Ruby stood waiting at the end of her street. She'd told her dad she was going to see Naomi but instead her friend was covering for her while she went to meet Finn. They were going to his flat, and he was cooking her a meal.

A ripple of anticipation ran through her as she wondered if tonight would be the night. They had been dating now for six weeks. He'd picked her up twice a week since her birthday, taken her out to dinner, to the cinema, and to a pub where they'd had a soft drink outside. One afternoon they'd walked around the park hand in hand, eaten ice cream and fed the ducks. He was such a romantic and fun to be with too, and every time she thought about him her stomach flipped.

He was her first proper boyfriend, and so much older than the boys at school. She'd sat in class dreaming about him, remembering his kisses, his gentle persuasion to try a little more each time they met. He was always patient with her when it felt too much though.

But she was ready. Tonight would be the night.

She'd been to his flat several times now. They'd had coffee

and watched TV. But this was the first time he was cooking for her.

As soon as she stepped inside after Finn had driven her back to his place, she could smell something delicious.

'There's a cottage pie warming in the oven,' he told her as she removed her jacket. 'My mum makes it all the time. She—'

'Your mum made it!' Ruby cried. 'I might have known.'

'No, wait.' He shook his head. 'I prepared it. I've watched her so many times when I was growing up that it's easy to replicate. And if I'm honest it's nice to cook for someone who can share it with me. Usually I make too much and end up freezing some or binning it.'

'It looks far too nice to throw away,' she admitted.

'I'll take that as a compliment.'

'Do you see your mum often?' Finn had told Ruby that his parents divorced when he was nine. His father had been a wastrel, always out looking for trouble, so it was no loss to either of them when he'd walked out. Finn rarely mentioned his mum, so it was a surprise to find out he'd spent time with her cooking when he was younger.

'I go every now and then,' he replied. 'She's all right, my mum.'

'You should visit her more often. You never know when she might not be around.'

Finn glanced at her and then gave her a hug. 'It must be hard for you.'

'It gets easier,' she admitted, realising she sounded a lot more grown up than she felt about it. 'I miss my dad, though. I wish I was closer to him but, like you, it is what it is.'

He kissed her forehead. 'Come on, the food is getting cold.'

Finn dished the pie out and it was indeed lovely. In no time at all she had finished her last mouthful and washed it down with a gulp of wine. She'd only had half a glass. Finn wasn't drinking because he was driving, and she didn't like the taste of it too much yet.

'I love having you here, Rube.' He reached across for her hand. 'I wish it was permanent.'

'Are you saying you want me to move in with you?' she teased.

'No . . . I—'

'Joking.' She covered his hand with her own. 'I love being here too.'

'It feels so strange to think I've only known you for barely a couple of months. It's like a light has gone on in my life since I met you. I swear I go to sleep thinking about you and when I wake up, you're the first thing on my mind. You give me a reason for wanting to make more of my life.'

Ruby grinned. She wasn't up on romantic chat-up lines but reckoned that would be one of the better ones. And she did love his company.

They moved through into the living room, leaving the table as it was. No sooner had they sat down on the settee, he turned and kissed her, his hand at the back of her neck pulling her close. It was tender at first, but then became more passionate. His hands were gentle, his manner too and she knew she could trust him not to hurt her. She could see from his eyes how much she meant to him.

One by one, he undid the buttons on her blouse and pushed it to one side. Kissing her neck, her shoulders, her chest, she leaned her head back and savoured the feelings running through her body right then. She freed the cuffs and removed the blouse completely. Reaching behind she unhooked her bra.

He gazed into her eyes and then brought her close again. Within minutes, they both followed the bra to the floor.

It wasn't all pain free but neither was it as awkward as she'd thought it might be. She touched him too, something she hadn't yet done. Unaware of the effect she was having, she was surprised when he moved her hand away. She'd been scared of bringing it up so was glad when he used protection. As they made love, for the first time she felt like a woman.

Afterwards she looked at him. He smiled at her. She could see such love and respect as he stared at her. So much so that she burst into embarrassed laughter.

'What's so funny?'

'I don't know.' She laughed again and he joined in this time. It was a mixture of happiness and relief that it had gone okay.

'Well, at least you're not crying.' He pulled her into the crook of his arm as they lay side by side. 'That would really ruin my street cred.'

They lay together, breathing returning to normal, relaxing in the afterglow of sex. Finn ran his fingers up and down her arms; she cuddled into his chest.

'Do you know what, Rube?' he broke into the silence. 'I think I'm falling in love with you.'

She put up her head and looked at him. Was this too soon? How would she know? The only thing she was sure of was her feelings for him. He made her feel so grown up, so alive, so . . . so loved.

'I think I'm falling in love with you too,' she replied.

'Really?' He looked shocked.

'Yes, really.'

He rolled over on top of her, pinning her arms up either side of her head. 'Well, that's good. Perhaps we can skip dessert and go for second helpings of each other instead.'

'What's for dessert?'

'Vanilla cheesecake. Something I definitely didn't make myself.'

'I'm quite partial to cheesecake.'

'Oh, like that is it?' He tickled her, making her gasp for air.

He gazed into her eyes, and it almost embarrassed her again. His look was so intense, as if a million thoughts were flashing through his mind all at once.

'I love you, Ruby Brassington,' he said.

She grinned. 'I love you too, Finn Ridley.'

As he leaned in to kiss her again, Ruby felt her heart would burst with happiness. Wait until she shared all this with Naomi.

TWELVE

In the empty relatives' room, Grace waited for Ruby to sit down before pulling a chair across the floor and sitting directly in front of her. She leaned forward, resting her elbows on her knees. There was no easy way to say what she had to so she just came out with it.

'The consultant I spoke to last night is saying that the injuries caused to Tyler from his fall don't seem to suggest that he fell head first.'

Ruby frowned. 'What do you mean?'

'He thought if Tyler had fallen over, he would most probably have landed on all fours, putting his hands out to stop himself. But Tyler's injuries seem to be consistent with a straight drop, as if he had been walking along the railing.'

'You think we had something to do with this?' Ruby shook her head. 'We didn't.'

'That's why we need you to go through what happened again, please.'

'You were there.'

'I was there *after* Tyler had fallen.'

Tears formed in Ruby's eyes and trickled down her cheek.

'I am truly sorry for your pain,' Grace started. 'I just need to cross the t's and dot the i's. Let's begin with an hour before the accident.'

'I was at home with the children.'

'That's Lily and Tyler?'

Ruby nodded. 'We were finishing tea when Luke came in.'

'What time would that be?'

She paused as if recollecting. 'About half past six, I think. The news was finishing. The kids had just had a pizza. Tyler had already eaten but he's always hungry.' A faint smile teased Ruby's lips before disappearing again.

'What happened then?' Grace urged.

'Lily and Tyler were playing in their room. Then we heard Lily yell. We went rushing into the hall to find the front door open and Lily looking over the side.' Ruby closed her eyes momentarily, as if to block out what she had seen. 'When I looked over the rail, I could see Tyler on the grass.'

'And what did Lily say had happened?'

'She said he'd been teasing her and pushing her and she told him to stop it. That's when he ran out of the room and got out the front door. Lily didn't realise – none of us realised – until it was too late.' She covered her face with her hands. 'Every time I close my eyes, I see him falling.'

'Was the front door locked?'

'Yes. But he does know how to open it. I just didn't think he'd be able to reach it.'

'Does he know the dangers of—' Grace stopped when she saw the look Ruby gave to her. 'I didn't mean to sound patronising. I have to write down the facts.'

'He's nearly three years old. Of course he doesn't know the danger, no matter how many times we tell him. Have you got children?'

'No.'

'Thought as much.'

It always irked Grace when people asked her that. Just because she hadn't got children of her own, it didn't make her heartless, nor unknowledgeable.

She let Ruby take a moment.

'There was a man seen rushing away from Harrison House shortly after the accident,' she said next. 'We're trying to trace him now. He could have been one of your neighbours, and may have witnessed what happened. Did you see anyone?'

'I might have seen someone when I looked over to see . . . to see if Tyler was okay.'

'Was it a man, or a woman?'

'I'm not sure.'

'Where were they?' Grace probed.

'On the path, running towards the main road.'

Grace made a note to check that out. CCTV cameras on Ford Green Road may have caught visuals if so.

'Is Lily still with your neighbour, Norma?' she asked next.

'Yes. We're going to fetch her soon, and we need a change of clothes too.' Ruby paused as if she was going to say something but then changed her mind. 'She's going to be lost without him for a while,' she continued eventually. 'We all will be. But we *are* going to take him back home.'

Grace paused. 'Was it Lily who pushed Tyler from the wall and you're afraid to tell us?'

Ruby gasped. 'It had nothing to do with her.'

'Are you sure? Because if you are covering for her, we need to know.'

'Lily would never hurt Tyler. How dare you come here and insinuate that our daughter had anything to do with it!'

Grace put up a hand. 'I just need to know what happened to Tyler,' she said gently. 'We owe it to him to get to the bottom of this.'

Ruby began to cry. Grace handed her a few tissues from a box situated on a low table and waited for her to calm down. She could sense the young woman was nervous about something. Ruby wouldn't look her in the eye, and instead her gaze dropped to the floor, as her skin grew more and more flushed.

Was she covering for Lily? Was her daughter involved in Tyler falling and if so, was it an accident or not?

'You're not in any trouble,' Grace told her after a few moments, hoping it would encourage her to start talking again.

'It was an accident,' Ruby insisted. 'I—'

The door opened and a young doctor came in.

'Hello. It's Ruby, isn't it?' He smiled.

Ruby's face crumpled as if she was expecting the worst.

Grace flashed her warrant card.

'Oh, sorry. Would you like me to come back later? There's nothing to worry about. Just here to let Mum know what's going on with Tyler.'

Grace stood up. It wasn't her place to be here right now, even though she was frustrated at the interruption.

'I'll leave you to it,' she said and left the room.

Outside in the corridor, she gathered her thoughts. It wasn't something she liked doing, questioning people who had other things to think about. But equally she had to be sure that Ruby Brassington was telling the truth.

And she was far from certain of that.

THIRTEEN

The hospital canteen was busy, only a few tables vacant. Frankie looked around as he stood in the queue. It was easy to spot the patients sitting in wheelchairs, with bandages or plaster casts, bruises and stitches, trailing drips behind them. But there were a lot of people without ailments. He wondered if they were here to visit sick relatives, or perhaps attending appointments themselves. Some could be waiting to hear devastating news, people they loved having gone out for the day, never to return as they were. For the most part, the human body was resilient and mended well under the most awful conditions. He hoped Tyler only needed a little time to recover from his ordeal.

Frankie bought two coffees and pointed to a table. He and Luke sat down. He pushed one of the cups across to him.

'Thanks, although I feel spaced out because I've been drinking too much of the stuff,' Luke said, busying himself adding sugar.

By the time he'd felt okay to take a sip of his own drink, Frankie noted that Luke had folded and unfolded his arms four times.

'You must be devastated,' he began. 'I have a son a similar

age and I can only imagine how I'd feel if something like this happened to him. He's hardly ever still, drives us mad at times.'

Luke gave a half-smile. 'They're all the same.'

Frankie smiled too. Then he started with his questioning. 'I need to run through with you again what happened last night. Let's begin with just before the accident. What were you doing?'

'I was watching the TV.'

'What was on?'

'The news.'

Frankie swiped a hand in the air. 'Go back a bit. Had you been in all day?'

'No. I was working at the club, stock-taking, you know.'

'The club?'

'Flynn's. I help out behind the bar, do a bit of this and that.'

Frankie nodded, writing the details down.

'And you got home at just after six?'

'Yeah. Ruby had cooked pizza for the kids and saved me some. I wasn't hungry as I'd had something earlier. She was annoyed. She said she wanted to sit down as a family at least one night a week.'

'You work at the club often?'

'A few hours here and there. I owe a favour to the club owner,' Luke was quick to say.

Frankie put down his pen, reading between the lines. 'Look, if you're working cash in hand, that's not great but I'm not here to investigate that. For now I need to know what time you finished work.'

'Half past five.' Luke hung his head. 'I keep seeing him lying on the grass.' He looked up teary-eyed. 'It's all my fault, isn't it?'

'Why do you say that?'

Luke was quiet then.

'Go on,' Frankie urged.

'Lily and Tyler were in their room. We heard them arguing, but that's nothing unusual. Tyler is always making noise and Lily likes to read. He must have slipped out, and before we knew it, he'd—' He looked away for a moment, running a hand through his hair.

'And Lily had nothing to do with Tyler's accident?'

Luke shook his head fervently. 'It was our fault. Tyler shouldn't have been able to get outside.'

Frankie waited to see if he would keep on talking but Luke wouldn't meet his eye as he finished off his coffee.

'There was a man seen running from Harrison House shortly after the accident,' Frankie decided to change the subject. 'Did you see anyone?'

Luke shook his head. 'Didn't really see anything after Tyler fell. I just ran to him.'

Frankie closed his notebook. 'Okay, let's get you back to your son. I'm sure you have a lot of things to do. I hope Tyler is okay.'

Luke nodded his thanks.

Frankie could see tears in his eyes again. There was no doubt he was worried about his child. But he wondered if the show of emotion was for Tyler, or for himself.

Because he knew Luke was lying. And he was going to find out why.

When Frankie and Luke got back to PICU, Grace was sitting in the corridor.

'Anything?' she asked him once Luke had gone to be with his family.

'Pretty much as I expected.' Frankie sat down next to her. 'The kids were in their room, Tyler got out and went over the railing before they could stop him. You?'

'The same. What about the man seen running away?'

'He said he didn't see anyone.'

Grace frowned. 'Ruby told me she'd seen someone.'

'Did she say what they looked like?'

'No. Said she was too far away to see if it was a man or a woman. She didn't mention it until I did, though.'

'Maybe he isn't anything to do with this?'

'Nevertheless, I'll get Sam on to CCTV. There should be sightings of him on foot we can look at. Then we start questioning. Someone must have seen something.'

2011

Ruby woke up and turned over in bed. Beside her, Finn was snoring. She moulded herself into his back and ran her hand up and down his leg, then his chest.

'Wakey, wakey,' she said. 'It's my birthday!'

'It's half past eight,' he muttered.

He had been to work the night before and although she didn't mind so much, now that he was here, she wanted him awake.

She giggled, continuing to caress his body.

Seventeen today. She remembered her sixteenth, how she had been full of hope and happiness after just meeting Finn, and now look what had happened during the past twelve months. Now she was living with him. Now he was her fella.

She'd managed to keep their relationship from her dad for four months but then she was spotted out in the car with him, when she should have been at Naomi's house after sixth form had ended for the day. Naomi had got in trouble with her parents for lying. Ruby had been told off by her dad for being with Finn and that was without saying she had stayed over with him once or twice.

But Ruby hadn't cared – she was in love.

Her dad had grounded her for a month, but she'd snuck out when he'd been at work. Finn always waited for her at the end of the street. Most of the time he could only spare an hour before he went to work anyway, so it was easy to fit in. And once she'd had sex with him, it was all they ever did.

But then it all came to a head with her dad.

'Where were you last night?' he asked her one morning.

'I was with Naomi at her house. We watched a film and had pizza.'

'I rang Naomi's parents and you weren't there. But Naomi was.'

Ruby blushed. She hated lying to him but how else could she go on seeing Finn?

'So where were you?' he repeated. 'Were you with that Ridley?'

'His name's Finn, Dad.'

'Don't change the subject.'

'Okay, okay.' Ruby nodded, knowing there was no point lying any more. They'd already argued twice about him. Her dad said she should finish her education before thinking of boyfriends. 'Yes, I was with Finn.'

'I told you not to see him again.'

'But you haven't even met him. You don't know what a nice person he is.'

'That's not what I'm hearing.'

'Then let me bring him home. If you spoke to him, you'd—'

'I said no, Ruby. I don't want you seeing him any more and that's my final word.'

'I'm nearly seventeen,' she objected. 'You can't tell me what to do.'

'I can while you live under my roof.'

'Then I'll leave.'

'Oh, don't be so absurd.' His temper rose. 'I want what's best for you, but can't you see you're ruining your life? You could still go to university if you knuckle down now. You could have a good job, a career. I don't want you throwing everything away.'

'If that's your way of saying you care about me, then you're too late.'

'What do you mean?'

'I know that you don't want to come home so you stay at work all the time.'

'That's not—'

'You should be happy for me that I've found someone nice to look after me so that you don't have to. I hardly ever see you and I'm fed up of being on my own. It's not my fault that I remind you of Mum. I miss her too and—'

'Don't you dare speak to me like that!' Before she could react, he slapped her across the face. 'Your *mum* would be turning in her grave. She would have expected more from you.'

Ruby touched her cheek, warmth emanating from where he had hit her. His words stung, coursing through her like shotgun pellets and shock made her well up with tears. He had never as much as laid a finger on her before. If she was brave enough, she would have slapped him too. She held in her tears for as long as she could before running out of the room.

'Ruby, wait. I'm so sorry,' he cried behind her, but she had slammed her bedroom door and stayed in there for the rest of the evening.

How could he think she was wasting her life with Finn? They were in love and as soon as she was eighteen, they were going to get married. Who cared about school, and college and getting a job? All she wanted was to have a baby and settle down. Finn was her life. She couldn't stop seeing him.

She wouldn't stop seeing him.

Her dad grounded her for two weeks. After that, she tried

to be more inventive with her lies, saying she had joined a youth club rather than asking Naomi to cover for her all the time. Stolen hours here and there were actually easier for Finn to fit around his work.

But after another row when she'd been found out again, she'd had enough. She loved Finn so much – her heart belonged to him, and if her dad couldn't handle that, then she would have to leave.

When she'd turned up at Finn's flat with a small holdall, he'd welcomed her with open arms.

'You must be prepared to be alone a lot while I work,' he stressed.

But she hadn't minded – at least it meant she could see him and they didn't have to sneak around any more. If she was honest, she'd gone along with it to get on her dad's nerves at first. He thought she'd come running back to him after a couple of nights but she hadn't. She'd stuck it out. A stubborn streak she'd inherited from him.

In the space of a month, she'd settled in as if she'd always been there. There were a few friends of Finn's that called now and then that she didn't much care for, but in the main it was good. Now, she lay next to him, happy and sad in equal measures. There wouldn't be a card or a present from her dad this year. In the space of twelve months, she had lost the respect of her father, but she was in a relationship with a man that she loved.

She hadn't told Finn yet that her period was late. They'd been careful, always using contraception, so she wasn't sure how it had happened. Maybe it was just the stress of the past few months.

She was happy about it though, and she hoped he would be too, when she told him.

FOURTEEN

Seth stood looking over the railing as he waited for Shelley to come home. The police being around so much was pissing him off but he needed to keep his cool. He'd seen both those detectives around too, knew she was a DS and him a rookie detective. He'd nicked Seth a few times when he'd been in uniform, he was certain.

He was keeping a low profile after what had happened last night. But he'd had to do it. He'd had to teach him a lesson and it had been the only way. Luckily he'd managed to escape in time. Now all he hoped was that Leon Steele didn't hear about it. It had been impulsive, but reckless too.

Seth had been working for the Steele brothers for a while now. There was Eddie who was thirty-nine and Leon who was thirty-seven. They were part of Stoke's criminal network, one that Seth belonged in but hadn't quite worked his way up the ladder far enough for his liking. He'd even tried getting in with their niece but that had come to a stop when she'd finished things. He'd been annoyed at the time but then realised it was better not to mix business with pleasure. So he'd slummed it and settled for shagging Shelley instead. It was all she was good for; he supposed she'd be okay until he found something better.

The thing with Shelley was she didn't mind his upbringing. She hadn't had it good at home herself so understood when he tried to better himself and it worked out wrong. Take getting involved with his neighbour, Luke. He thought he'd played it clever by lending him some money and then recruiting him to do his own bidding when he couldn't pay it back, but he'd been more trouble than it was worth. The jobs he'd set up for him were only fetching and carrying as a driver, but he'd complained so much that Seth had taken him off one or two for fear he'd cock up. And that wouldn't do. He wasn't going inside again for no one.

Seth had been on the wrong side of the law for as long as he could remember. Now twenty-three, he'd been put into care at the age of five when his mum had overdosed on heroin, his father having disappeared a long time earlier. There was no one else to have him so he'd been shoved in a children's home. After three foster homes hadn't worked out, social services seemed to give up on trying to match him to anyone else and he'd become a permanent resident at the home, ruling the newcomers and the old timers who lived there with him.

At the age of thirteen, he'd started boxing at Steele's Gym. That was where he'd met Leon Steele. Leon had been on the lookout for smart lads like him, he'd said. He'd started to work for him, delivering stuff on his bike – packages, envelopes, phones, even the odd message.

He'd paid him well, looked after him too. Leon was a good person to have on side, and Seth wanted to be an equal to him one day; work alongside him, not for him. But lately, he could sense Leon was losing patience with him. He wondered if it was because he was muscling in on his patch. Well, if he didn't pay him enough, did he think he was going to work for nothing?

He did long enough hours on the doors at Flynn's. That wasn't part of his plan to get in with the Steeles. There was work to be done, money to be made. He wanted to gather together enough to set up on his own, so he didn't have to give Leon a cut of anything. He was old enough and smart enough to do it now. Leon didn't own him. No one told him what to do any more. His reputation as a mean bastard was second to none, he thought.

So he'd have to get his story right about last night if Leon came calling. And get his money back from Luke. He shouldn't have involved him in the first place. Why wouldn't he ever learn?

He looked down when he heard a car door. Shelley had arrived back in a taxi, which meant she'd got some money from somewhere. Seth liked her but wasn't sure he fully trusted her. She was getting far too big for her boots. Just lately he had caught her watching him, staring at him, as if she had some hidden agenda. She'd better not be playing him. If she wasn't careful, she'd be in for a beating too. He didn't care who got the wrath of him.

He took one more drag of his cigarette and threw it to the floor before going back inside.

'Have you found out anything about that man yet?' Seth asked the minute Shelley stepped foot inside the flat.

Hi, love, how are you? Want me to make you a cuppa? She sighed. Had he ever been interested in her, or what she had to offer? Or was it all about what she could do for him? Still, two could play at that game.

'Nothing yet. There was no time when I was alone with her.' Seth paused. 'Are you cooking something for lunch?'

'I bought oatcakes. You want some with cheese?'

'Yeah, ta.'

She went through to the kitchen, sighing again when she saw the mess he'd left it in. Honestly, it was worse than living with a pig at times. She had been the skivvy at her mum's house, knowing if she didn't clean up no one else would, and here she was doing it again. Being with him was harder work than she'd thought.

'Make us a brew too,' he shouted in.

She bet he hadn't moved from the sofa he was lounging on this morning. She wouldn't want to be as lazy as him, having everyone do things for her. She'd be so bored, even though she didn't go to work like he did. He didn't get his hands dirty until at least the afternoon every day. But she supposed he was out until late each night.

She grilled the oatcakes and gazed out of the window while she grated cheese to put on top of them. Through the gap over the concrete railing, she could see there was still police activity outside, which she thought odd given Luke and Ruby's story of it being an accident. Obviously she knew something had happened, but she wondered now if anyone had seen the man running away. She couldn't be the only person who saw him, could she?

She added the cheese to the oatcakes and popped them under the grill again. Tea was made once they were ready and she took everything in to Seth on a tray.

'What are you doing this afternoon?' she asked as she handed it to him. 'Do you fancy coming into town with me?'

'What for?'

'I don't know. A look around the shops? A pint in Wetherspoons?'

'Don't have time. I need to sort out the boys' deliveries before I go to work tonight. Got to be careful now the feds are close.'

'You said you were working this evening, not all afternoon as well.' She gave out a loud sigh.

'Change of plans. I can't turn work down. It's not the done thing, you know that.'

Did she? Maybe she should find time to go to Flynn's and see what he was up to. And if it was what Shelley thought it was, then she would rat him out to the Steele brothers. She had to get her debt paid off as soon as possible. She wasn't going to live from hand to mouth for very much longer. Life may have delivered her a cruel start but she had the power to make the future whatever she wanted it to be.

And really, that didn't include Seth at all. She had her eye on a bigger fish.

FIFTEEN

Grace arrived at Harrison House with Frankie in an unmarked pool car. It was midday, so most of the residents were up and about.

'Let's do the first floor. You take one side of the block and I'll take the other,' she told him as they went towards the communal stairs. 'That way we can see each other if anything kicks off.'

Grace knocked on several doors before she got lucky. A man in his sixties answered from flat 105. He had a face that was in need of a good wash, and half of his breakfast down the front of his stripy jumper; socks on his feet but no slippers.

The smell of cats assaulted her when the door opened and she all but took a step back.

'Staffordshire Police.' She flashed her warrant card. 'I was wondering if you can tell me anything about the incident that took place last—'

'You'd better come in.'

Not offended by his abruptness, Grace went inside.

'Are you moving?' she asked, stepping sideways to get around the mound of cardboard boxes stacked against the wall.

'No, more's the pity. Why would you say that?'

'There's so much stuff.'

'It all belongs to me and everything in them is paid for.' The man picked up a tabby cat that was sitting on top of one of them.

'I don't doubt it. I was just thinking it was a fire hazard.' Grace grimaced, hoping she could get out of here soon. Cat hair, the stench of the animal itself as well as its pee sometimes sent her off on a sneezing fit.

'Sit down if you like.'

'I won't take up too much of your time.' Grace decided to stand after seeing a thick layer of hair on the cushion. 'Can you tell me what you saw, Mr . . .?'

'Wellington. Derek.' He sat down. 'It was before everything kicked off, so I guess around half past six. The news had just finished. I let Charlie out.' He nodded his head at the cat now in his lap. 'That's when I heard the noise. Something was going on in the car park, lots of shouting. It sounded like a fight. But then I heard the woman scream, so I was watching what happened to the little boy.'

'You saw the incident?' Grace queried.

'No, I just saw the boy on the ground afterwards. I was too busy trying to see what the noise was about. There seemed to be some kind of fight and I was worried about my car. It's always getting vandalised down there. Still, that's nothing compared to the poor boy's injuries. I wish I had paid more attention.'

'Yes, it's tragic,' Grace empathised. 'Is there anything else you can recall?'

He paused to think. 'There was a young boy who came screeching in on his bike.'

'A motorcycle or a pushbike?'

'Pushbike. A red one, like a BMX or something similar. Red helmet too, I saw him skid to a halt. He was still for a moment and then he turned around and tore out of the car park.'

Grace nodded. 'Can you describe the boy for me?'

'I'd say early teens. He was small, but he had his scarf wrapped around his mouth. It's so cold out there, and so slippy underfoot. I nearly came a cropper yesterday.'

Grace smiled in sympathy. 'Have you seen the boy before?'

'A few times. He goes to see that Forrester lad.'

Grace's eyes narrowed at the mention of the name. Seth Forrester was someone she had warned her half-niece, Megan, away from last year, after finding out he was trouble.

'Do you know what number he lives at?'

'Somewhere on the other side of floor one at the end, I think. It hasn't been the same since he moved in a few months ago. He has a lot of visitors.'

'Oh?'

'Several men and boys come to the property. And I don't mean he's a pimp either.'

'You think he's dealing?'

'He's up to something.' He coughed to clear his throat. 'Not that you heard that from me.'

'Of course not.' Grace nodded in understanding. 'Do you know his name, the boy on the bike?'

'No, sorry. Although there's a lad who calls often and his name is something like Cain or Kyle.'

Grace took a moment to gather her thoughts while she wrote a few words in her notepad. It was interesting to hear about the visitors to Seth Forrester, something she could look into at a later date. She'd only met Forrester a couple of times but didn't care for him at all.

'You said you've lived here a long time?' She got back on track again.

Derek nodded. 'Twelve years.'

'Do you know the parents of the little boy?'

'I see them around, say hello, that kind of thing. They look decent enough, and the kids are nice. The young girl is really pleasant and good mannered. The boy is a bit of a handful but they are at that age, aren't they? My great-grandson is two and a half and just the same.'

Grace sniffed as the smell of cats began to get to her.

'Do you ever see anything that you perhaps feel uncomfortable mentioning? Like maybe both of them going out together, perhaps the children left alone?'

'That wouldn't go down well with the folks here. They mostly keep themselves to themselves but they'd grass for something like that.' He shook his head. 'But they don't strike me as the type. You can often get a sense of a person after one or two meets, even casually.'

'And you've seen no one around acting suspiciously lately? Apart from visitors to Seth Forrester's flat.'

'Nothing any different from usual. You know these flats. Everything goes on but no one sees anything. But this . . .' He shuddered.

She closed her notepad and stood up. 'Thanks for the information. I may need you to come to the station and give a statement too.'

He nodded. 'I'm tired of certain people bringing this area down. We're not all bad.'

'We don't all tar you with the same brush.'

'Maybe. I just hope I don't get a clout for sticking my nose in.'

'Please contact me if you feel threatened in any way.' Grace handed him a card with her details on it.

'As if that's going to defend me from fists and boots,' he joked.

Grace smiled as she showed herself out. The public – a copper's best friend sometimes and worst enemy at others. Thankfully she had come out of the chat with some intel. She'd pass on the information about Seth Forrester and also ask Sam to check out the CCTV again for her. The lad on the bike could be a potential witness.

2011

Ruby was spending more and more time with Finn. She had started to pull away from her friends, much to Naomi's annoyance. Sometimes Ruby missed her company; other times she just wanted to be with Finn. So when she was with Naomi now, although she enjoyed it, she could sense they were growing apart. She wondered if this was something that would have happened eventually anyway.

After sixth form, she'd gone home to the flat and prepared a meal with Finn. With limited time as he was due at work, they showered together and hopped into bed. Their lovemaking had improved over the time they'd been together. Ruby had come out of her shell, trying things she'd never dared to think of doing up until now. Finn was always gentle with her, teaching her what he enjoyed and learning how she liked it.

But once they were back in the living room, his mood had turned sombre. 'I need to talk to you,' he said.

Ruby had news too, but she didn't know how to tell him. She wasn't sure how he would react. So she let him go first.

'You're at my flat permanently now. Well, I have to tell you about a few people I'm trying to stay away from.'

She looked at him with a frown. 'Stay away from?'

'You know you don't like some of the men who come to visit me.'

Ruby nodded. She didn't like any of them, if truth be told. They always seemed to be either leering at her or having a go at Finn.

'Well, I . . . I'm a member of a gang.' He seemed to spit it out, as if he were afraid to say it aloud. 'I've been trying to leave for a while now but they won't let me.'

'I don't understand.'

'I've done some bad things in my past, Rube. I'm not proud of them but I want out now. It started when I was twelve but now I'm nearly twenty, it's not something I want to be involved with any more. I'm older and wiser and now I have you, I want to live a good life. Not one full of violence and—'

'Violence?' Ruby pulled her head back.

He leaned forwards and planted a kiss on her forehead, as if to negate what he'd said. 'I started hanging around at my local park, you know the one across the grass from my flat? I was lured in by some of the older kids. They told me how much money they were making delivering and collecting packages.'

'You mean drugs?' Ruby suddenly began to feel uncomfortable. It was as if her bubble was about to burst. She knew she and Finn were too much of a dream come true.

He nodded. 'I'm ashamed to admit it, but that was only one of the things I'd do. The older recruits would buy us things – T-shirts, watches, phones, bikes. Then when they had you, you had to do jobs for them and they'd give you money until you were under their control. We also had to dish out violence to anyone who crossed the leader. His name is Dane and he's the worst of the lot. He's beat people up, glassed some in their faces; done worse than that to others. That's why I'm telling you all of this. Because he knows I want to leave and he's been having a go at me for it.'

'Why don't you go to the police?'

He shook his head. 'You don't get the feds involved, Rube. That would land me in even more trouble.'

'But he can't be allowed to rule you. Okay, you were into all that stuff when you were younger but you should be able to leave whenever you want.'

'It doesn't work like that. Dane gets pissed off when anyone tries to. He says we should work for him forever, like we're family. I've tried to get away several times but he always pulls me back. He says I'll owe him forever, which is ridiculous. But if I don't do as he says, he'll send people after me.'

'To hurt you?' Ruby was scared now.

'Yes. I don't know what to do. I really want to leave.'

'Can't you just keep away?'

'I can try but he'll come after me.'

'Then I'll protect you.' It was a silly thing to say but she didn't know what else she could offer.

'If you stay with me, it might get a bit tough until I can cut ties completely.' He cupped her chin with his hand. 'I'm not sure I can handle you being caught up in that.'

'Are you saying that we have to end?' Ruby sat up with a gasp. He was the best thing that had ever happened to her. She couldn't lose him.

'No,' he cried. 'I'm just saying we have to be careful. He might come after you to get back at me. Or he might just have a go at me. I need you to know that I'm trying my best to get out. It's time for me to grow up. I want to be with you, have a normal life.'

Ruby sat still, quiet while she took everything in. Finn was her dream man, her one love, but all that could change in the blink of an eye. Here he was sounding as if he wanted to settle down with her, and she should be happy. But inside, she was terrified and wondering what she was getting herself into. Did she love him enough to stand by him? She looked at him now as he gazed out of the window, thinking of their situation no doubt.

Yes, she did. She would see this through. It was time to tell him her own news.

'Finn,' she said, taking a deep breath. 'I'm pregnant.'

He turned to her sharply. The look on his face changed three times in as many seconds – shock, amazement and then a smile. He came across to her and took her hands, pulling her up and into his arms.

'That is about the best news I can have.' Finn hugged her tightly, almost slow dancing with her. 'I have to get away from him. My responsibility from now on is you, and our little bean.' He waited for her to look up at him. 'You've just made me the proudest man on earth.'

They were the words she wanted to hear. Ruby had been so nervous about telling him. They'd planned to start a family but not until later, not until they were married. Now she couldn't wait to have his baby. They would move if necessary to get him away from Dane. Finn was clever enough to get another job somewhere else. She wouldn't mind that. A chance to start again somewhere; an opportunity to raise the family she longed to have.

SIXTEEN

Shelley had just made a cup of tea when there was a knock at her door. She opened it to find a man in a navy jacket and smart dark jeans, with short red hair. Even if she hadn't recognised him as the woman's sidekick, he had cop written all over him. The woman wanted everyone to join in her meetings and become friends. Like that was ever going to happen in Harrison House. Still, it was nice of her to think of trying, she supposed. Most people in authority seemed to have given up on them.

'DC Higgins, Staffordshire Police.' He held up his warrant card. 'We're looking into an incident that happened last night. Wondered if you saw anything?'

'You mean the commotion in the car park?'

He frowned.

'It sounded like some kids were having an argument, lots of shouting but I didn't see anything.' Then it dawned on her. 'Oh, you're talking about what happened to little Tyler.'

'Yes. Did you see anything?'

'Not until after it had happened. I came onto the walkway when I heard the sirens but he was on the grass then. It wasn't nice to see, although I'm glad it wasn't concrete he landed on.'

'And there was no one else around but the parents?'

Shelley paused. 'I did see someone running across the green. A man, I think. I'm not sure if he had anything to do with it, though.'

'Was that from the commotion in the car park, do you think?'

She shrugged. 'It could be.'

'Did you see what he looked like?'

Shelley shook her head. 'He was too far away.'

'Where did you see him?'

She pointed over his shoulder. 'He ran towards the main road.'

She waited as he wrote in his notebook. Then she smiled at him as he looked at her again.

'Do you know the parents?' he asked next.

'Ruby is a friend of mine. We have coffee every now and then.' She paused. 'What are you fishing for? They're good people. Their kids are always playing out on the walkway. Not downstairs on the grass where most parents dump theirs and don't care if they can't see them to keep an eye on them. Ruby is a good mum.'

'And Lily?' He took more notes. 'What's she like?'

'She's lovely. Such a sweet girl, quite shy really. Nothing like I was at her age, I can tell you.' She grinned but it wasn't returned. 'They're good parents,' she said again.

He gave her a nod and then closed his notepad. 'Thanks. You live here alone, do you?'

'Why? Do you want to come in for a . . . coffee?'

It was fun to see him blush at her intense stare.

'I wanted to know if there was anyone else I could chat to.'

She tutted. 'It's not my flat. It's my fella's.' She turned away from him and shouted. 'Seth.'

'What do you want?' he said as he joined them.

'Police are here, wanting to know if you saw the incident that happened last night.'

'Or even what happened in the car park.' DC Higgins raised his eyebrows in question.

'I was at work.'

'What time would that be?'

'I told you. I saw nothing. Now, if you don't mind, we're busy.' He closed the door in the officer's face.

'What did you do that for?' Shelley snapped as she followed him back into the living room. 'He seemed really nice.'

'He's a fed. We don't trust any of them.'

'*You* don't, more like. I've never had any trouble with them.'

'And what were you telling him about the car park for? The less people know about that the better.' He grabbed her by the arm, his fingers digging into her flesh.

She squealed. 'Let me go!'

'If I find out you've been saying things you shouldn't—'

'I haven't said anything.' Shelley shrugged off his grip and marched into the kitchen with a slam of the door. She rubbed at her arm where he had manhandled her. Then she lit a cigarette. Stuff her no smoking indoors rule. She needed one to calm down. The bastard couldn't treat her like that.

It was so hard, getting enough information for Eddie Steele so that he'd wipe her debt clean. Seth wasn't that bright but he didn't let her in on anything. In the meantime, she had to put up with his moods, the occasional burst of a hot temper, and his paranoia.

She wished she could walk out right now, but she'd give Seth his comeuppance one day.

Grace waved Frankie over and he joined her.

'Anything?' she asked.

'Not unless you can count Seth Forrester slamming the door

110

in my face.' He rolled his eyes. 'I thought he lived here some-where but a woman answered the door. I was chatting to her and then she tells me that it wasn't her flat and that he's in. He didn't want to speak to me though. Said he saw nothing.' He smirked. 'Tosser.'

'Indeed.'

'A couple of people mentioned a commotion in the car park, which seems to have been separate to the fall. From what I can gather it could be kids just mucking around screaming. Oh, and the woman in Forrester's flat said she saw someone running along the path.'

'Any description?'

He shook his head. 'She wasn't sure where he came from either. I'll check it out, though. How about you?'

'Same about the commotion, plus a young lad pedalling away on a bike. Could be something to do with either incident. Also, Forrester's having a lot of visitors, apparently.' She threw a thumb over her shoulder. 'I'm going to grab something to eat from the shop. Do you fancy a break?'

'Sure.'

They took the path that led them to Ford Green Road. Grace glanced up as they went past the spot where Tyler had fallen.

'I can't imagine how much pain that little boy was in yesterday,' she said. 'It beggars belief.'

'I can't stop thinking about him falling either.' Frankie thrust his hands into his pockets. 'Even though I wasn't there.'

'Me too. I guess it will play on our minds for a while.' Grace nodded. 'Which is why we need to get to the bottom of this as soon as possible.'

SEVENTEEN

Once they'd bought lunch, they walked back and sat on the wall at the entrance. Grace looked around. If it weren't for them being there, you'd think nothing had happened the night before. It was such a weird incident. It might never turn out to be a crime. It might always have been an accident. But getting the details that they were after would decide how the case was treated afterwards.

She always liked this stage of investigations. Trying to crack who was lying, and if so, why. People often covered for others too.

'Bloody hell, it's cold,' she said, watching the icy breath from her mouth. 'I thought January was bad but February has been worse. My bum is getting numb already.' She pointed over to the flats. 'If Tyler didn't fall, I wonder if his parents are worried what he will say when he wakes up? I know he won't be able to articulate it all, but he could be anxious.'

'I couldn't imagine Ben being quiet.' Frankie sniggered. 'He'd want to tell everyone about it, good or bad.'

Grace smiled. She could see the love he had for his child, and envy ripped through her. She'd never had the chance to have children with Matt, something they had both been looking forward to until his cancer diagnosis. Now, even with a fledgling relationship with Simon, she felt she'd missed her chance. She wasn't secure enough with Simon, long-term enough even, to want that kind of commitment yet. And she knew he didn't want any more children. If she stayed with him, it meant shelving any dreams of motherhood.

She often looked at other people's children, wondering if she would ever regret missing out on the feel of her own child growing inside her. The sound of its cry as it took its first breath. She pushed the thought away, at times the intensity becoming too much.

She shook her head: where had that little maudlin chain of thoughts come from? She was happy, wasn't she?

Frankie interrupted her thoughts. 'Ruby and Luke seem like normal parents to me, though, boss.'

'Yes, I can see their love for their children.' Grace had told Frankie that Luke wasn't Lily's biological father. 'I still think they're covering up something though.'

'You don't think it was an accident?'

'Do you?'

'No. I guess we'll find out eventually, especially now that he might pull through okay.'

'Which is wonderful news.'

They ate their sandwiches and sipped at the coffees in amicable silence, ignoring the odd stares from residents coming and going. They really didn't like a police presence at Harrison House, even though it was down to the two of them for now.

'I wonder how many illegal things we've stopped happening here since we started investigating.' Grace grinned.

'We've probably upset Seth Forrester. He seems to have a lot of swing around this block of flats.'

'He might think he does but we'll be on to him now it's been brought to our attention.'

'Don't you miss all the murder and mayhem of Major Crimes, Sarge?'

'I can always watch TV or read a novel if I do.' She rolled her eyes. 'Although neither will be true to our jobs or else they wouldn't make good entertainment.'

'You know what I mean. Being on the front line, chasing down the villains.'

'That's what we do here.'

'I guess but what I'm trying to get at is, isn't this all a bit domesticated for you?'

She thought about how to answer him. Yes, it was tame after hunting down serial killers and murderers, but equally, she'd taken a lot of that home with her over the years. It marred you, there was no doubt about that. Sometimes it was easy to compartmentalise something, switch the computer off at the end of the day and never think about it again. But other times, it was really tough. Painful to think about, harder to forget. The nightmares, the images, they all stayed in her head. She had seen a lot in her years on the force, but nothing more than when she'd worked in Major Crimes. How to put all that into words – especially when she didn't want to?

'It's more than a job to us, Frankie,' she decided on. 'I do miss being in the thick of things but I also enjoy what we do too. It's all down to the tiny details. The criminals who slip up, ensuring we're one step ahead. The lying, the deceit. I like digging into all of that.'

'And you can outrun any criminal in Stoke because you do so much running on your treadmill. I think that's a skill in itself.' He laughed. 'So you don't miss your job then?'

She sniggered. 'Not one bit.'

He nudged her. 'Having a cool boss makes everything so much easier for me.'

'Hey, stop crawling just because I bought you a cheese and onion bap and a lukewarm coffee.'

They sat in silence again. She liked that they could, that she felt comfortable enough to do so with him. And she was grateful to have this opportunity to work with him on a closer basis. He was young, had a keen eye and was eager to learn. He would be a great asset to the Major Crimes Team when there was a vacancy. He wouldn't be with her for long.

'Right.' She wiped one hand against the other. 'Let's crack on.'

She spotted a figure walking towards them. She smiled, recognising the stance. It was Simon. He was wearing the thick woollen coat she'd chosen for him when they'd been out shopping the previous weekend, and carrying the same leather satchel which had been part of his attire since they'd met. His dark floppy hair was covered by a thick black beanie hat with the logo on for *Stoke News*, his lips looking a little blue in the bitter cold.

Those lips found a smile for her as he drew nearer.

She'd been lucky to find Simon, even more so to keep him. Their relationship hadn't got off to the best of starts when she'd come to Stoke from Manchester and almost immediately been involved in a serial killer case involving her estranged family, the Steeles. From that day, Simon's line manager had seemed hellbent on getting Grace for something, assuming she was corrupt too. But he had nothing on her.

'Got anything for me?' he asked.

'Nope.'

'I meant food, not intel.'

'Same here. I was starving, sorry. I think you might find a few breadcrumbs if you look closely.'

'See how she treats me?' Simon turned to Frankie. 'I hope she isn't as hard on you.'

'She's a slave driver.'

Grace playfully swiped Frankie on the arm.

Simon sat down on the wall next to her. 'What're you up to?'

'Just trying to find stuff out.'

'No luck, I gather?'

'Hey, ye of little faith.'

Simon waited and neither of them spoke.

'You didn't get much then.'

'Not that we're sharing with you. Unless you have any gossip for us.'

Their banter was comical. They both knew they wouldn't cross the line, but loved teasing each other about it. Many people at the station hadn't trusted Grace when they'd first got together but in time she had won them over. She was loyal to anyone she worked with, and fiercely faithful to Simon. It just took different ways of doing it.

Frankie stood up to go. 'I'll leave you to it.'

'Don't worry.' Simon leaned over to Grace for a sneaky kiss as Frankie sat back down. 'I have to go anyway. People to interview, you know.'

'Now that you can't get your own way.'

'Exactly that. You mean nothing to me otherwise.'

'So you didn't come over here just to see me?'

'Not at all.'

He stood up before she could hit him this time, and walked away laughing.

'You'd better leg it, mister, or I'll be after you.'

Grace sat on the wall for a moment. At least now their relationship seemed cemented. And she loved how he made her feel with a wink of an eye or a smile that made her stomach flip.

In their line of work, it was nice to have a little light within the dark days.

2011

Telling Finn that she was pregnant had been far easier than letting Naomi know. It was a Saturday afternoon and Ruby was in the garden of her friend's home, enjoying the summer sunshine. The sun was high but for some reason the mood was low.

After dumping Gareth, Naomi had been seeing Darius Pickford for six months, so even though things had been icy between them when Finn had come along, now they were both going out with someone they liked. It meant their evenings together were planned and treasured.

Ruby still wasn't comfortable telling her what had happened, but she wanted to share everything with her best friend. Besides, she was bursting to tell someone, especially as she hadn't mentioned anything to her dad yet. She was wondering how to broach the subject as she knew Naomi would be mad. But sitting here in the garden, time was running out before the pregnancy was visible anyway.

'Jeez, I'm dripping.' Naomi fanned a hand in front of her face. She was wearing shorts and a skimpy vest, her arms and legs the colour of caramel after a few days of hot weather.

Realising this might be her cue, Ruby took off her T-shirt. 'I thought I'd show you my bump.'

Naomi looked at Ruby's stomach and then gasped.

'You're pregnant?'

Ruby nodded, and grinned.

But Naomi didn't smile.

'How far gone are you?'

'Fourteen weeks.'

'So when did you find out?'

'For certain? A few weeks ago.'

'You knew all this time and didn't tell me?' The tone of Naomi's voice made it apparent how upset she was.

'I wanted to be sure first.' Ruby clasped her hands over her bump.

'But we tell each other everything.'

Ruby lowered her eyes for a moment. 'I just – I just didn't know how to.'

'Why not?'

'I thought you'd be mad at me.'

'For skipping sixth form all the time and getting pregnant, living in a council flat and going out with a loser?' Naomi laughed harshly. 'Why would I be mad?'

'That's not a very nice thing to say.' Ruby sat up and put her T-shirt on again. 'I never have a go at you and Darius.'

'That's because he comes from a decent family. His dad is a GP and his mum owns her own dental practice. They have reputable careers. Darius will have good prospects.'

'And Finn won't?'

'He wouldn't know where to start.'

'Why are you always attacking him?'

'I'm not.'

'Yes, you are. Is it because you're jealous that I live with him and he drives so we're not stuck in a parents' house all evening unable to do what we want?'

'That's not it, at all.'

'Then what is it?'

Naomi sat up on the lounger. 'He's no good for you, Rube. You've changed since you've been going out with him.'

'No I haven't,' she snapped.

'Yes, you have! Look at you, all on the defensive. You never used to be like that.'

'You're just jealous that I have a man and you have a school-age boyfriend.'

'I'm not. I just hate how everything is so secretive with you now. You could have told me ages ago but you chose not to. You could have even told me that you *suspected* you were pregnant. I would have supported you but you didn't want to tell me.'

'I was embarrassed, that's all.'

'You should be. You're so clever and I thought you wanted to go into physiotherapy? You had plans to go to college.'

'I can still do that.'

'It won't be easy with a baby.' Naomi gnawed her bottom lip. 'I'm not being funny but pregnant at seventeen isn't what I expected from you.'

'Well, that's it, then. Friendship over.'

'Don't be angry with me. I'm worried about you, that's all.'

'Because I'm having Finn's baby?'

'Yes. You're so young. Can't you at least think about what you're doing?'

'You mean have an abortion?' Ruby sat up and swung her legs round to the floor. 'I might go home.'

'No! Let's talk,' Naomi insisted. 'How will you cope? I know I couldn't.'

'I have Finn. I thought I'd have my best friend to help me too, but it seems not.' She stood up.

Naomi followed suit. 'I'll be there for you, you know that.

But if you're with Finn all the time, why would you need me? Besides, he scares me and I'm afraid for you.'

'You're a snob,' Ruby cried. 'He's not good enough for you, is he? That's what this is all about.'

'He's dangerous and I hear lots of things about him.'

'No, he isn't. He's not the man you think he is. He's kind and gentle and . . . and he loves me.'

'I only want what's best for you.' Naomi reached for her hand. 'Please stay for a while.'

'As long as you don't ask me to choose between you because you might be offended at who I pick.'

Ruby lay down again, closing her eyes and pretending to sunbathe. But she was fuming. Naomi had no right to speak to her like that. She didn't understand how much her life had changed, how much she had grown up. How much she wanted to have Finn's baby.

When she left Naomi's house that night, she never went back. Naomi was heading off for university in September anyway. What did she care if she wasn't happy for her?

Except that she did care. Naomi was like a sister. They had shared so much growing up. She was going to miss her. Perhaps things would calm down and they could get over it. But it wasn't going to be her who made the first move.

Back at the flat, Finn was home. He made coffee. 'Did you have a good afternoon?' he asked.

'It wasn't great,' she said, a huge sigh following. 'We fell out when I told her about the baby.'

'Oh.'

'She didn't seem happy for me. I'm sad about that.'

'I know I'm no substitute for Naomi but you don't need anyone else.' Finn drew her into his arms. 'I love you enough for everyone. I can be your best friend.'

Ruby nodded. He was everything to her. Maybe telling her

dad could wait until after the baby was born too. She didn't want to go through that humiliation again.

'I can do girlie things with you.' He flickered his eyelashes. 'I'll paint your nails, do your hair.'

'No you won't.' She threw a cushion from the settee at him. 'That would be my biggest nightmare.'

'Seriously, Rube. We're a team. You, me and the bump.' He placed a hand gently over her stomach. 'I can't wait to see our baby.'

Ruby smiled at him. He was right. He was going to be a dad and she was going to be a mum. In one way, everything would change as soon as the baby was born anyway. Maybe falling out with Naomi was part of both of them growing up, moving on.

She had what she wanted right here.

EIGHTEEN

The news from the hospital was good. Tyler was doing well for now, though they were still running tests and observations. When Luke suggested going home to change, Ruby hadn't wanted to leave, but the consultant had given her the reassurance that their son was stable. They decided to go and pick up Lily together.

Panic began to seep into Ruby as Luke drove them back to the flat. She didn't know what to do, knowing the police would see through her soon. When things started fitting into place – or, rather, were *out* of place – that's when everything would come tumbling down.

Once at Harrison House, she held on to Luke's hand as they made their way to the main entrance. Even though no one knew they were due home, she felt eyes on her everywhere. A ripple of whispers seemed to go around the flats, residents popping heads over the walkways, leaning on the rail.

It was raining a little, a sharp nip in the air, but warmer than it had been of late. There were several vehicles in the car park, the usual residents who didn't go to work or were home from night shifts. Ruby pulled her coat a little closer, unsure whether she was shielding herself from the cold or from the people. The sense of someone watching, being followed, covering her back, would never leave her and it wasn't any different now.

They got inside the communal entrance quickly.

'They're blaming us, aren't they?' Tears slid down her cheeks. 'They don't have to say anything. I can feel it.'

Luke wiped at her tears. 'I don't care. We did nothing wrong.'

He squeezed her fingers a little more as they continued up to the first floor. But Ruby was frightened, scared for her life yet again. She couldn't keep doing this. It wasn't fair.

She was desperate to see her daughter now; to hold her in her arms after the events of yesterday. Before she'd got together with Luke it had been her and Lily taking on the world. There was a strong bond between mother and daughter, and Lily loved her little brother, which was good. Because once Tyler had come home, Ruby would have to make plans for their future. She didn't feel safe now.

They both spotted the detective going door to door on the opposite walkway and quickly went into the flat.

'What is she still doing around here?' Luke hissed as soon as the door was closed.

'I'm not sure. No one saw what happened though, did they?'

'I don't think so. Did they mention a man running away to you?'

Ruby nodded. 'I told them I saw someone but that I couldn't see what they looked like.'

Luke balked and began to pace the living room. 'I told them I didn't see anyone. They're going to think one of us is lying.'

'We were both worried about Tyler.' Ruby made a mental list

of things to take back to the hospital with them. 'No one could blame us for not taking notice of everything going on around at the time.'

'We can't let the police find out that it might have been something to do with us.'

'I'm not lying again!' she cried.

'But—'

'You're going to land us in trouble if you think like that. It's easy to slip up, so we must say as little as possible. I just said I saw someone running towards the main road. It could have been anyone.'

'I suppose. I never saw where he went, did you?'

'No, not after he dropped over the railing himself. And I was desperate to see how Tyler was by then.'

Luke flopped onto the settee. 'He could be anywhere by now.' Then he sat upright. 'You don't think he could be watching the flat, do you?'

'Luke, you're scaring me!'

'But we have to think of the possibilities. This is a nightmare. And we still don't know what we're supposed to give him. Are you sure you didn't recognise him?'

'Why would I know who it was?' Ruby couldn't look him in the eye, knowing she was lying.

'Because I don't. I can't understand why we're being targeted, what he wants.'

Ruby turned to the door. 'I have to fetch Lily. She's been on her own with Norma for too long. She must be worried sick by now. And that Detective Allendale might call and I want to be ready to go as soon as we can. I don't want to leave Tyler for too long.'

'We need to talk to Lily, too. In case the police want to question her, to see what she saw.'

'I'll do it, when we're at the hospital.'

Really, Ruby wanted to get out of Harrison House with her family. Already she didn't feel safe here. The flat certainly didn't seem like home any more. She doubted it ever would again. It had been tarnished.

At least they would all be safer in the Royal Stoke. She hated lying to Luke but surely no one would come after them in such a public place?

Grace saw Perry's car turning into the car park and went across to see him.

'Hey, what brings you here?' she asked as he got out of the driver's side.

'That assault we spoke about this morning, that came in overnight. A young kid named Milo Benton. He's in a pretty bad state, broken ribs and a face full of bruising. I spoke to him with his mum; he told me he was beaten with a baseball bat and that it had happened outside here around six to six thirty p.m.'

'Ah, I wonder if that's the commotion in the car park,' Grace said. 'So there were two incidents happening here last night. That makes sense a little. It's a pity it was so dark. People might have seen more. A lot of the security lighting is triggered by sensors, but there must have been lights over that area on all the time. Did he say who attacked him?'

'It was just the one bloke but he wouldn't tell me his name. Said he'd be dead if he did.' Perry shook his head. 'These kids. They only have to cross each other, never mind double cross each other and they're all fists and knives.'

'Was he scared?'

'You could say that.' Perry held up his hand and shook it vehemently. 'He was that nervous.'

'Can we get to him again? Find out more?'

Perry nodded. 'I was planning to go back. Seth Forrester

likes to use a baseball bat, I'm told. Also, Milo is known to the Steeles.'

Grace groaned. 'In what capacity?'

'Intel says he's a runner for Leon. So I'm wondering if this has anything to do with him.'

'Interesting. Thanks for letting me know, I appreciate it.'

She did too. When she'd first arrived in Stoke, and bowled head first into a case involving her estranged family, Perry hadn't taken to her at all because of it. Now, she had his trust and she liked that he was loyal to her. Despite some initial rumbles from the station that she had been on the Steeles' payroll, things had settled down because it had been clear nothing was going on. She would never be disloyal to the force. Her job was her livelihood. The Steeles weren't family to her. She knew where her loyalties lay.

Her mind getting back to the task in hand, she wondered what the significance of Perry's information would be. More worryingly, it seemed that the Steeles may be rearing their ugly heads again. Would she ever do anything in this city without one of them being involved? The sooner they were brought down, the better. And she hoped to be in the thick of it when it happened. She wanted them off the streets of Stoke.

NINETEEN

Even though Tyler was still unconscious, Ruby had wondered if she should bring Lily in to see him. But her worry that she would be upset was unfounded. Lily said hello to her brother as if Tyler could talk back to her and, after a barrage of questions, had pulled up a chair and read him a story from a book she'd purposely brought with her.

At that moment, Ruby couldn't have been prouder of her daughter. She had her mother's strong will, that was for sure, and it was great to see. Especially when she needed to have a firm talk to her as soon as she could.

After an hour with Tyler, the consultant came over to them.

'I've a bit of good news for you, Mum and Dad,' he said after introducing himself to Lily. 'Tyler's vital signs are good and we're going to bring him out of the induced coma this evening.'

Ruby put a hand to her mouth, still unsure what that would mean. As if reading her mind, the consultant continued.

'If he is able to breathe on his own, we can assess him again then.'

'And if he doesn't?' She pressed her nails deep into the palms of her hands.

'Then we will reassess accordingly. But for now, we remain confident.'

Ruby gulped back a sob but it escaped regardless. Luke reached for her hand and gave it a squeeze.

'If you have any questions, don't be afraid to ask.' The consultant turned to leave. 'He seems to be one lucky boy. Hopefully you'll be telling him to be quiet again soon.'

His smile warmed Ruby's heart and she wiped away her tears. She gave Lily a quick hug.

'Let's go grab some cake from the canteen and bring it back here,' she said.

Lily stood up and Luke reached for Ruby's hand again. There were tears in his eyes too, tears of relief. She wanted to smile at him but realised it wasn't over yet. Not by a long shot.

On her way down to the canteen, Lily chatted away and Ruby carefully picked her moment to talk to her daughter. She'd noticed an indoor children's play area this morning. It was empty as they got to it.

'Let's sit here a moment.' Ruby walked over to a bench and patted it.

Lily sat down next to her.

Now that things were looking better for Tyler, it was imperative that she spoke to Lily, made her understand how important it was to say that she saw nothing. She glanced at her daughter, hating that she had grown up before her time. Ruby had let her down so much because of everything that had happened over the years. They'd constantly been on the move, never settling anywhere, always living in fear.

'What is it, Mum?' Lily asked after they'd sat there for a while.

Ruby wanted to say that this was all her fault. She'd known her past would catch up with her one day. She would have to throw the police off the scent until she could pack her things again and leave. She would have to tell Luke everything now as well, but not until Tyler was home – they needed to get through this trauma first. She had become too safe, too complacent at hiding away, at thinking she wouldn't be found. Now she had to be clever again.

Wiping her tears away, she pulled Lily close once more.

'Lily, I have something to ask you and I need you to be grown-up about it.'

'Is it about Tyler?'

'Yes, what exactly did you see?'

'I was in my room until I heard you screaming. I crept out and looked over the railing when you and Luke ran downstairs.'

Ruby closed her eyes momentarily. Lily was too young to see all this.

'I saw Tyler lying on the grass. He wasn't moving, and I knew something was wrong because he's never still, is he? He wasn't making a noise either. That's when Norma took me into her flat.'

Lily began to cry.

'It's okay, darling.'

Ruby's heart was breaking. How could she let her children suffer so much? Enough was enough. She had to end this once and for all, give him what he wanted.

First, she needed to ask Lily to lie. She didn't feel good about it but it was for everyone's benefit. It would also give her time to think what to do next.

They sat for a moment before she pulled away.

'Okay, poppet, I need you to be brave and trust me. If the police speak to you, I need you to say that you were playing with Tyler, and he slipped out and you didn't notice.'

'But—'

'Please do as you're told!' As Lily's face crumpled, Ruby

hugged her again. 'We'll be in trouble if you don't keep to that story, and you don't want that, do you?'

'What would happen?'

'I'm not sure but I don't want to chance it. I don't want to be apart from you.'

'What do you mean?'

'Nothing, darling.' Ruby stroked the hair on her child's head, hoping to soothe her. It broke her heart to see Lily upset like this. But even though she hadn't voiced it aloud, she had always known that one day they would have to move location again. She hated what her past catching up with her was doing to her daughter. No eight-year-old should have to live in constant fear.

How could she keep putting her children through this? It was more of a prison sentence than he'd got.

For now, she would pretend everything was okay. If Lily kept to what she'd told her to say, the police would stop digging and she could get her children and Luke out of Stoke as soon as they could take Tyler home.

'Remember, Lily,' she whispered. 'I will always love you. And I will always, always protect you.'

TWENTY

Grace knocked on another door, wondering if she was going to get sworn at, or have the door slammed in her face, or be told to mind her own business. Maybe someone might want to talk to her. Perhaps somebody even *saw* something.

Still, at least she and Frankie would have enough by the end of the day to put to Allie in the morning.

'Just a minute,' a voice called out.

The door opened and Grace turned back with a smile. The woman looked to be in her late sixties. Her hair was short and silver grey, and her teeth seemed a bit too large for her mouth. Her eyes weren't smiling but they weren't exactly unwelcoming. Grace could see fear in them, and speculated why.

'Hi, Staffordshire Police. I was wondering if I could have a chat with you about the incident that took place here last night?'

The woman gained her composure and smiled. 'Come on in off the doorstep, won't you?'

As she waited for her to close the door once she was inside, Grace noticed her quickly glance around. She wondered whether the woman was looking to see if anyone was watching.

She went into a pleasant living room and sat when urged to.

There were numerous photos in frames of two young children and two older men. She spotted knitting needles pushed in a ball of Aran wool by the side of the chair, and was immediately reminded of her mum. She used to knit all the time, said it gave her something to do with her hands. Grace wasn't sure her mum's hands had ever stopped shaking since the day they'd left Stoke when she was twelve. She, too, had been scarred by George Steele.

'I'm sure you heard about the incident last night?' Grace began, getting out her notebook. She only mentioned the one occurrence to see what the woman would offer.

'I did, yes. It was a terrible shock. That poor little boy.'

'May I take your name?'

'It's Mary Stanton. You can call me Mary.'

Grace wrote it down. 'So last night? Were you home?'

Mary wrung her hands in her lap. 'I was poorly so I didn't see anything.'

Grace sighed inwardly. She'd been hoping to get something from her but Mary seemed somewhat nervous. Was it speaking to her that she didn't want to get in trouble with the neighbours for?

'It's okay,' she soothed. 'I know what it's like around here, but really, there's nothing to be afraid of. If it was purely that the little boy was playing around and he fell, then that's all well and good.'

'Do you suspect that?' Mary began to scratch her chest, creating immediate red welts.

'It's hard to say what happened without witnesses. I'm sure someone must have seen something though.'

'Not me.'

'Ah, right.' Grace wrote this down, seeming to have come to another dead end. It was then that she spotted the toys in a basket by the side of the settee.

'I look after some of the local kids,' Mary explained. 'I get lonely and I'm known as Granny Stanton. Sometimes the parents need an hour or two to go to an appointment or just to have a break. No one abuses my good nature though,' she added. 'It's just that sometimes I miss a bit of company since my Bill died seven years back. We used to look after the kiddies together then. It was nice. I don't have any family nearby.'

'Have you ever looked after Tyler or his sister, Lily?'

'No, their mother always did a good job of that.' She sat forwards. 'They're good parents. I'm sure no one is at fault.'

Grace nodded her understanding. 'Do you ever see them going out as a couple?'

'Not very often, but then again I'm not staring down and looking around all of the time.'

'I didn't mean that how it sounded.'

'I'm sure you didn't. I wish I could help you more but I didn't see anything. I only came out when Peggy a few doors down told me what had happened. Is he going to be okay? Usually I can hear him screaming as he plays on his bike up and down the walkway.'

'We'll know more later. Did you hear anything last night? There's talk of something else going on in the car park around the same time.'

Mary shook her head. 'No, sorry.'

Grace hadn't missed the blush that had covered Mary's face. 'Okay, thank you for speaking to me.' She stood up. 'In the meantime, if you do hear anything or if there is something you'd like to tell me, please call me.' She got out her contact card and handed it to her.

Once Grace was out on the walkway again, she smiled. 'Thank you. You've been a great help and I—'

'No problem,' Mary cut her short. 'I hope you find out what you need to know.' And with that she closed the door.

Grace moved back, shocked by her sudden departure. She recalled Mary looking around before she closed the front door. It was clearer than ever that she didn't want anyone to see her talking to the police.

She pushed her notepad back into her pocket and went to rejoin Frankie.

Mary sat on the settee, staring at the card she had been given by the detective. She had invited her in so there was less chance of getting seen talking to her. So why then hadn't she told the truth?

She had never spoken to the police before; never thought she'd one day find herself in a position to have to lie to them. She had always been discreet, despite being dragged into all sorts at every opportunity with Peggy.

Mary wasn't a gossip, nor would she ever be. Yet she had kept something from the police and it didn't sit right with her. She wasn't sure she could live with herself if anything happened to Tyler and she hadn't been truthful. She would sleep on it that night, and decide in the morning whether she should tell the police more.

But what if she was wrong?

No, she shook her head, wiping away angrily at her tears. She wasn't wrong. She knew what she had seen, and it would haunt her to her dying day.

Mary played with the card, toying with her conscience. Was she too scared to say anything? That detective was nice. She'd be okay with her. She couldn't go to prison for perjury or whatever they might charge her with, could she?

Because the man involved looked like her neighbour Seth Forrester. Maybe she could use this to her advantage . . .

2012

When she heard the doorbell ring, Ruby pulled herself from the settee. Eight months pregnant now, she was struggling to stay awake. She wondered who it would be this time. There were so many visitors coming and going, so many of Finn's so-called friends. She never liked any of them, especially Dane, and tried to avoid them all as much as possible. Despite Finn's best intentions, he was finding it hard to get away from the gang. Every time he said no, he was given one last job. But it always led on to another.

Ruby didn't like it but she realised he was trying his best. It would take more time than they'd thought but he would be free of them soon. But Finn did say he was doing fewer jobs now, so it was only a matter of time. She sensed his frustration but also his fear. Dane was not someone you should cross so she couldn't blame him for being anxious. She only hoped it was sorted before the baby was born.

She opened the door.

'Dad!' She pulled her cardigan around her to hide her bump, knowing it would be impossible really. But she didn't want him to be disappointed in her. She'd been worried he'd find out the

135

further along she went, yet still she couldn't bring herself to visit and tell him.

She hadn't been home since she'd found out she was pregnant just before her seventeenth birthday. Her dad had rung her several times when she'd first moved in with Finn, but less so over time when she stopped calling him back. Maybe he realised as much as she that they were better off this way. He didn't need to worry about her now, even though he and Finn had never been introduced – she hadn't wanted him to pick fault any more than he had already.

She'd also been anxious that he might try and persuade her not to keep the baby. He'd want what was best for her and would be sad she'd given up her chance of a career, a life of her own. But to Ruby, becoming a mother would be the best job in the world. She loved this baby that was growing inside her and she knew Finn would be a good dad, like her own.

Seeing him standing there, looking shocked as well as embarrassed, all she wanted to do was run into his arms. Yet he couldn't even look her in the eye.

'I wondered why you hadn't come to see me,' he said. 'Edie Bridges told me. She saw you in town.' Edie lived next door but one to her dad.

'I was scared of what you'd say.' Ruby clung on to the door frame, afraid to look him in the eye.

'Can I come in?'

She checked her watch.

'It's okay if he doesn't want me to. I'll be gone in five minutes.'

'He would be fine seeing you here, Dad.' She wasn't lying to him. Finn was always trying to get her to reconcile with her father, even though he was adamant he could take care of her and the baby.

She opened the door wide for him. He went past her, leaning

forward as if to kiss her over her bump and changing his mind at the last moment. She felt a jolt in the pit of her stomach. This was her dad, who until her mum died had been everything to her. Why hadn't she been able to stay close to him? Maybe grief had made them push each other away.

They went through to the tiny living room. The chocolate-brown settee she'd been sitting on stood against one wall, an armchair by the side of the door. The coffee table held a stack of her magazines in a pile and two coasters near to. The wooden fireplace had been painted cream, two photos of her and Finn above it. The picture window looked out onto the main road and a row of council-owned garages.

The flat wasn't much but she prided herself on keeping it clean and tidy. She wondered if he was expecting her to live in a hovel, then chastised herself. He would never think that of her.

'Would you like a coffee?' she asked for want of something to say.

'No, I won't stop long. I just came to give you this.' He reached into his pocket for his wallet and pulled out a few notes.

'I don't need your money.' She shook her head. 'I can look after myself.'

'I'm trying to help.'

'I'm fine.' She rested a hand on her bump. 'We're fine.'

'What has happened to you, Ruby?' A loud sigh followed. 'You used to be my little girl. And now you're nearly eighteen and about to become a mum yourself. I wish things had turned out better for you.'

'What makes you think I'm not happy?' She folded her arms.

'You had dreams to go to college, university.'

'I changed my mind.'

He hung his head down for a moment. 'Was it my fault?' His eyes were glistening when they caught hers. 'Wasn't I there

137

enough for you? I found it hard when your mum died. She did so much with you. I was lost. I'm sorry.'

'You were strict, Dad, but that wasn't it. I just met Finn and fell in love. I'm having his baby. You should be happy for me.'

It wasn't all lies but neither was she content with it all. She hadn't expected to fall pregnant so soon, and so young. But she was determined to make the relationship work, for the baby growing inside her belly. She would look after him or her to the best of her ability.

Dad reached forward and took her hands in his own.

'Come home with me, Ruby,' he begged. 'It isn't too late. I'll keep you safe, help you with the baby. I can—'

'No, I'm staying with Finn. I love him. He loves me and we're happy.'

'Well, if you ever change your mind, whatever time of day or night, you only have to ring. I'll be here as soon as I can. Do you understand? I'm always here for you.'

'I know, Dad.'

He drew her into his arms as best he could. His love surrounded her and she struggled not to cry. It was his way of apologising for things, even though it was too late. She hung on to him for a while until he prised them apart.

'Does he treat you well?' he asked.

She nodded.

'Then that's all that matters, I suppose.' He pulled away completely. 'I'd best be on my way. I'd love to come and see you again, especially when the baby is born but I'd settle for you coming to visit me instead? I miss you, Ruby.'

'I . . . I'll be okay, Dad.' She couldn't promise something she might not be able to do. But surely, it wouldn't hurt her to keep in touch a little?

Ruby watched him as he left, his shoulders seeming to have

the weight of the world on them. They used to be so close. He was beaten – had she done that to him, leaving him alone?

But he had pushed her away too. She realised now she was with Flynn how much losing a person could mean. Her dad hadn't ever got over her mum's death, she could see that now.

She wanted to shout him back but she couldn't. She had made her bed; she had to lie in it.

In the kitchen, her tears came freely. She did love Finn but missed the life she used to have. Everything was so much harder and she was lonely when he was working. Like Naomi had said, it wouldn't be easy with a baby. She'd dropped out of sixth form, unsure of the point in continuing if she was going to have a child to look after. She could always pick college up again when the baby was older.

But the one thing she was certain of, she did love Finn. It was nerves, that's all. Wasn't it?

TWENTY-ONE

When Grace got back to the station, it was four thirty, already dark and bitterly cold. Icy patches were forming underfoot. So much for the weather warming up.

'Any updates?' Allie came over to her as she sat down at her desk.

'Only that there were two incidents. There was an altercation in the car park at the same time as the accident, which Perry is dealing with.'

'Ah, yes, Milo Benton. He's in a bad way, apparently.'

'Him against a baseball bat.' Grace wiggled her mouse to wake up her computer so that she could log on to the system. 'But I don't think it has anything to do with the attack on Tyler Douglas.'

'But that wasn't an accident, though?'

She shrugged. 'Technically if someone didn't keep an eye on Tyler – negligence from the parents. Or something else happened. I want to know who this man seen running away is.'

'If they are involved, the first thing they're going to do is try and cover their backs. So we listen and we watch.'

As Allie went back into her office, Grace checked her emails to see if Sam had found anything yet but there was nothing for her. Sam wasn't at her desk, but she was sure she'd spotted her when she'd come back in.

She took a sip from a scalding mug of coffee and grimaced before putting it down and turning to Frankie.

'We have something going on in the car park, a man running from Harrison House and we have a young boy on a pushbike seen pedalling away, round about the same time Tyler fell,' she said. Then she spotted Sam in the distance.

'Anything useful coming up on CCTV?' she asked as Sam sat down at her desk.

'There's no one coming out on the main road from the path. I can't see everything though – the cameras don't cover that far.'

'But we have two witnesses who said they saw someone and also a tip-off. That's a bit strange. Did you spot anything else?'

'There are several people coming and going. Some went into Harrison House, some came out, and two used the back door to the entrance. I recognise one of them but the quality isn't all that good.' Sam pointed at the screen.

'Isn't that Seth Forrester?' Frankie asked.

'The very same. Handy with his fist and his mouth, and currently out of jail,' Sam explained. 'He's also rumoured to be involved with the Steeles.'

'But nothing on him right now?' Grace asked, trying to hide the blush appearing on her face at the mention of her estranged family.

'No, but I wouldn't be surprised to hear he was involved in the assault.'

'That was mine and Perry's thoughts. He lives in flat 116?' Grace looked at Frankie for confirmation.

'Yes,' he replied. 'With Shelley Machin: she's one of the witnesses who saw the man running away.'

'We need to chat to him. If he lives that close he could have walked past and seen what happened, and be giving us the old "I saw nothing". Frankie and I can pay him a visit tomorrow.'

Caleb hadn't dared go out since the police had issued an alert for a witness to come forward. He'd been keeping an eye on the *Stoke News*, and listening to the bulletins on the radio. The boy on the bike: he knew it was him they were looking for.

But after receiving another message from Seth, he'd had to go out. Seth wanted him to bring the package to him.

He pedalled fast even though most of the road was on an incline, and was in the car park of Starbucks just as Seth arrived in his car. A shiver ran through him when the window went down. Seth curled his finger and beckoned him over. Caleb rested his bike on the side of the wall and climbed into the passenger seat.

'Caleb, my man!' Seth enthused, holding out his hand.

Caleb shook it, half expecting him to grab him and put an arm around his neck. Seth's enthusiasm unnerved him but he kept calm.

'You have something for me?' Seth wanted to know.

He got the envelope out from inside his coat and gave it to him.

Seth checked inside it and smiled. 'That's my boy. Now, tell me, why did you rush off last night? One minute I saw you – the next you were gone.'

'I got scared, that's all.'

'What about?'

Caleb stopped to think. If he said he'd seen what happened, Seth might not like it. But if he let him think he hadn't seen it, would that be any better? He couldn't work out the logistics so he lied.

'I saw you beating up Milo Benton.'

'Ah. Did you see anything else going on? There was some trouble with a boy who went over the side of the railing.'

'No,' Caleb said. 'I saw nothing.'

Seth smirked at his words. 'Okay, okay. Now piss off and I'll be in touch when I next need you.' He handed him a twenty-pound note. 'For your trouble.'

'Thanks.' Caleb took it from him, ashamed he would do so but at the same time unable to refuse. It wasn't the first time he'd realised he was in too deep. It was over now though. He wasn't going near Harrison House nor Seth ever again.

The roads were fairly busy on the way back, the city's evening rush-hour about to start. As he pedalled, his head was full of the conversation with Seth. Would it be best to tell his mum he had lost his phone so he could get one with a new number? She would be mad with him but that would be better than crossing Seth, and at least he didn't know where Caleb lived – as far as he knew.

He freewheeled a little before turning into Minor Crescent, a few minutes from his home. It was a narrow road, cars parked either side, a blind bend ahead of him. The street lights gave out ample light as he pedalled along.

A blast from a horn made him jump. He saw a car behind him and flicked up his middle finger. He had every right to be on the road and it was wide enough for them both. Once he'd got past the parked cars, he could get on the pavement out of the way.

He turned his head slightly when he heard the car revving up behind him. Then he heard it again, but this time it was louder. The car was coming at him!

He looked to see if he could squeeze between two parked cars and get onto the pavement but the gap wasn't big enough.

The driver continued to rev the engine behind him. It was inches away from him.

'Watch out, you dickhead!' he shouted. Out of the seat, pedalling hard, he caught a glimpse of the driver just as the car bumper rammed into the back wheel of his bike.

Caleb was thrown into the air and over his handlebars, the bike smashing to the ground. He landed with a thump, rolling with the momentum. Finally finding a bit of clear pavement, his thick coat and gloves took the brunt as he slid to a halt against a garden wall.

He cried out in pain, lifting his head to see his leg at an awkward angle underneath him. Only now did he realise how important it was to wear a helmet. It wasn't cool, and it messed up his hair, but it could have saved his life if he'd hit his head on anything.

Then he saw headlights flash on full beam. He could see the car sitting with the engine idling. A screech of tyres. The car mounted the kerb and came at him. He put up his arms and screamed. But before hitting him again, the vehicle dismounted the pavement and drove off.

A man was running towards him from one of the houses nearby.

'Are you okay?' He bent down level with him. 'I saw what happened but didn't get a number plate. The car was too fast. I'll call for an ambulance.'

'No!' Caleb screamed. 'No ambulance. Please, I need to get home.' He tried to move the injured leg, but the pain was too much and he turned to the side to vomit.

'You're in no fit state to move,' the man said. 'I'm calling the police too.'

Caleb wanted to protest about that as well but he couldn't. He knew he needed help, no matter what the consequences. The bastard had probably broken his leg.

Worse, he knew that had been a warning. He could have been crushed up against the wall. He could have had his legs run over. He'd been lucky, although right now, he didn't think so at all.

Because the driver had been Seth Forrester.

TWENTY-TWO

Ruby was drained as they parked at Harrison House. It was getting dark, she was tired and emotional after spending time with Tyler, and they only had an hour before they were going back to see him again. It seemed as though life was on hold as they waited to see how he was. As if they were living in a bubble.

A sense of dread crept up her spine as she felt eyes on her once again. She looked across the way to the path that led to the main road. She tried not to gasp aloud as she saw a man standing stock still, in full view, hands in pockets, coat collar turned up.

It was him.

She tried to still her panic as she walked upstairs with Lily's hand in hers, Luke coming up behind them. How would he feel knowing the truth? She couldn't begin to understand how it would hurt him.

Because everyone was going to find out pretty soon that she was lying about knowing who the man was. But she couldn't bring herself to tell Luke, nor the police; not after what she had done and the real reason he was coming after her.

Had *kept* coming after her all these years.

Luke was opening the front door now, his back to the outside. She looked to the man again. He hadn't moved an inch.

He was watching her; he was watching her family, and he wanted her to know. She thought he might have left after what had happened to Tyler. But he was still here, right in front of her.

She lowered her eyes, pretending that she hadn't seen him while she gathered herself. Now she knew he had stayed in Stoke after what he'd done to Tyler, he could be after hurting them all. And he wouldn't stop until he got to her this time.

She shouldn't give in to him but she couldn't stand up to him either. She was on her own again. Getting away was the only way to go now. If she didn't, he would kill her.

She was sure.

It was half past eight and Mary was trying to watch a rerun of *Midsomer Murders* but her concentration wasn't the best. Ever since she had spoken to the police, she'd been on edge. So the banging on the door had her jumping in fright. She never had visitors this late in the evening.

She went to answer it, putting on the chain before she opened it. There was someone with their back towards her.

'Yes?'

He turned around and she gulped when she saw his face.

'I'm not going to cause you any harm,' he said. 'But if you don't let me in, I will break down the door. There's no one around now to help you.'

Mary faltered. She didn't trust him not to follow through with his threat. It would take her a long time for a response from the police if someone was sent to her, and that was if she got the chance to make the call. He could have done all sorts to her by then.

She didn't trust him. 'I can't.'

'Best make it quick, then.' He slid a small padded envelope through the gap.

'I don't want it.' She shook her head. 'I saw nothing.'

'That's good to hear!' Still he pushed the envelope at her. 'Take it,' he urged when she froze.

'No.'

He glared at her for a moment and then posted it all the way through the gap at the side of the door. 'Five hundred pounds. That'll get you a nice holiday. Make you forget what you saw, what do you say?'

'I keep telling you. I don't want your money.'

'Call it compensation. I give you that and you keep your mouth shut and your big nose out of my business. You get me?'

She nodded her head vehemently, knowing it would end badly if she didn't.

He pulled up his shoulders and smiled. 'Good, we are at last in agreement. I'll be seeing you around, Mary. It's imperative you keep to your story now, okay?'

'I saw nothing.'

'There's a good girl. And not a word to anyone otherwise.'

He stared pointedly at her for a moment before finally walking away.

Mary closed the door, pushing the bolts across top and bottom. She couldn't believe he'd gone without so much as putting a hand on her. She realised she wouldn't be so lucky the next time.

Her breath calming, she took the envelope through to her bedroom. She pulled out the clothes in the second drawer of her cabinet, shoved it at the back with the rest of them and covered it over.

It wasn't the first time he'd made her take money from him. It was the fifth envelope he'd given her over as many months.

Five hundred pounds each time, whenever he thought she'd seen something that would threaten his livelihood. But she hadn't spent a penny of it.

He had to be setting her up for something. Why would he be giving her more money rather than just a warning to keep her mouth shut? Maybe it was time to get rid of it all.

WEDNESDAY

TWENTY-THREE

It was half past eight when Grace's desk phone rang that morning. She took the call and then turned to Frankie.

'One of the residents of Harrison House who I spoke to yesterday has come in to see me,' she said. 'Mary Stanton, flat 108.'

Frankie moved his chair slightly so he could see around his monitor comfortably. 'Did the duty sarge say what about?'

'No, but Mrs Stanton was cagey yesterday, as if she needed to tell me something yet didn't want to say too much for fear of what might happen.' Grace grabbed her lanyard with her ID card attached to it and placed it around her neck. 'Best go and find out.'

'Want me to come with you?'

'I think she'll be more comfortable speaking to just one of us.' She grabbed her jacket from the back of her chair. 'I won't be long.'

Downstairs, Grace went into the soft interview room, which they used to help people feel more at ease. There was a settee and two armchairs, a coffee table and a few knickknacks: a potted plant that was in need of water, an imitation Monet framed photo and a *Game of Thrones* wall calendar.

Mary was sitting in one of the armchairs, her hands in her lap. She wore a thick black coat, the scarf around her neck tucked into its collar. Sensible boots on her feet.

'Hi, Mary,' Grace greeted as she sat down across from her on the settee. 'You wanted to see me?'

Mary said nothing at first so Grace thanked her for coming. She could see a shake to her hand and her eyes racing around the room, landing anywhere but on her own. What was she so worried about?

'Mary, is there something you want to tell me?' she began again. 'Did you see what happened to Tyler Douglas?'

'I'm not sure.'

'Oh, I can imagine. I don't think I'd be too sure from that distance either.' Grace smiled kindly.

Mary ran her fingers across her bottom lip.

'It seems a few people saw a man running along the path in the direction of the main road. Is that what you saw?'

Mary nodded fervently. 'Like I said, I can't be certain. But I think . . . I think it was Seth Forrester. Although someone told me there was a fight in the car park too.'

'Seth Forrester?' Grace sat forwards immediately. Could this link him to either incident? She sat quietly, wondering if Mary would offer anything else. But the woman stayed quiet.

'Did you see him on the walkway before the accident, Mary?'

'I . . . I don't think so,' she said. 'But then again, I'm not always looking.'

'But you were when Tyler *fell*?' She emphasised the last word purposely.

'I was at the kitchen window,' Mary said quickly. 'I can't see everything from there.'

'Can you see the path?'

'Well, no. I . . .'

Grace realised that Mary had sensed she knew she was hiding something.

'It doesn't matter if you didn't tell me everything when I visited yesterday,' she tried to reassure her. 'I just need to know what happened. Did you see anyone hurt Tyler Douglas?'

Mary looked pained when she spoke. But finally she nodded. 'Yes, I don't think it was an accident.'

'Why do you say that?'

'I saw Seth on the walkway, and then I saw Tyler on the ground. I don't know what happened in between. I only looked away for a second.' Mary nodded. 'Seth was outside the flat where the little boy lives. I saw the boy run into his arms and he picked him up. I saw his parents talking to Seth. And then I must have looked away for a second and the next thing I know, the little boy was on the ground.' Her eyes filled with tears. 'I don't know what happened. But I will never forget the screams of his mother for as long as I have left to live.'

Grace had been taking notes but stopped. Was the incident about to turn into a serious crime? She hadn't thought for a moment that anyone outside of the family would be to blame. It seemed unbelievable that someone could do that to a helpless child. And for what reason? For now, she decided to rule out a few things.

'Did you see a little girl there?' she asked. 'Tyler has a sister.'

Mary shook her head. 'She wasn't on the walkway.'

'And you're certain you saw both parents?'

'Yes. I'm sorry I didn't tell you straight away.'

'There's no need to apologise. You came to us today and I'm sure this will be a great help. Is there anything else you'd like to add?'

'No.'

Grace wasn't convinced. 'You're sure it was Seth Forrester that you saw?'

Mary shook her head, as if now having second thoughts.

'Well, I can't be one hundred per cent certain. There was a pillar in the way, but it did look like him.'

'If he's causing you problems, I can have a word with him. I can also speak to Trent Housing Association. I could—'

'No, no.' Mary stood up, checking her watch. 'There's nothing else.'

'Okay, I'll write this up as a formal statement and you can sign it and then be on your way.'

'I have to go now – a doctor's appointment, you see.'

'Well, you can come back and sign it for me at a later date. I could bring it to you but I don't want to antagonise anyone.' By that, they both knew she meant Seth Forrester. 'I'll call you once it's done.'

Grace showed Mary out but back at her desk she thought on her words. There were so many contradictions that nothing she said could really be used. But why had Mary only just thought to tell her about seeing Forrester? And why the almost change of heart when she did eventually say something? Was she afraid of Seth for some reason?

Perhaps there was more to this. She needed to do some digging.

2012

Ruby woke up with terrible cramps in her stomach. She'd hardly slept at all for the past few nights – her due date for the baby was four days ago. It was two a.m. Finn wasn't home. She tried his phone over and over until eventually she could stand the pain no more.

As she got out of bed and into the bathroom, her waters broke. After trying his phone for a final time, leaving an irate message, she called for a taxi.

Having no one with her was the loneliest she had ever felt in her life. She didn't have a birthing partner – no friend, no mum and she couldn't ask her dad to come, even if she had kept in touch with him. She wanted someone to hold her hand, rub her back, say soothing words to her. She was so scared, so uncertain. Luckily she had a terrific midwife whose patience and soothing calm were second to none.

'Come on, Ruby,' she coaxed. 'You can do this.'

'I can't!'

'You can.'

'No, I really can't.'

'Let's get this baby out into the world.'

Ruby grimaced and groaned as she pushed again, holding on to the midwife's hand. 'I can see the head,' the midwife said, as Ruby shed tears of joy intermingled with pain and frustration. 'Not long now, Ruby. Just one or two more pushes, there's a good girl.'

Ruby took a few deep breaths and pushed again. Minutes later, another push and then it was all over as she heard her child take its first breath, crying out as it entered the world. She had never heard anything so sublime.

'You have a daughter and everything is looking well. Congratulations.'

Ruby cried as much as her baby, but this time they were tears of relief. The baby was handed to her and she stared in wonderment at what she and Finn had made. Her daughter, her beautiful baby girl. They had chosen Lily for her name. She had her mum's eyes, her dad's chin. She reached for her phone and took a photo of her, then sent it off to Finn.

Lily screwed up her tiny face and tried to scream but it came out as a snuffle. Both mother and child were exhausted.

'I'm going to take care of you, Lily,' she whispered. 'I'm going to be the best mother you could wish for. I'm going to—'

The door to the room burst open and Finn came rushing in.

'Rube,' he cried, holding a large teddy bear. He kissed her long on the lips and then placed his hand on Lily's head. 'Oh my, she's beautiful.' He glanced at her. 'I'm so sorry I couldn't get away. That bastard Dane wouldn't let me finish. I couldn't even sneak out as he was with me the whole time. I told him you were in labour too.'

'You didn't answer your phone.'

'I had to put it on silent. I was in charge of a poker game.'

'You said you would keep it on because I was due.'

'It doesn't matter.' He kissed her lightly on the forehead.

'Because things are going to change from now on. They have to.'

Ruby wasn't so certain of that. Over the past few months, Finn had tried to distance himself from Dane and his cronies and nothing seemed to have worked. He'd come home several times with black eyes and bruising to his torso but he'd laughed it off, saying someone had tried to force their way into the club while he'd been on the doors. She knew it wasn't that. Dane wouldn't let him leave, wouldn't let him walk away. It was as if he took great pleasure in making Finn suffer.

Yet she couldn't help but smile at him as he took Lily from her and held her in his arms.

'She's perfect,' he whispered, running his finger across her cheek. 'Just like her mother.'

Ruby nodded in agreement. Maybe now he had seen her, maybe now he was a father, he would be there for them. Being a dad would suit him.

'No matter how hard it will be, I'm quitting,' he said as he handed Lily back to her. 'I promise we'll find a way to get away from Dane, as a family.'

'That's right.' Ruby rested her hand on the side of his face. 'We are a family. And not even Dane can spoil that.'

TWENTY-FOUR

Shelley was on the doorstep having a cigarette when Luke came out of his flat with Lily. She bobbed back inside so he wouldn't see her but as soon as he was off the walkway, she closed her front door and walked along to flat 114.

Ruby answered soon after her knock. She wore no make-up and her hair needed washing, which would have been unusual had she not got a child in hospital.

'You looked wretched.' Shelley's shoulders dropped. 'Is there anything I can help you with?'

'Not really.'

Ruby let her in and she followed her through to the kitchen.

'How's Tyler?'

'Doing fine, thanks. He's been brought out of the coma. He woke up but he wouldn't settle. We were there until eleven last night but thankfully he was sleeping when we left. Luke's gone to take Lily to school and run a few errands before we head back. I'm exhausted but I'll be at the hospital soon.' Ruby yawned as she flicked on the kettle. 'I've just made a coffee. Would you like one too?'

'Thanks, that would be great. How's Luke coping?'

'Not good. He's edgy all the time.' Ruby sighed. 'Can't say I blame him. This whole thing, it's a nightmare.'

Shelley wondered how to play it. Maybe she should just blurt it out, see if Ruby denied it.

'Do you want to tell me what really happened on Monday?' she started. 'I was having a cigarette in the doorway and I saw it all.' It wouldn't hurt to fib a bit to get the truth out of her.

Ruby almost spilt scalding water over herself as she missed the mug she was pouring it into.

'Hey.' Shelley moved towards her.

'You won't tell anyone, will you?'

'Of course not! It must have been awful, though. Do you know him?'

Ruby shook her head. 'How could anyone do that to a child? Tyler was so helpless.'

Shelley's ears pricked up. She wanted to know more but had to tread lightly for fear of giving the game away that she hadn't *actually* seen everything.

'I thought he might have been one of Seth's men but I didn't recognise him,' she said. 'But I don't think any of his cronies would hurt a child. Do you think it was intentional?'

'I'm not sure. Tyler was wriggling so much.'

Shelley stayed calm. Was she saying the man had dropped Tyler purposely? What kind of an animal did that?

Ruby picked up the mugs and they moved through to the living room.

'So you don't think it had anything to do with Luke, then?' Shelley posed the question tentatively.

Ruby turned to her sharply. 'Why would you say that?'

'Well, it can't be to do with you, can it?'

'No.' Ruby looked away for a moment. 'Luke's a good man.'

'I like him,' Shelley said. 'From what I know of him, he's pretty decent.'

'He's a diamond.' Ruby paused. 'Earlier you said . . . why would it be one of Seth's men?'

'I didn't think it was my place to tell you.' Shelley put down her mug. 'Seth's been calling to see Luke a lot lately.'

'I knew it. I . . . I think he's been borrowing money again. I asked him about it earlier in the week. I wanted to know if he'd run up more debt but he said he hadn't.'

'Did you believe him?'

Ruby shook her head.

'Oh, Ruby. I know he is. There's not much I miss when I'm at home. It's always good to keep ahead of Seth if you can. When did he last come to your flat?'

'Monday afternoon. He wanted to see Luke but he wasn't home. I had to tell him to ring Seth as soon as possible. I went ballistic when Luke got home, but he denied it all.' She bit her bottom lip before continuing. 'Luke told me Seth worked for the Steele family, and that you don't want to cross them. Is that right? Who are they?'

Shelley's eyes widened at the mention of the Steeles.

'What?' Ruby queried.

'You've never heard of them?'

Ruby shook her head.

'They're one of Stoke's criminal families. There are two brothers and there was a sister but she's been jailed for murder. Eddie and Leon are a law unto themselves. They do what they want, when they want.'

'Oh no.' Ruby clutched a hand to her chest.

'I hope they have nothing to do with this.' Shelley shook her head. 'They don't take prisoners. Seth works for Leon. He's the younger of the two brothers and worse than Seth.'

'What do you mean?'

'They come down heavy on people if they don't pay their debts off pretty sharpish.'

'But Luke doesn't owe money to Leon.'

Shelley raised her eyebrows. Things were getting interesting. Ruby paled.

'Seth is his debt collector,' Shelley explained.

'How do you know?'

'I do the books for Seth.'

'The *books*? You mean like an accountant?'

'Don't look so shocked. I do have exams in maths and English, you know.'

'I didn't mean—'

Shelley waved the comment away with her hand. 'I just do the adding and subtracting.'

'So you know how much everyone owes?' Ruby's eyes widened.

'I do, but I'm really sorry, I can't tell you anything.'

'Please! We're broke. I need to know.'

Shelley shook her head and got up. 'You'll have to talk to him. I've said too much already.'

She got to the door before Ruby spoke again.

'Thanks, Shelley,' she said.

'I'm glad you know now.'

'Yeah, me too.'

Shelley walked back to her flat. Even though she hadn't learned a lot, she couldn't help feeling sorry for Ruby. In better circumstances, she could see them being great friends. Ruby was a real sweetheart. She seemed kind and loyal, like she would look after you. She supposed that was the mothering instinct in her.

And it would be nice to have one good friend. Shelley had plenty of acquaintances around Harrison House but no one to call a bestie, someone she could share everything with and know it wouldn't go any further. Her mate Mandy was okay but she didn't trust her that much, and there wasn't anyone else remotely possible. Stoke was a funny place for that. Split into six towns, your friends were often where you lived. People frequented local pubs, worked nearby and knew each other. Even moving a few miles away had left her with no one but Seth and a few of his friends' girlfriends who she didn't much care for.

But Ruby was gullible, even though she seemed savvy. Seth wouldn't let her near the books.

Seth wasn't going to be very happy about this when she told him. Luke could kiss goodbye to ever feeling safe again, unless he paid his loan off, which she knew he wouldn't be able to do if they had no money. That was the nature of the beast: borrow, not be able to pay back, borrow more, repeat and then repay the debt in other ways. Which meant being drawn into the criminal world.

Still, Seth would be pleased with the information she'd acquired, which might keep him off her back until she'd found out more about where *he* was getting the money from.

Ruby sat on the settee, contemplating her next move. She'd hated confiding in Shelley, didn't trust her as far as she could throw her. Although she was always nice to her, she was Seth's girlfriend and he was shifty. She avoided him as much as possible. But she'd had to see if her notions about Luke were true.

Finding out they were had been bittersweet.

Had he started to gamble again? That would explain his agitation when she'd told him Seth had called last week. Luke had promised he wouldn't get into more debt. There was at least one casino in Stoke she knew of, but then, there was bound to be one in every city. He had been getting in late on a few occasions, but he'd always blamed that on his work.

On top of everything else, this was the last thing she needed so she would have to park it for now. Her children were her top priority at the moment. She loved Luke so much, and she would eventually voice her thoughts, but he was the least of her worries right now. He could look after himself, to a certain extent.

But she wouldn't be letting him get away with it, once she had time to deal with it.

TWENTY-FIVE

Grace was coming out of the supermarket before a visit to Harrison House, her arms full of sweet treats to take back to the office, when she almost collided with a man in her rush to get out.

'I'm so sorry,' she said. 'My fault. Are you—'

'Nice to bump into you, Grace. Literally.'

Grace looked up and groaned inwardly. It was her half-brother, Eddie Steele, with her sixteen-year-old half-niece Megan. She and Eddie hadn't been on friendly terms since she'd come back to Stoke. Him being part of a criminal fraternity was not something she was comfortable with even if she wasn't a serving police officer. Besides, there were units at the station looking into their activities and she didn't want to jeopardise anything.

It never failed to amaze her just how alike she and Megan were. They were both slim build, with long dark hair. Each had deep-set eyes and full lips, though Megan wore way too much make-up for her liking, accentuating everything that Grace didn't, and she was wearing the latest fashionable gear.

Eddie, too, had the same eyes and mouth. He reminded her of their father the last time she'd seen him. That was bittersweet.

Be nice, Grace.

'Hi!' She smiled, not really wanting to stop and talk. 'How are you both?'

'That's the most civil thing you've said to me since you arrived in Stoke,' Eddie smirked.

'Stop it, Ed.' Megan nudged him. 'Or she might leave quickly. Do you have time for a coffee, Grace?'

'I . . .' She was completely stuck for words. Although she and Megan had left things on good terms the last time they'd seen one another, it was a long time ago now. It was disappointing in one way as she would like to get to know Megan better, but good in another as it meant she could keep away from the family. Work and pleasure definitely didn't mix in this combination.

'No, sorry, I really don't.' She hoped she sounded disappointed about fobbing them off.

'Another day, perhaps?' Eddie moved aside as a woman came past with a trolley.

'Perhaps.' Grace stayed non-committal. The shopping she had in her arms began to slide out of control and she managed to do a rendition of a juggler before some of it crashed to the floor.

'I should have got a bag,' she muttered as they all bent down to pick things up.

'Ginger nuts!' Eddie grinned, handing her the packet. 'My favourite.'

Why was it that it felt like even if he was being nice it sounded as if he was taking the piss? She never knew if Eddie was being genuine or not, a thing she reckoned he felt the same of her. She wondered if they'd ever get to just like each other for sharing a brutal beast of a father, or if his chequered past and her job would always get in the way.

'I'd best be off,' she said as soon as they'd piled her arms high again.

'Let me see you to your car,' Eddie suggested.

'I'm fine.'

'It won't take a moment,' he insisted. 'I'll meet you inside, Meg.'

'Okay.' Megan nodded. 'Nice seeing you, Grace.'

'You too,' Grace replied, that bit at least genuine. After getting to know Simon's daughter over the past few months, she felt she was at one with teenage girls now.

She was probably nothing of the sort.

Eddie grinned at her as they crossed the car park towards her car, and she realised they were still wary of each other. It made sense, she supposed. For now, it was the way it had to be.

At her car, he took the shopping from her arms again and, almost awkwardly, she got her keys out and opened the boot. He placed the groceries inside, next to all of her police paraphernalia.

'Thanks,' she said, waiting for it. He was bound to want something as he hovered around.

'Grace, I—'

'Don't tell me, you need a word.' She slammed the tailgate down.

'You know me so well.' He laughed.

They both looked to their right when a horn blasted and someone gave a pedestrian an angry gesture as they walked in front of their vehicle.

'What do you want this time?' she said, turning back to him.

'It's not what I want but something I need to tell you. It's about Seth Forrester.'

'Oh?' He had her full attention as he continued.

'He lives in Harrison House, where that little boy fell over the side of the walkway.'

'Yes, I know.'

'Such a shame that happened. I hope he's okay.'

Grace noted his seemingly genuine tone of concern. 'As far as I'm aware, he's stable.'

166

'Good. But Seth . . . I hear he's lording it up, saying he beat someone up that night with a baseball bat.'

Grace displayed her poker-face, recalling details from her earlier conversations with Perry and Sam. 'And why would he tell you that?'

'Showing off, innit.' He laughed. 'He's quite good at picking on people who're younger or less able than himself. That's the coward's way if you ask me.'

'So who is he supposed to have beaten up?' Grace was all ears.

Eddie shrugged. 'He didn't brag that much but I got the impression he knew more than he was letting on.'

'Why?'

'Gut feeling.' Eddie paused. 'Perhaps you could have a word?'

'Thanks for telling me how to do my job,' she said as she raised her eyebrows.

'Just doing my duty as a loyal citizen.'

'Even if you have only bumped into me by chance?'

'I can hardly call in to see you.'

'You *can* always leave me a message at the station.' She moved round to the driver's door. Before opening it, she turned back to him. 'Thanks for that. I'll check it up. Rumours have a nasty way of being true.'

'I'd best be getting back to Megan.' He rolled his eyes. 'If I know her, she'll have put half of the clothing aisle in the trolley by now.'

Grace smiled. 'It's good to see her happy.'

He nodded, waving as he walked off. 'I'll see you around.'

Grace watched him go for a few seconds, standing still. If only things had been different, she would have family of her own. Sadness fell upon her. She almost wanted to shout him back, invite him to her place to have a drink with Simon and Teagan. Then she sighed and got into her car. How laughable was that? It wasn't going to happen. He was part of the Stoke criminal network that she would never condone. And while he might be nice on the surface to her, she was well aware of the things he was linked to, scrapes he had got himself into. She wouldn't want someone like that in her life anyway. Which is a shame, as she would have liked to spend more time with Megan.

She started the engine and drove off; at least she might now have a lead. It was imperative she spoke to Forrester to see what he had witnessed – or done. Because he hadn't come forward with that information. He clearly wanted to protect himself.

Yet she couldn't help but wonder, had Eddie given her the name deliberately to throw her off the scent of something else? Was he setting her up? It seemed too easy, even if she had bumped into them by chance.

Or was she overthinking things because of their relationship?

At Harrison House, she made her way across to Seth Forrester's flat but there was no reply when she knocked. She pushed through a contact card with a note asking him to ring, but she doubted she'd get a response. She'd head over there again that afternoon, try and pick him up then.

Her phone rang. It was Frankie.

'Hit and run you might want to know about, Sarge. Minor Crescent, a lad by the name of Caleb Campbell was knocked off a red BMX yesterday around four p.m. Someone at Harrison House mentioned seeing a boy on a bike, didn't they, with a similar name?'

'Yes. Where is he now? Do you have an address?'

'I do but I doubt he'll be at home. He was taken to the Royal Stoke on blue lights, admitted to a ward with serious injuries.'

2012

Ruby was in her element as a mum and, since Lily had been born, Finn was playing the doting father to a tee. Nothing was too much trouble. Ruby had half expected him to leave her to do it all, but he'd surprised her by wanting to help out as much as possible.

Lily was three weeks old and it almost seemed like it had happened in a flash. Ruby was kneeling next to her, changing her nappy on the mat on the floor as Lily kicked out her feet.

Finn came into the room with his coat on. He glanced at her sheepishly, picking up his car keys.

'Where are you going?' she asked.

'I have to do a job with Dane.'

'I thought you weren't doing any more.'

'It's only the one.'

She wasn't happy with him doing anything for Dane at all. Things hadn't gone smoothly when he'd tried to leave again. She recalled the way he'd arrived home after another beating two days after Lily had been born. She'd told him she wanted to move out of the area straight away and they'd had a row.

Even though he said they would leave, Finn was still too scared to cross Dane.

'What will you be doing?' She lifted Lily and held her against her chest.

'I'm only going to be the driver, the lookout.'

'But what if you're caught? I'll be left with Lily on my own and you won't see your daughter growing up. I don't want you to go.'

'I have to. Can't you see? I have no choice.'

'Yes, you do.' She picked up Lily and held her close. 'You said we would move. He wouldn't find us then.'

Finn shook his head. 'You don't know him like I do. He likes the chase, and then he likes what he does to you. I've seen what he's capable of first-hand. It's best I do as I'm told.'

'But you said—'

'Please, Ruby. Leave it.'

She tried to make him change his mind, to the point that they argued again, but he'd still gone. Ruby sat in distress all night until he came home. His face told her things hadn't gone to plan.

'It's all gone pear shaped,' he said as he stood in the doorway, resting his back and head on the frame. 'I fucked up big style.'

'What do you mean?'

'I was supposed to be the lookout. It was quiet, dark, no one around. So I got out my phone to ring you. I spotted Lily on my home page and started flicking through images of her, photos I'd taken. I was so engrossed I missed the police car until it was too late. Mikey Stuart got arrested. He's Dane's right-hand man. If he goes down, I'm for it.'

'Will he say that you were there? You're not going to get into trouble, are you?'

'This isn't about me! He got caught because I messed up. I

wasn't paying attention and they all know. I'm in for another kicking.'

'They can't do that. We won't let them in.'

'I'll just have to take it.' He pulled her into his arms.

'I know you don't want to hear it again, but we can't keep living our life in fear of Dane. Let's just get out of here before they catch up with you.'

When Finn said nothing, Ruby began to cry. She wasn't sure what Dane and the others would do to him and she didn't want to ask for fear of what Finn might say.

'I messed up, Rube,' he spoke, eventually. 'Not you. Let them do what they have to. I'll get over it. Because I'll still have you and Lily. They can't take you away from me.'

He planted a kiss on her lips and she cuddled into him on the settee. But with the threats hanging over them, it was hard. Finn was her life; she didn't want anything to happen to him.

TWENTY-SIX

Caleb was sitting up in bed when Grace located him on ward 17. There was a woman sitting next to him who she assumed was his mum, owing to the likeness. Like Caleb, she was blonde, but her hair was long to his short-cropped style. She was thin, attractive and hard to put an age on. Mid-thirties, if Grace hazarded a guess.

The nurse pulled the curtain around them for privacy and then left them to it.

'Mrs Campbell?' Grace showed her warrant card. 'I'm DS Allendale. If it's okay with you, I'd like to ask Caleb a few questions about what happened yesterday.'

'You should be out looking for the idiot who did this,' the woman said. 'I can't believe this has happened. He might need an operation and plates in his leg.'

'I'm sorry to hear that. But if I can have a quick chat with Caleb, I can be on my way doing just that.'

Mrs Campbell paused for a moment and then sat down in a chair.

Grace stood next to the bed. The boy wouldn't meet her eye at first and when he did, she could sense his anxiety.

'Caleb, can you tell me what happened?'

'I'd been to the shop and I was going home again.'

'He was supposed to be too ill for school,' Mrs Campbell retorted.

'Go on,' Grace went on.

'This car came out of nowhere. I heard the engine revving up, and when I turned to look back, it hit my wheel and I flew over the handlebars.' He held up a bandaged hand and pointed to his leg. 'I fell funny on my leg and I couldn't get up. I tried to but I couldn't.'

'Did you see who the driver was?'

'I didn't see his face.'

'Not even enough to tell if it was a male or female?'

'I think it was a man.'

'Why do you say that?'

'I could tell by how he was sitting in the car.'

'So you should be able to tell me what he looked like.'

'I can't remember.'

'What car was it?'

'I'm not sure.'

'Colour?'

'Black, I think.'

'Does Seth Forrester have a black car?' Grace asked next, noting his resistance to tell them anything.

At the mention of his name, Caleb's eyes widened. It took him a few seconds, glancing from his mum back to her, before he nodded.

'Was it him?'

'I told you, I didn't see who was driving.'

'And I told you to keep away from Forrester,' Mrs Campbell said. 'He's nothing but trouble.'

'Was there only the driver in the car?' Grace went on.

'Yeah.'

'Don't push him. He's in a lot of pain and he's in shock too.' Mrs Campbell spoke to Grace this time. 'If I get hold of whoever it was, I'll . . . what kind of a monster does this to a child and then disappears without stopping to see what they've done?'

'One who might have thought that Caleb saw something happen at Harrison House.' Grace kept her eyes on the teenager. 'Isn't that right, Caleb?'

Caleb looked away.

'What do you mean?' Mrs Campbell looked confused, then she turned to her son. 'Are you saying you know who did this to you?'

Caleb had clammed up.

'Caleb?' Grace's voice was softer now.

'I saw it,' he said.

'The assault in the car park?'

'I didn't see any assault. I saw what happened to the boy.'

Grace pulled up a chair and sat down. She tried to stay calm but was anything but. He could be their first witness.

'That little boy is in hospital too,' she told him. 'It would be incredibly helpful, and brave, if you could tell me everything.'

'I was going to see my mate.'

Grace wanted to ask for a name but instead let him keep talking.

'I was supposed to be there for half six but I was a few minutes late. I heard a scream and looked up.' Caleb winced as if in pain. 'There was a man, hanging the boy over the side.'

'Sorry?' Grace sat forwards.

'He was holding the kid over the edge. I heard the woman scream again and then . . . he let go. I just pedalled away as quick as I could.'

'The boy on the front page of the *Stoke News*?' Mrs Campbell gasped. 'You saw what happened? That's why someone knocked you off your bike?' She glared at Grace. 'You need to sort this, and quickly. Someone is trying to kill my son! I want him in witness protection, or whatever it is you do. A safe house, that's what we want.'

Grace didn't respond. Despite the woman's distress, her focus was on Caleb. But he had gone quiet again. She put down her notepad.

'Look, I know you're scared of repercussions, but believe me. Not telling the police who you thought dropped a child from a first-floor walkway will have more serious implications. I need you to think long and hard. If it's Seth, I need to know.'

Caleb tried to sit up. 'He'll kill me if I grass on him.' His voice was raised.

'Okay, son, calm down.' Mrs Campbell threw Grace a filthy look. 'You should be harassing the person who did this, not my boy.'

Grace waited for Caleb to sit back again. 'Just one final thing. Is the man that you saw drop Tyler Douglas from the first-floor walkway at Harrison House the same man you saw in the driver's seat of the black car?'

Caleb was silent for a moment before nodding.

'And you think it was Seth Forrester?'

He nodded again.

'And he was the friend you were meeting.'

Another slight nod.

'If he's out to hurt Caleb, I want him charged,' Mrs Campbell insisted. 'And if he's harmed that poor child, he needs punishing.'

'Please! Everyone, keep your voices down.' A nurse came from behind the screen. 'If I can hear you, so can other people. Any more and I will ask you to leave.'

'I'm sorry,' Grace told her before turning back to try one last time. But before she could speak, Caleb beat her to it.

'I'm scared of him.' He looked at her with unease in his eyes.

'We'll do our best to apprehend him as soon as possible,' Grace replied.

She left them alone then. There was no point in pressurising the boy. There might be some house cameras on Minor Crescent, but she was going to speak to Seth Forrester regardless.

In the hospital foyer, she rang Frankie to update him.

'Both Ruby Brassington and Luke Douglas have been lying to us,' she said, updating him on what Caleb had told her. 'Why haven't they told us what happened? What are they scared of?'

'Or covering up?'

'We need to speak to Seth Forrester. It would have been easy for him to drop the boy and then run back to his flat.' But Grace knew he was supposedly the perpetrator of the attack on Milo Benton in the car park, according to Eddie. And why would Seth be threatening Ruby and Luke anyway?

'Exactly – why?' Frankie echoed her thoughts.

'I'm not sure yet, but something doesn't add up.' Grace walked through the large doors to the outside. 'Can you meet me at Harrison House to pick Forrester up? Before that, can you ask Sam if she can look for the car please? She should be able to cross-reference anything that appears at or near to both crime scenes if she can find footage of the car around Minor Crescent.'

'Yes, boss.'

'We need to speak to the parents as well. I want to know why they were lying to us. What they're so scared of.'

'Or what they've done to upset someone enough to do that?'

'Exactly.'

As Grace disconnected the call, she swallowed bile in her throat. Their case had just blown wide open in the most hideous of ways.

Little Tyler's fall was no accident.

TWENTY-SEVEN

Monday evening

Ruby had been watching the news when her worst fears came true.

The children were in their room. She could hear Tyler playing with his cars, making engine noises as he pushed them around the floor. Lily would no doubt be trying to read a book.

'What time are you working tonight?' she asked Luke who was sitting in the chair across from her.

'Seven fifteen till midnight. Need to get going soon.'

'But you've only just got in, less than an hour ago.'

'Needs must, you know that.'

There was a knock on the front door. Before either of them could react, Tyler came running in, almost tripping over the hall rug in his haste. He righted himself and flew into his mum on the settee.

'Door, Mummy.'

'I'll go,' Luke said.

Tyler grabbed his dad's hand and pulled him along the narrow hallway.

After glancing through the spy hole, Luke turned back to Ruby. 'I don't know who it is.'

Ruby pushed Lily towards the door. 'Lily, take Tyler and go into your bedroom. Stay in there until I come and fetch you.'

'No,' Tyler cried.

Lily shook her head. 'I want to stay with you, Mum.'

There was only one entrance to the flat, only one escape route. Ruby pushed her again, too far away to grab Tyler.

'Go,' she said.

Watching her daughter's face crumple didn't make Ruby feel good but at least she was safe for now.

Another bang came on the door this time. 'If you don't come out, I will kick it down.'

'You go into the kitchen,' Luke said. 'Take Tyler in there.'

'Be careful,' she told him. 'Tyler, come here.' Ruby reached for him but he dodged her hold.

Luke opened the door. 'Can I help you, mate?' he asked.

The man was tall, with the build of someone who pumped iron often. His head was shorn, a tattoo on his neck of a skull, his features a mess of battle scars. Beady eyes stared at them both in turn before he spoke.

'Yeah, you can. I want what's mine.'

Luke frowned. 'I don't know what you're talking about.'

'Oh, I think you do,' the man smirked. 'And I want it back.'

Ruby moved to stand behind Luke, reaching for Tyler's hand. 'Go to your sister,' she told him.

'No.' He pulled from her grip again and ran towards the man.

The man scooped up the boy and smiled at him. 'Nice little chap you have here. What's your name?'

'Tyler, and I am nearly three!'

'Nearly three-year-old Tyler, hello.'

Ruby didn't dare move. He had her child in his arms and until she had Tyler back, she was saying or doing nothing.

Luke, however, had other ideas.

'Come here, son.' He held out his arms. 'You don't want to be bothering this man.'

'Oh, he's fine with me.' The man nodded. 'He's a little treasure, isn't he? I suppose all kids are precious cargo to their parents.'

'Did someone send you?' Luke asked.

'You could say that.' He stared at Luke, and then at Ruby.

'Well, if you give me some sort of clue what you're after, I can perhaps help you out.'

Ruby could sense Luke putting on a brave face but she could see how his body was shaking. He must be as terrified as she was. She prayed someone would come out onto the walkway soon and stop whatever was happening, nip it in the bud. Only then could they regroup and decide what to do next.

'Perhaps this will remind you.'

Before either of them could react, the man dangled Tyler over the side of the railing by the back of his jumper.

'Tyler!' Ruby screamed.

'What do you think you're playing at!' Luke cried, stepping forward. 'Let him go.'

'Come any closer and I'll drop him,' the man threatened.

'Please!' Ruby burst into tears. 'He's only a little boy.'

Tyler began to cry too, his arms and legs flapping about. 'Mummy!' he sobbed.

'This is a warning,' the man said, tightening his grip on Tyler's hood. 'I want what's mine by Monday. If I don't have it, I will harm you and your children, one by one.'

'We don't know what you're after.' Luke put his hands on his head. 'Please, don't hurt him.'

'Give him to me.' Ruby pushed past Luke, lunged at the railing and tried to reach Tyler, hoping to bring him back to safety.

Tyler began to flounder more. 'Mummy,' he shouted, his cries turning into sobs. 'Mummy!'

She almost got a hand to him, but he wouldn't stop wriggling. In horror, she watched as the man lost his grip and her son fell to the ground.

Ruby was left with only the sound of her own scream.

2012

'Do you fancy a takeaway?' Finn asked as they drove along the main road. 'I'm starving.'

'You had something to eat less than an hour ago.' Ruby laughed. 'You can't be hungry yet.'

'I'm a growing man.' Finn flexed his muscles. 'Working out at the gym is paying off but it leaves me with an appetite.'

'For burger and chips?'

'Well, yes, as long as you're my dessert.'

He parked the car on a piece of waste land and turned to Ruby. 'I won't be a minute. Love you.'

Ruby smiled at him. 'Love you more.'

As she waited, she stared in awe at the bundle of pink wrapped up in her baby seat. She still couldn't believe she was a mum, that this little girl, now a month old, was hers.

Once he was back in the car, Finn pulled Ruby into his arms and began to nuzzle playfully at her neck.

'Hey, your daughter might see us,' Ruby joked. Then she caught a movement out of the corner of her eye. Three men were walking towards the front of the car.

'Finn,' she said.

'What?' He started to tickle her.

'Stop it.'

But he didn't stop.

She pushed him away roughly. 'Finn!'

Finn glanced in the direction she was looking. 'Lock your door quickly.'

He reached to start the engine as she thrust down the door lock button. The locking mechanism clicked into place and she breathed a sigh of relief. Until there was a loud bang on the window beside her. She screamed. Dane was by her side and he was carrying a metal bar. She recognised the two men as visitors to the flat, both of broad build and menacing.

'What's going on, Finn?' Her lip was all of a tremble.

Dane walked around to the driver's seat and made a circling motion with his finger.

'Drive away!' Ruby cried.

'I can't.'

She would never forget the look of fear in Finn's eyes.

'I have to speak to him,' he whispered. 'I don't want them to harm you.' He wound down the window slightly.

'Finn, my boy,' Dane cried. 'Whatcha up to?'

'I don't want any trouble, Dane.' Finn's voice came out a little squeaky.

'Who says I'm going to cause trouble? I just spotted you here and came to say hello. I've been meaning to call at your gaff anyway.' Dane sneered. 'Your actions could have got me sent down so I've had to lay low for a few days.' He stared at Ruby. 'Pretty thing, ain't she? Let's hope she stays that way.'

'No, please—'

'*No, please.*' Dane mimicked his voice. The other men laughed.

Ruby clasped her hands around Finn's arm but she didn't dare look at Dane. He could smash the window and unlock the car in an instant, pull Finn out onto the ground, and there was no one in their vicinity right now. She held her breath when he looked across at her again.

'This is your first warning. Either you show up for work this weekend, and take what you get as your punishment, or I'll come after you properly.' He pointed at Ruby. 'And then I'm coming for her.'

With a swing of the bar, they began to attack the vehicle. Metal crunched and glass broke, the noise deafening. Ruby covered her ears with her hands, pulling her feet up close to her chest. Lily woke up and began to scream.

It was over in less than a minute but it seemed to last forever. As suddenly as it had started, it stopped. The men walked away, laughing with each other.

Ruby flew into Finn's arms and burst into tears.

'It's okay.' Finn stroked her hair. 'They're gone now.'

'But they'll be back. What are we going to do then?'

'I don't know. I may have to do more work, to keep them off my back.'

'No. You'll get drawn in again.'

'I don't want them to hurt you, but . . . Maybe it's better to stay on his good side, for a while longer. You're my main priority, you and Lily, and they know it. I won't let them hurt you.' He pulled away and looked at her.

Ruby could hear her friend Naomi saying 'I told you so' inside her head. Naomi was right. He was trouble. But Finn was *her* trouble. And she loved him. And she would stick by him no matter how frightened she was.

'I'm not going anywhere,' she told him. 'It's you and me forever.'

He hugged her tightly. She didn't say a word when she felt wet tears on her face, and knew they weren't coming from her.

TWENTY-EIGHT

Mary pushed on the door to floor one but instead of turning her usual right to go home, she made her way left, to the end of the walkway and across to the other side. Outside flat 114, she tried not to think of what she'd seen two nights ago when the little boy had fallen. She wanted to knock on the door and ask how he was but she suspected the parents would be at the hospital anyway. And she didn't want to stay on the walkway outside their flat for long in case anyone saw her.

At flat 116, she stopped and looked around. There were a few people about but no one was looking at her. She wondered why she was bothered so much. People only cared about themselves.

She lifted the letterbox and pushed the envelope through. Hearing it plop onto the floor, she turned and rushed away as quick as her legs would allow. She didn't want to be there when he saw it.

The money had played on her mind for months. He said it was for her to keep quiet about what she saw. Just because she spent a lot of time looking over the railing didn't mean she was a busybody. Yes, she had noticed a few things but she hadn't mentioned them to anyone.

When the first envelope appeared, he'd posted it through her letterbox with a note. But last night was the final straw. She had to make sure he knew she wasn't his to do as he wished with. She would not be a pushover.

Shelley's ear pricked up when she heard the letterbox go. She went through to the hall and saw a large envelope on the mat. She picked it up, frowning when she saw the writing on it.

I WILL NOT PLAY YOUR GAME

She opened the door and stepped outside on the walkway. In the distance she could see someone. It was that woman from across the way, Mary. Seth was always giving out grief about her; said she was too nosy for her own good, but Shelley couldn't see any harm in her. Maybe she had seen too much every now and then and Seth was worried she would grass him up, but if he thought about it, if she was going to do it she would have done it by now. Shelley reckoned Mary would keep her mouth shut about anything. She seemed a good sort from what she knew of her.

But the message was intriguing enough for her to look inside the envelope. It wasn't sealed shut anyway, so she wasn't really snooping. She hurried back inside and opened it.

It was full of money, twenty-pound notes.

She frowned again, wondering where it had come from. Quickly she counted it. It added up to nearly three thousand pounds.

The envelope was obviously meant for Seth but what did the message mean? What game was he asking the older woman to play? It didn't make sense.

She made a coffee, had a cigarette on the doorstep while she looked across at Mary's flat. Was she watching her now, wondering if Seth had got the envelope or not? She put out the cigarette and went inside again. Then she took the envelope and popped it in her handbag. That sort of cash wasn't for sharing. She would deny ever having seen it.

TWENTY-NINE

Uniform had picked up Seth Forrester and brought him in. Grace left him stewing in interview room three while they had a quick look at what Sam had found on CCTV. Finally, she and Frankie went in to see him.

'Oh, it's dumb and dumber.' Seth rolled his eyes before folding his arms. 'I believe you wanted to see me.'

Grace ignored his comments while she set up the room and read out the necessary details to start the interview.

'You're not under arrest but we want to question you under caution about a number of things.'

'As long as you don't intend to fit me up for something I didn't do.' He sneered at Grace. 'I hear you're good at that. And I hear you've been warning people away from me.'

Grace held his stare before dropping her eyes to her notepad. He was referring to her having a quiet word with Megan about him being bad news. Her grandmother, Kathleen Steele, had asked Grace to encourage Megan to stop seeing him.

'Perhaps you ought to ask yourself who wanted me to warn her off,' she countered.

He visibly sank back as he caught her meaning. Forrester

was no match for the Steeles. She gave Frankie a surreptitious glance. Maybe Seth wouldn't be so cocky now.

'Can you tell me where you were around four p.m. last night?'

'I was at home.'

'Alone?'

'No, I was with my woman. I was on a late shift so me and Shelley were in bed until about half six, if you catch my drift.'

'I do but I'm not sure I want to. So you left your flat at what time?'

'About quarter to eight.'

It was still possible that he had knocked Caleb Campbell off his bike. Grace would have to ask Sam to check the CCTV again.

'There was a hit and run last night that appears to involve a black BMW, and I believe you have one of those?'

'Yeah, but—'

She showed him the CCTV image that Sam had found. 'Is that you in your car?'

It was a long shot. The image was blurred and they couldn't be certain yet. The number plates weren't clear either. Grace watched intently as Seth studied it.

'No, that's not me. I told you – I was at home.'

'But you can see our predicament?' Grace pointed to the image. 'This looks like your car.'

'It isn't me. So don't even think about setting me up for it. I'll have lawyers on to you so fast you—'

'Oh, quit with the threats,' Grace snapped. 'Like I said earlier, you're not under arrest.'

'So can I go yet? I have things to do, places to be, you know? If you don't have anything else?'

He could tell they hadn't, Grace was sure. But she did have one more thing to mention.

'What about Monday evening, around six p.m. for an hour or so?'

187

He sat forward. 'You mean when that kid fell over the railing?'

'We have a witness who says they saw you around the time Tyler Douglas was attacked. We also have CCTV of you leaving the building.'

'I was outside on Monday.' He paused to stare at her again. 'I went to my car to fetch my gym bag. I'd left it in the boot when I got back from the boxing club. The next thing I knew there was a crowd, an ambulance and cops everywhere.'

'Did you see what happened?'

'I told you, no. If I had, I wouldn't keep that to myself. What do you take me for?'

'Do you know Ruby and Luke well?'

'Not really.' His eyes shifted to the left and back again quickly. 'I see her out with her kids every now and then and I see him around, in the pub, maybe out on the walkway if we pass. But nothing more than that.'

'So you didn't see anything happening on the walkway on Monday evening?'

'No.'

'And you didn't see the altercation in the car park that happened the same night?'

He shook his head. 'It was all quiet when I was there.'

'And we won't find out your car was involved in the hit and run?'

'I'm telling you, it wasn't me.'

Grace glared at him for a moment. Even though she had information about him being in the right place, she didn't have any evidence to back it up other than hearsay. She let him go, hoping what she'd told him would get him thinking about what he was doing. Which was lying to the police.

Outside the station, Seth took deep breaths to keep his temper at bay. He hated being cooped up in an interview room. It brought back too many bad memories of his times in the cells. But even if it was an occupational hazard, this wasn't of his doing this time.

He walked along Bethesda Street, past the museum and up Albion Street towards the taxi rank.

What the hell was going on? Had that bloody nosy cow across the way been talking about him? She'd be in for it if she had.

But then he realised he'd better be careful what he said because the only reason he couldn't be sure if he saw anyone or not was because it would implicate him in the attack on Milo Benton and so far the lad had kept his mouth shut about who had beaten him. Unlike Caleb Campbell, who must have been the one who grassed him up. Seth needed to see him. He'd pay him a visit tomorrow.

He pulled up his collar against the cold and stomped up the bank, deciding to ring Shelley. Perhaps she could tell him more.

'Everything okay?' she asked.

'They let me go after we'd had a chat.'

'That's great! Because wait until you hear what I found out this morning.'

Seth's smile widened as he listened. 'This man you saw running away. What did he look like?'

'I told you. I couldn't see. He was too far away.'

'It wasn't anyone you know?'

'I can't be sure. Why?'

'Because if I find out that you're covering for someone, I—'

'I'm not, honestly! Who would I be doing that for?'

The line went quiet for a moment.

'Are you coming home?'

'I'm going to the club for an hour and then I'll be back.' Seth stopped in his tracks, a woman behind him almost bumping into him. He scowled as she passed.

'Come home now. I can—'

'I'll be there when I'm done.' He disconnected the call. Let the stupid cow stew for a while.

Shelley cursed loudly as she realised Seth had ended the call. Then she typed out a quick message:

'Police have been talking to Seth. I'll let you know more as soon as I see him. He's heading your way, going to Flynn's.'

THIRTY

Seth decided not to go to Flynn's nightclub. He strode through the corridors of the Royal Stoke in search of ward 17. He was thinking he'd be safer visiting in the afternoon slot. Maybe Caleb's mum would be at work. He didn't want to bump into anyone.

He recalled what he knew about Caleb, how his dad had left when he was nine and his older brother was fourteen. He knew his mum worked hard and Caleb thought a lot of her even though he was doing something she wouldn't be happy about. Seth had thought he was okay until he didn't show on Monday. He should have delivered his package. It only made sense now why he had got to Harrison House and panicked.

He reached the nurses' station and put on his best smile. 'I'm looking for Caleb Campbell?'

'He's in bay two, bed three,' the nurse said after checking her computer. 'Try the day room if he isn't there.'

'Thanks.' Seth made his way across the ward to see bed three empty, so went to the day room.

Caleb was alone, sitting in an armchair, his leg up on a footstool, his head down as he scrolled his phone.

'Hey.' He sat down next to him with a thump.

Caleb almost jumped off the seat with fright. He looked towards the door that Seth had closed behind him.

'I— Hey.'

'I came to see how you are after your little . . . accident.'

'I'm . . . I'm okay, thanks.'

Seth smiled. 'That's good to hear. I assume you told no one that you saw who was driving the car.'

Caleb shook his head.

'Really? I hear you've been talking to the cops about me.'

'I didn't tell them it was you. I swear!'

Seth pressed his hand onto Caleb's bandaged wrist and began to squeeze.

'Ow, man you're hurting me,' he squealed.

'If you say anything else about me, I will dangle you over the *second* floor of Harrison House and drop you.'

'I'm sorry! That woman detective put words into my mouth. I never told her anything.'

'Great.' Seth clasped his hands together. 'So when you're out, and up and about again, you can start work. I have some jobs lined up for you that I'll have to get someone else to do for now, but even so, there's lots for you to do.'

Caleb pretended to be more interested in his phone.

'Are you listening to me?'

'I don't want to do it any more,' he spoke quietly.

'I don't give a flying fuck. You owe me.'

'But—'

Seth squeezed down on Caleb's wrist again. 'Listen here, youngster. If you ever cross me again, you might not live to regret it. You work for me now, and you don't have any choice in the matter. This isn't something you can start one day and finish when you feel like it. You do as I say. Do you understand?'

'Yes! Please let me go. I—'

The door opened and a young girl with short purple hair and wearing a striped onesie smiled at them. She pushed along a trolley with a drip attached to it.

'Hi, Caleb,' she said, sitting down on the other side to Seth. 'I didn't know you had a visitor. Hi, I'm Nancy.' She waved at Seth. 'Have I missed the beginning of the programme?'

Not wanting to bring attention to himself, Seth stood up to leave.

'Remember what I said, Caleb,' he muttered. 'Come back to work as soon as possible. In the meantime, I'll come and see how you're doing every now and then.'

He left the room, pretty pleased with how his meeting had gone. That little bastard wouldn't get the better of him. He would give him a month and he'd better be on his bike again.

In the hospital toilets, he snorted a quick line of cocaine, pinched his nose and went back to his car. Now to sort out Luke Douglas.

Caleb sat staring at the door long after Seth had gone. His eyes brimmed with tears and he wiped at them furiously to stop them falling. What had he got himself into? He thought he'd be able to earn enough cash for his bike and then stop. He wasn't stupid; knew what he was carrying was dangerous to transport. If he was caught with it, he would be in trouble with the police. But he didn't want to be stuck working for Seth forever.

What was he going to do? Should he tell his mum? No, she would go mad with him. More to the point, she would be disappointed in him and he'd hate to see that.

He would have to tell her though. She would know what to do. He couldn't hack this on his own.

'That was good, wasn't it?' Nancy said.

Caleb had almost forgotten she had come into the room.

He nodded. 'Oh, yeah, it was cool.'

'Do you want to play a game of cards or something? I'm so bored.'

Caleb shuffled to his feet and reached for his crutches. 'I'm tired. I'm going to have a nap.'

On the ward, he lay on his bed, curled up on his side, his back to everyone. That way no one could see him crying.

2012

Ruby was at home. It was eleven a.m. and Lily had kept her awake for most of the night. She yawned as she cradled her in her arms, staring out of the window. The weather was cold but bright and breezy so she decided to take her out. It would do her good to get some fresh air. She popped her into the pram, tucking her in tightly.

They were about to leave the flat when there was a knock on the door. Ruby opened it and before she could see who it was, she was pushed up against the wall, her head slamming into it.

It was Dane, the man who had come at them in the car last night. His eyes flicked from hers to her mouth and she felt her heart skip a beat. His face was ravished with evil. She couldn't tell if he was high or if that was his usual look. Why hadn't she thought before letting anyone in?

'Where is he?' he asked, spittle covering her face as he moved in close.

'He's taken the car to be fixed,' she replied, her voice coming in fits.

His arm was across her chest and she yelped in pain as he pushed on it.

'Tell him I want to see him.'

She tried to nod her head but it hurt.

Dane looked into the pram.

'Please don't do anything to her.' Ruby began to cry. 'What do you want?'

'Finn needs to be taught a lesson about loyalty.' He ran a finger down the side of her cheek.

She screwed her eyes shut, trying not to see herself face down on a bed with him pumping into her from behind.

'That attack on your car last night? It was nothing compared to what I'll do to him when I see him again.'

'Please, leave us alone. We don't want any trouble.'

'You don't get it, do you?' He pulled her closer. 'If he continues to mess me about, there will be repercussions. And you don't want that.'

'Let me talk to him,' she pleaded, hoping to get more time. At least if she had Dane out of the flat, she could get away.

Finally, he let go. He leered at her, then nodded.

'You tell him once he's in, he's in for good. And don't even think of leaving. Because I will find you, and when I do, things will be much, much worse than if you had stayed, do you understand?'

She nodded fervently. She wasn't sure she could speak anyway. Terrified, she waited for him to leave. Then she sank to the floor and rang Finn.

Finn came rushing through the door twenty minutes later. Ruby fell into his arms.

'He threatened you and me,' Ruby said through her tears, her hands shaking with fear. 'And he's mean enough to hurt Lily, I'm sure of it.'

'What did he say to you?'

'That he'd be back soon if you didn't continue to work for him.'

'That bastard.' They sat down. 'I can't cope with this any more. He's never going to let me go and I can't risk him hurting you. It doesn't matter if he chases us. Let's get out of here on Friday as soon as I'm paid.'

Ruby nodded, wiping her eyes. As they planned their escape, it couldn't come quick enough.

THIRTY-ONE

By the time Ruby heard the key go in the door, she was fuming. Even though it gave her the opportunity to throw the attention from herself, Luke had promised her he wouldn't gamble again. He'd run up debt two years ago and it had taken them an age to pay it off.

'What the hell has been going on?' she barked, as Luke joined her in the kitchen.

Wrong-footed, he seemed confused, as if he was trying to figure out why she was shouting at him.

'I've just found out that you owe money to Seth Forrester.'

Luke's demeanour seemed to shift. 'What happened on Monday had nothing to do with me.'

Ruby poked him in the chest. 'Have you been gambling again?'

She watched his face drop. 'Who told you that?'

'Don't lie to me. It's written all over your face. Shelley told me that you owe money to Seth, and that he works for the Steeles. She says they're not a family to cross. If someone is after us, I don't think I can take any more. I have enough to worry about with Tyler.'

Luke's shoulders dropped at the same time as his eyes. Ruby groaned, wanting to slap him hard. But equally she was at fault too.

'How much?' she wanted to know.

He shook his head.

'How *much*?'

'Just shy of five thousand.'

She gasped.

'I'll pay it back as quick as I can.'

'How exactly are you going to do that? We don't have that kind of money.'

'I've been doing extra hours at the club.'

'Which led to you gambling?'

Luke went quiet.

'You promised.'

'I know, but—'

A hard rap on the door interrupted them.

Luke glanced through the spy hole and cursed. He ran a hand through his hair and pulled the door open.

Ruby groaned inwardly when she saw it was Seth.

'What do you want?' Luke said.

She watched as he held his shoulders high, trying to make himself look taller. He was at least six inches shorter than Seth and had nowhere near his muscular capacity.

'I suggest you remember who you're talking to.' Seth's face was straight in Luke's. 'I call the shots around here and if I'm not mistaken, it's you that owes me something and not the other way around.'

'I nearly lost my son because of you.' Luke threw a balled fist, landing it on Seth's nose. 'You sent someone here, didn't you?'

Seth responded, punching Luke in the mouth, followed by two swift hits to the stomach.

'Stop it!' Ruby cried. Luke had never been a fighter, and he'd certainly never dared to have a go at anyone like Seth before. But he had every reason to be angry after what had happened.

'Shelley told me about the man who came to see you,' Seth said. 'But I had nothing to do with it.'

'You would say that,' Luke said between gasps for breath.

'It's the truth. But I wonder what the cops would think if they knew what really happened. Why you never told them he was dangled over the edge and—'

'You'd better not say anything or else—'

'Or else what?'

Luke ran at him again. He grabbed Seth around the waist and pushed him into the wall. But Seth pressed his hands down onto his shoulders and forced him to move away. Luke cried out in pain as he squeezed hard.

'Leave him alone,' Ruby tried again, seeing Luke overpowered.

'You need to tell him to stick to his payment plan.' Seth looked from Ruby to him and back again. His smile was snide. 'She doesn't know, does she?'

'I've just found out,' Ruby replied.

Seth nodded. 'He owes me money and he thinks that your boy went over the railing because I sent a thug to do my dirty work for me. *He* needs to realise that rumours have a nasty way of spreading and if I hear anyone saying that I had anything to do with that fall, then I'll push you over the railing myself.' He grabbed Luke's jumper and pulled him close. 'Do you understand?'

'Yeah.' Luke's lip was bleeding. 'I hear you.'

'Let him go,' Ruby pleaded. 'You're hurting him.'

Seth glared at Luke. 'You've been nothing but trouble since I first met you. I want my money back by the weekend. All of it.'

Luke balked. 'I don't have it.'

'Then I suggest you get it from somewhere.'

'I can't—'

Seth punched Luke in the stomach and he doubled over. Ruby cried out in anguish.

'The weekend, remember.' Seth left as quickly as he'd arrived.

Ruby sat down beside Luke. 'Are you okay?'

Luke shrugged her hand away. 'I'll be fine.'

She pinched the bridge of her nose, trying to contain her anger as this wasn't all his fault. 'What did you do for him?'

'I fetched and carried a few things, and then he wanted me to do more. I said no but he wasn't too accommodating.'

'You put our family in danger!' Ruby couldn't hold back her fear. This was like history repeating itself. Bile rose in her throat at the thought.

'I'm sorry. I thought I had it under control. I borrowed a bit from Seth and you know how it is, I couldn't pay him back and so he offered me more.'

'That's the game they trap you in. Why didn't you tell me?'

'I was too embarrassed, and I thought I could sort it out without you knowing. But now he wants me to do other jobs for him to reduce the debt. That's what he's been calling round for.'

'What kind of things?'

'Still fetching and carrying for him. The odd driving jobs.'

She shook her head. 'Our son is in hospital. You should be thinking of your family, not Seth!'

'I have to pay off the debt.'

When he wouldn't look at her, Ruby stood up. Despite her feelings for him and the pain he was in, she couldn't deal with this too. She was even more fearful about what would happen now.

'I'm sorry,' Luke said. 'I never meant for this to happen. I'll go to Gamblers' Anonymous or something.'

'You said that before.' Ruby prodded him in the shoulder. 'I moved to Stoke with you so that we could start again after you messed up. We took a loan to repay your debt and we moved away to get you away from temptation. I liked it in Sheffield – I had friends and a job. I left it all behind because of *you*. And now look what you've done.'

'Ruby, I—'

She held up her hand. 'I can't bear to be in the same room as you right now. I'm going to the hospital to see Tyler and then I'm going to collect Lily from school. I don't want to see you until I get back. And come to think of it, I might not want to see you then either.'

'But—'

She shook off his hand and stormed into the bedroom. She sat on the bed, holding in tears, shoving her fist against her mouth in case she screamed. She'd said she was going to confide in him. Why couldn't she?

And she was telling so many lies, she was bound to trip up soon. She didn't leave Sheffield because of Luke. No, she'd been constantly looking over her shoulder and when it had been clear that she was in imminent danger, she had persuaded him to go, using what he'd done as an excuse to start somewhere else afresh. And now she was scared that her past was catching up with her again.

She was getting in deeper and deeper, but she shouldn't take her anger out on Luke. None of this was his fault. Okay, she'd found out about the money, but she was as deceitful as him.

Because this was all her fault, not Luke's.

She had to find it in her heart to trust him with the truth at some point.

THIRTY-TWO

After updating Allie, Grace had rung Ruby Brassington to see if she was at home. She'd arranged a time where she could speak to her and Luke together. She wasn't looking forward to questioning them again, but things had changed.

'Right, Frankie,' she said as they parked up yet again in the car park of Harrison House. 'I need you, myself too, to strip out the emotion and just do our job.' She held up her hand as he went to protest. 'I know, I know. I sound callous, but we'll be nothing to anyone if we miss things by allowing this to get to us. Let's sort this out for little Tyler.'

Frankie nodded. They walked up to flat 114, residents checking them out as they stood watching on the walkways.

'Is it true?' a man asked as they went past his door. Grace turned to see he was in his thirties at the most, but with a lived-in face of someone in his sixties.

'Is what true?' she asked, stopping level with him.

'That the boy didn't fall? That some mad bastard hung him over the railing and dropped him.'

'When did you hear that?'

'Just now.'

'From who?'

'It's all around the flats. How could anyone do that? You caught him yet?'

'I can't comment on the case, but rest assured we're following up our enquiries.'

Grace continued on her way and was soon sitting in Ruby and Luke's living room.

'How is Tyler?' she asked when they were all seated.

'Much better, thanks.' Ruby smiled. 'The consultant says he can come home tomorrow if he's still doing well. He's amazed at how quickly he's bounced back.'

'There's a bit of bruising here and there, and his ankle is in a cast,' Luke added. 'There don't seem to be any brain injuries to worry about but they're keeping him in for one more night for observation. He didn't shut up while we were there this morning, though.'

'That's great news, I'm really pleased.' Grace's smile was almost there. 'But regarding his fall, I do need to ask you both some further questions. Clear up some anomalies.' She paused. 'Why did you lie to us about Tyler falling? We have witnesses coming forward to say something totally different happened. Are you sure there isn't anything else you want to tell me?'

Shifty looks passed between the couple but then they shook their heads.

'A man was seen dangling Tyler over the walkway before dropping him,' she continued.

'And you believe people from Harrison House over the boy's own mother and father?' Luke answered. 'He fell.'

'I'm not—'

'I can't do this any more.' Ruby held her head in her hands. 'We have to tell the truth.'

Luke threw her a warning glance.

'It all happened so quickly,' she began. 'There was a knock

204

on the door. We told Lily to take Tyler into their bedroom but he was hard to catch. Luke answered the door and before we could stop him, Tyler ran outside. There was a man standing on the walkway. He spoke to Tyler and he ran into his arms. We've warned him not to go to strangers but he's only young. The man picked him up and was laughing with him, tickling him and then all of a sudden, before we could stop him, he hung him over the railing.'

'Are you sure this is the truth?' Grace questioned, wanting to be certain.

'Yes,' Ruby replied. 'It's the truth.'

Luke sat forwards and ran a hand over his face.

'Did he say who he was, or what he wanted?' Grace asked, catching Frankie's fist clenching and unclenching as he sat next to her.

But Ruby didn't seem to have heard her as she continued.

'I begged him to leave Tyler alone,' she sobbed. 'But then he began to wriggle, and as we argued, he . . . he slipped out of the man's grip. Before any of us could grab him, he had fallen.'

'So you don't think it was intentional?' Grace probed.

Ruby shook her head. 'He didn't drop him purposely, but it was his fault.'

'Why did he do it? You must have some idea.'

'We don't know.'

Grace held in her exasperation. 'Well, can you tell me what he looked like?'

'Tall, white. He wore a black jacket, hat and gloves, jeans and black boots.' Furtive glances passed between Luke and Ruby.

'And you didn't recognise him?' Grace couldn't help but frown. 'Is there anything that you saw on this man that would identify him? Tattoos, scars etc?'

Ruby shook her head. 'It all happened so fast.'

'Do either of you know anyone in Stoke who would do that?'

'No.' They spoke in unison.

'Anyone outside of Stoke?'

Luke shook his head. Ruby said nothing.

Grace sighed loudly, unable to hold in her annoyance. Her heart went out to them, she could see they were scared about something, but she needed them to work with her too.

'So some random stranger knocked on your door, picked up your son and held him over the railing for no reason?'

'We don't know!' Luke held his head in his hands.

'Why did you both want to put the blame on Lily?' Frankie asked.

'We didn't, but it was the only thing we could think of,' Ruby said. 'We were so scared that the lie came tumbling out. And the guilt was unbearable. We let someone put our son in danger.'

'But you had us chasing up leads rather than find out who did this,' Grace said. 'Why?'

'Because we were scared of what he might do next!' Ruby's right foot began to bob up and down as if she couldn't keep still.

Grace wasn't convinced by that at all. She could almost see them cowering when she mentioned certain things. What were they so afraid of? Or who – especially if this had been an accident.

'How well do you know Seth Forrester, Luke?' She turned her attention to him again.

'He's a neighbour. I see him around.' He grimaced. 'It wasn't Seth. The man who did this didn't have a local twang.'

'Do you recognise what accent he had?'

'I'm not sure but it might have been London – Cockney. But he definitely wasn't a Stokie.' His voice cracked. 'We were in a panic. We were more interested in sorting Tyler out.'

'Threatening someone by using their child as bait is an

offence that needs investigating, regardless of the outcome. This man could be anywhere by now. What would have happened if Tyler hadn't survived?'

Neither Luke nor Ruby replied.

'Tell me his name.'

'We don't know it!' Luke cried.

Grace reeled in her temper, losing all of her empathy entirely. She'd seen it all before, men and women crying. Not for the loss of a loved one, but because they had lied and been found out.

She looked first at Ruby who seemed fit to burst, wringing her hands as her eyes flitted everywhere but towards Grace. Then she glared at Luke who sat back now with his eyes momentarily closed. She wanted so much to help them, to believe in them, but she'd had enough.

'You can both come to the station with us. We need to clarify a few things, get you to look at some photos and see if we can identify this man.'

She and Frankie were almost out of the front door when there was a shout from Ruby.

'Wait. I do know who it is.' She looked at Grace with a pained expression. 'His name is Finn Ridley.'

2012

The night after Dane had threatened her at home, Ruby was watching TV with Finn, cuddled up next to him on the settee. Lily had been asleep for half an hour, giving them time to relax. Yet they were both on edge, unsure if Dane would come at Finn again. She placed her arm across his torso and gave him a squeeze.

'Things will work out okay,' she told him as he did the same to her shoulder. 'Dane will get fed up of hounding you eventually, won't he? Especially now we're going.'

'I'm not so sure, but at least we'll be out of here soon.'

They were still planning to go on Friday. Even though it was Wednesday, they didn't want to pack anything until the last minute. Ruby would be sorry to leave some things behind; they could only take what they could carry in the car, now fixed after its recent attack. But she wouldn't miss living in constant fear of a knock on the door, or a visit by Dane or one of his cronies. Or Finn coming home covered in bruises.

They sat in silence with their own thoughts for a while. Ruby sensed Finn's apprehension but she couldn't wait to leave.

'We'll be fine as long as we have each other,' she said, trying to convince herself as much as him.

Twenty minutes later, there was a bang in the hallway. Ruby knew instantly that someone had kicked the door in and got into the flat.

They both leapt into the air and Finn pushed her towards the armchair. She jumped over and hid behind it. She could hear Lily screaming in her cot but she couldn't do anything. She had to stay still, so that they thought she wasn't there.

'You owe me, Ridley. The only way you'll leave here is in a body bag.'

'No, Dane,' Luke cried. 'Please!'

Ruby heard the sounds of fists and feet, groans coming from Finn. Covering her mouth with her hand in case she cried out, tears poured down her face as Finn took hit after hit.

And then it went quiet. She waited as long seconds turned into a minute, listening to the cries of her daughter and yet not daring to move. Finn had sounded terrified and it had been torture to hear it happening. But she had to make sure they were gone.

After a few seconds, she heard Finn groaning her name. Hopeful that Dane had left, she scrambled over to him.

'Finn! I heard Dane's voice. Look what they did to you.'

'I'm hurting.' He held up his hand and groaned. 'Stomach.'

'I'll get help.'

She had to lean close to him to hear his voice. 'Knife.'

With his blood pooling as it leaked out, Ruby reached for her phone. Her hands were shaking as she called the emergency services.

'Police. Ambulance. We need help!' she yelled. 'Someone help us!'

THIRTY-THREE

'Go on,' Grace urged Ruby.

'Finn is Lily's father,' Ruby told her. 'We met just before my sixteenth birthday.'

'You knew who he was?' Luke balked.

'Keep talking,' Grace said when Ruby had been quiet for a moment.

'He was okay when I first met him but then he started pushing me around. A slap here and there. The odd verbal abuse, then the shouting and the swearing and the beating down with attitude. He acted as if he owned me. He worked as a bouncer at a nightclub and I hardly ever saw him. I was glad of that in the end because he was really cruel. He wasn't good for me but I got pregnant with Lily when I was seventeen.'

Ruby stopped for a moment to catch a breath.

'I was always wary of how he would be when he came home,' she went on. 'One minute he was the loving person he should be; the next he was an uncontrollable beast. In the end, I began to dread seeing him more than I looked forward to it.'

'Why didn't you tell me?' Luke asked.

'I couldn't tell anyone.' Ruby's eyes glistened with tears.

'So why didn't you leave him? You could have done that at any time.'

'No, I couldn't. You don't know what it was like. I left and went home to my dad once, but Finn threatened to hurt him if I didn't leave with him. I believed him; he was so nasty to me. When I did go back, he kept saying that he'd change. He was all right for a few days and then he'd revert to normal.'

Grace knew very well what it would have been like for a young woman with a baby and a coercive controlling partner. She would have had no choice, felt trapped, isolated, out of control. Unloved.

It reminded her of her own mother, stuck in a relationship with a maniac who used everything in his power to make her life a misery.

'How long did you stay with him?' she asked.

'Until Lily was two years old. I was only nineteen and I was so scared of him. I didn't think I'd ever dare to leave. When I found out I was pregnant with her, I thought he'd calm down to some extent but I knew what I was in for once the baby was born. I was trapped. After a beating one night, I'd had enough. I packed our things up the next day and left London. There was a bus in the station and I just jumped on that.'

The room was in silence again. Ruby wouldn't move her eyes from the floor and Luke was staring at her, clearly hoping she'd make eye contact. Grace felt sorry for him all of a sudden. It seemed he was in the dark as much as they were.

'Where did you go then?' she wanted to know.

'Manchester. I was put up in a B&B and then a women's hostel for a few months until Finn found me and I had to leave. That's when I went to Sheffield. I've been on the run from him ever since.'

'So you knew who it was all along who hurt Tyler?' Frankie echoed Luke's earlier question, his face dark.

'I was scared! I panicked. You don't know him like I do. He's evil, and he's dangerous.'

'You're certain it was Finn Ridley?' Grace questioned. 'You haven't seen him for a few years.'

Ruby nodded.

Grace stood for a moment, contemplating what to do next. She was tempted to let them stew while she did more digging into Ridley and his whereabouts. But she couldn't.

'I want you to come to the station to make a statement,' she said.

'Lily will need picking up from school soon.'

'I'll fetch her,' Luke said.

'You have to provide a statement too.'

'But what about Tyler?' Ruby cried. 'I have to go to my son.'

'I understand that but I want you in the station within the hour. I won't keep you long but it's imperative we do this properly. Do I make myself clear that if you don't arrive there, I will have to come and get you and you may be arrested for wasting police time?'

'I'll see if Norma can fetch her and mind her until we're done.' Ruby looked at her with watery eyes. 'I'm so sorry.'

Grace said nothing. She was finding it hard to swallow at the moment. But as soon as they were out of the flat and out of hearing range, she turned to Frankie.

'How could Ruby not tell us the truth?' She stopped to look around them and rested her hands on the railing. Looking down she could see where Tyler had landed after his fall. To think that it had been done deliberately was beyond her comprehension. 'She should have trusted us.'

Frankie shoved his notebook in his pocket. 'The world gets a little more tainted every day. I hope we never have to police anything like it again.'

'At least the boy is safe.'

'You don't think they'd harm their kids, do you?'

'Not at all.' She shook her head. 'But Ruby's clearly on the run from someone who might.'

As soon as the police had gone, Ruby grabbed her keys and marched to the front door. She knew Luke was going to be as mad as hell and she wanted to get away. She also needed to think about what to do, and say, next.

'Where are you going?' He stopped her at the door.

'To ask Norma if she will collect Lily. I want her home and safe.'

'It seems like no one will ever be that again as far as you're concerned. Why didn't you tell me about him?'

Ruby placed her hand on his cheek and looked at him. She loved him so much but she had lied to him too.

'I'm so sorry.'

'You blamed me when all along you knew who he was!'

'I didn't know what else to do.'

'Couldn't you have talked to him, told him not to do anything?'

'He's dangerous, don't you get it?'

'So you let our son go through all that, all the while knowing the man who attacked him? And then you didn't say anything.'

'I couldn't tell you because—'

'You don't trust me enough?'

'No. It's because I've always been afraid that no one will believe me.'

Ruby could sense that Luke was ready to explode and she didn't blame him. But what else could she have done? She had to protect him – and Lily and Tyler – from the danger she had put them in.

He was still watching them. He would harm them all if he

didn't get what he'd come for. She didn't want to do anything that might endanger them further.

'What does he want?' Luke said. 'Do you know that too?'

She shook her head as she lied again.

'That's just great. So we'll have to wait and see, won't we? Tyler will be home soon. He'll probably come back and finish off the job.'

'Don't say that! He won't find us if we keep moving.'

'We're in the middle of a police investigation. Do you think they're just going to forget everything now? They'll get Children's Services on to us for putting our kids at risk. You should have told me.'

'Don't you dare blame me for all of this.' She prodded him in the chest. 'You lied too.'

Luke stepped back, momentarily stunned.

'You borrowed money again. If I hadn't found out this morning, would you have told me about it?'

'That's different.'

'It's exactly the same. You were trying to protect me. So don't have a go at me for keeping something from you.'

There were inches between them as they stood breathless glaring at each other. Ruby was cornered, her back literally against the wall. She had nowhere to go, no one to turn to and now she had lied to the police again. No one would ever believe a word she said in the future if she kept covering up the truth all the time.

'He's dangerous,' she said. 'And I've always felt safe with you.'

'Yet you couldn't tell me.'

'I've been living on the edge for years.' She burst into tears. 'Scared for my life, for my children's lives and for yours too.'

It was a moment before Luke took her in his arms, but it gave her time to realise that she should have trusted him. He should have been honest with her too. They were both to blame.

But right now, it had to be all about keeping their family together.

'Have you told me everything, Ruby?' he asked as he held on to her.

She nodded, knowing that she could never do that. It was too much of a risk. And she hated herself for it.

But she hated herself even more for lying about Finn.

THIRTY-FOUR

Mary pulled the front door shut and popped her keys into the pocket of her coat. She began the walk towards the stairs that would take her to ground level. Even though it was just before five p.m., everywhere was shrouded in a cloak of darkness.

She'd thought it best to go out later in the day. There was less chance of her being seen, even though the lamplight on the side path would keep her illuminated. It would mean she would feel safe, though, and in full view of other people. It would also take her to the main road.

After the accident with Tyler Douglas, the police presence was less now, almost non-existent. She was still worried that there might be repercussions because she'd handed the money back, and although she'd rather avoid Seth altogether, she needed a few provisions – milk, bread and coffee.

She hadn't slept well for the past two nights. She'd sat indoors for ages thinking about everything, but she was glad she'd spoken out. It was the right thing to do and her conscience was clear. She'd hated herself last night though, for not doing it earlier. She had been scared, but having that money had made her fear him even more.

After shuffling down to the end of the walkway, she pushed on the door that led to the stairs. At the halfway point, she stopped to catch her breath on the concrete landing, holding on to the rail for support before taking the next flight of steps.

As she moved forward again, she saw someone up above. It was a man, his face covered with a hat and a scarf. Fearful as she held on to the rail, she pushed her feet down onto each step gingerly. The man jogged down the steps, stopping behind her. There was ample room for him to pass her but he didn't.

She dared take another step down. Another one and she wondered if he had gone back upstairs rather than come down. She hazarded a quick glance round to see. But he was still there.

'Do you want to go past?' she asked him. 'Your legs are a lot younger than mine.'

Before she realised what was happening, he punched her full in the face. She stumbled backwards with its power. Her hand grappled for the rail but she missed it in her panic. Her head took the full force of the concrete steps and she flipped on her side as she fell. The wall in front came crashing towards her, and she banged her head again. Her vision began to blur.

She hoped he'd leave her alone then. But she could see him coming towards her, then towering over her. Stooping down, he pressed his hand over her mouth and nose.

'Oh, Mary, Mary, Mary. Always watching, listening and saying too much,' he chided as she struggled to take in air.

Her arms flapped about and she tried to claw at his gloved hands. But he was too strong for her. All of her life she had tried to help people, be a good neighbour, and now she was in trouble because she had done the right thing. Her head was throbbing, her leg bent awkwardly beneath her. The pain was unbearable, her breath almost gone.

As he disappeared from her vision, her world went black. But she knew one thing. Seth Forrester was evil.

She had been right to blame him for something he hadn't done.

Back in his home, Seth could hear Shelley in the bathroom. He lit a cigarette and took three quick bursts for a hit of nicotine. He removed his hat and gloves and ran a hand over his head as he paced the living room.

That stupid woman! He was only going to give her a shove, a scare even, but as she'd been lying there at the bottom of the steps, helpless, bloody, he'd wanted to get rid of her so much. He hadn't meant to kill her but she'd made him lose his temper. Putting his hand over her mouth and nose seemed like the simplest thing to do. He should have stopped at giving her a warning.

Yet for months now she had been on his back, spreading rumours, complaining to the housing association about him, watching every move he made. She hadn't even been satisfied with the money he'd given her to keep her quiet.

He stopped. The money! Shit, it was in her flat. He'd have to go back and get it. She must have her keys on her as she'd left the flat. If he was quick no one might have found her yet.

But then he reasoned with himself. He couldn't go back.

Sirens rang through the air. He rushed to the kitchen window to see blue flashes slicing through the dark. One of the nosy fuckers must have called the police already. That was the trouble with Harrison House. People say they saw nothing but they weren't too slow on reporting anything amiss.

He needed her dead now. If she wasn't and he could be ID'd, then he would be going back to prison. Fuck, he wasn't going there again, no matter what.

'What's going on outside?' Shelley came in behind him.

Seth turned to see her wrapped in a white dressing gown, pink toenails on her bare feet.

'Don't know.' He shrugged. 'Someone's called the police again.'

Shelley paused. 'Are you okay? You're sweating so much. I hope you're not coming down with that flu bug that's going around. Everyone I know has it, and I don't want to catch it as— Hey!'

Seth pushed past Shelley and made his way into the bathroom. He couldn't stand listening to her wittering on. He had other things to think about. He'd have to come up with something as to why Mary had the money.

He'd used gloves today but his prints could be on the envelope or the notes.

2012

The paramedics arrived at Finn's flat and two police officers followed a few minutes later. Finn was unconscious and they were trying to stem the bleeding before they moved him. By now a crowd had gathered at the entrance to the flats to see what was going on.

Ruby sobbed in the background. 'One minute we were talking, the next he was being attacked,' she tried to explain to an officer.

'And you didn't see who did it?'

She shook her head and pointed to the armchair. 'I hid behind there.'

'Why? Was someone after him?'

'I . . . I don't know. It was just something he told me to do.'

She wasn't sure they believed her but they didn't pressurise her. A woman officer tried to move her away but she stayed put.

'It's better if you're not here,' she justified. 'Give the paramedics more room to work.'

'But he's dead, isn't he?' Ruby shook off her arm. 'He's not coming back.'

'He's alive at the moment. Let them do their job.'

Eventually, Ruby was shown into the back of the ambulance. The paramedic wrapped a silver blanket around her shoulders as she clung to Lily, who was in her arms.

'Do you know who it was that attacked him?' a different police officer asked. 'It's okay if you're frightened to tell me but it would help us. It was quite brutal.'

Ruby shook her head.

'Did you see if it was one person? Two? More?'

Ruby shook her head again, afraid to say anything.

'Not to worry. And there's bound to be CCTV nearby so we'll be checking that too. Are you sure you're okay? You don't need to be looked at in A&E yourself?'

'No, I'm fine.'

It was then she looked down to see she was covered in Finn's blood. It was all over her hands, her clothes, underneath her nails. She hugged Lily closely. All she wanted was to get the men who had hurt Finn. But first she needed him to stay alive.

At the hospital, they were taken through into the emergency area. Behind a door was a long corridor with several cubicles leading off them. While they worked on Finn, she was shown into a side room where she waited for news and was given a cup of tea.

It was just past midnight. Her hands shook as she tried to drink the sweet liquid. The police still wanted to talk to her and she wondered how much she should say this time. She wanted to tell them everything but Finn had warned her enough not to. She was concerned about getting him into trouble too. It wasn't a fight that had escalated beyond the point of no return. Dane and his men meant to kill him.

Tears slid down her cheeks. Lily stirred in her lap and she held on tightly to her daughter, praying that Finn would be okay, that he would stay alive.

She closed her eyes as she thought back to his laboured breathing.

A woman in blue overalls, her hair scraped from her face in a ponytail, came over to her.

'Are you a relative?' she asked.

'I'm his girlfriend. Is he going to be okay?'

'Finn has been stabbed, several times.' The woman took her hand. 'The scan showed internal bleeding so we've taken him down to theatre for emergency surgery. He'll be assessed while he's there.'

Ruby gasped. 'Is he going to die?'

'There's no way of knowing that until the surgery has been completed. He was bleeding heavily so has lost a lot of blood. Also, knife wounds can look superficial on the outside. It's the damage caused inside that we have to investigate. I'm sorry I can't tell you any more than that for now. Let's wait to see how he does before making assumptions.'

'He is, isn't he? He's going to die!'

'Is there anyone I can call for you?'

She shook her head. She had no one to help her. She couldn't burden her dad with this, not after so long away from him. But how she wished she could.

'Please tell me he isn't going to die.'

When the woman said nothing, Ruby pushed a fist against her mouth and sobbed.

He couldn't die. She couldn't live without him.

Ruby sat with Lily in the side room for what seemed like hours, but in actual fact only fifty minutes had passed. She watched the hands of the clock going round and round, shredding a tissue, her eyes so sore she could barely see out of them.

All the time she waited for the door to open. For someone to come in and tell her more news of Finn. That he was still alive.

Please don't let him die.

She didn't want those bastards to win.

When the police arrived to question her again, she told them nothing. Finn said he could handle the gang himself. They were going to leave so she didn't want to make matters worse. He'd been threatened with his life before, and now it had been carried out. She broke down again, curling up in the uncomfortable chair with Lily.

What was she going to do if she lost him?

THIRTY-FIVE

When her interview with Ruby Brassington finished, it was half past five. Grace grabbed a sandwich and a bag of crisps from the canteen and headed back to her desk. Sam had left her a note to say there were no security cameras on any houses in Minor Crescent so they were none the wiser as to who had carried out the hit and run on Caleb Campbell. Grace wondered if Caleb had been followed and deliberately targeted in a quiet street.

She was about to check up on Finn Ridley when there was a shout from Allie's office. Grace popped her head up as she came over to them.

'Suspicious death,' Allie told everyone. 'A woman has been found at the bottom of a flight of stairs. Dave Barnett has been called out too.' She looked at Grace. 'It's Harrison House.'

'You're kidding!' Grace shot out of her seat.

Allie shook her head. 'Thought you could come with us.'

'Yes, of course.'

They were out of the building and on their way in less than five minutes. As Grace raced through the traffic she spoke to Frankie, who was beside her.

'Do you think this could be connected to our case? Surely it's too much of a coincidence that two crimes would be committed so close together, for them not to be linked?'

'I guess, but until we know who the woman is we can't be certain.'

Grace kept her eyes on the road then. At the flats, the area being cordoned off was a hive of activity. Uniformed officers tried to keep a growing crowd behind the crime scene tape. Residents were dotted around in their groups of twos and threes, mouths going nineteen to the dozen. Grace knew they would be surmising, presuming, supposing. But she was only interested in the facts.

'I'm glad we had Ruby Brassington in the station when I heard the news,' she told Perry as they donned the necessary protective gear. 'If we hadn't, I would have assumed someone had got to her. Even so my heart was in my mouth when I was told.'

They signed the log to say they were attending the crime scene and walked towards the communal staircase where the body had been found, where a woman had lost her life. The area had been sealed off, hidden behind a white sheet as a tent was unable to stand. Spotlights had been lit to illuminate the scene.

'Residents are complaining that they can't use the entrance to get to their flats,' Allie said as she went up the first set of steps.

'We've already been in touch with the council, Ma'am,' an officer told her. 'For now they can enter from the side, the fire escape. It's not ideal but this is the only way in.'

They drew level with the body and Grace closed her eyes momentarily to shut out the sight.

'It's Mary Stanton, from flat 108,' she said eventually. 'I've interviewed her twice this week in connection with Tyler Douglas's accident.' Guilt flooded her as she wondered if Mary's visit to the station had anything to do with her death.

Dave Barnett, the senior CSI, was stooping over the body. He stood up when he realised they were behind him, pushing his glasses up his nose.

'It's a bit of a nasty one,' he said. 'At first it looked as if she'd taken a tumble, but on further investigation, she's been hit in the face. With a fist most likely, causing her to lose her balance and fall backwards judging by her stance.' He pointed to the side of her head where there was a deep gash. 'She caught the edge of a step there, and then there's the thud she took when she landed. If it wasn't for that nose bleeding, and the marks appearing around her mouth, I would have said it was an accident, until further inspection.' He looked at them from the corner of his eye. 'But then you're the detectives, I guess.'

Grace couldn't even give him a quick eye roll. She liked Dave and a sense of humour was always a great asset in their jobs, as long as the general public didn't see any of them laughing when someone had been murdered. But this was playing heavily on her conscience right now.

'And no signs of anything missing?' Perry asked. 'Do we know who found her?'

'A neighbour,' Dave replied. 'He lives on the same floor as our victim. He called for the emergency services.'

'Did she have anything on her?'

Dave pointed to an evidence envelope containing a set of keys and a purse. 'No one else has been up or down since I've been here.'

Allie nodded. 'Grace, come with me and Perry.'

'Yes, Ma'am.' Grace turned to Frankie. 'Can you liaise with uniform and set things up for me? I'll join you once I've given her home the once-over.'

Frankie nodded and went downstairs.

Grace took a deep breath and followed quickly behind Perry and Allie. She was not looking forward to this at all.

THIRTY-SIX

Whoever had murdered Mary Stanton had waited for her to leave her flat. Two days ago it would have seemed tricky with such a large police presence but now it had been pared back, it was easier to get around.

Inside, the first thing Grace spotted was the woman's knitting that she'd seen when she'd visited before, and felt sad that whatever Mary had been making would now never be finished. They searched carefully through drawers in units, kitchen cupboards, wardrobes and bathroom cabinets, looking for next-of-kin details.

They continued to look around but there seemed nothing out of place, nor any indication as to why the woman had been killed almost on her own front door step. Was someone taunting the police, doing things right under their noses? It took her back to her previous case where two women had been strangled in open spaces. The killers were behind bars now but the case had been difficult as there weren't many clues, and the murders had happened so quickly that forensics hadn't come back before the second woman had been attacked.

When she had seen enough, Grace came out of the flat and stood on the walkway. Most of the neighbours were outside too, despite the bitter cold, gawking at the goings-on.

She beckoned Perry to her.

'Mary Stanton could see the Douglas's front door.' She pointed. 'Do you think someone was trying to shut her up, now we know Tyler's fall wasn't an accident?'

'I think it's a valid question. Maybe she'd seen something that her killer thinks she shouldn't have.'

'She said she saw Seth Forrester hanging Tyler Douglas over the wall.'

'Which we now know may not be true, since Ruby told us that it was Finn.'

'Which also means that it could be Seth who attacked Milo Benton as he said he was in the car park to get a gym bag from his car.' Her brow furrowed. 'You don't think Seth is responsible for this, do you? And why, if he had nothing to do with the Tyler Douglas case?'

Perry sighed loudly. 'Your guess is as good as mine. He's done some nasty things in his time, and I'm sure he's capable of it.'

'Do we have enough to bring him in?'

'Not yet.'

Grace nodded. If it wasn't Forrester, could it be Finn Ridley? She had updated everyone about him that afternoon, and how it was alleged that he had dropped Tyler over the walkway. Was Ridley involved somehow in the murder of Mary Stanton, now that they had a positive ID? Although, to be fair, they only had Ruby Brassington's word for it so far and she'd cried wolf far too many times for Grace's liking.

Mary could have seen everything if she was out on the walkway and someone had clearly wanted her to keep her mouth shut. What they needed to work out was whether the suspect had meant to kill her or if they just went too far? Either way, that poor woman had lost her life.

Grace turned as Allie joined them, removing her forensic mask and taking in a deep breath of fresh air.

'The residents are going to be up in arms about this,' she said.

'I wouldn't blame anyone for thinking ill of us,' Grace replied. 'It could have been my fault. She'd been talking to me.'

'You didn't push her down the stairs.'

'Even so, I feel responsible. And I bet no one saw anything, as usual.' Grace shook her head in disdain. 'It's so galling. When Tyler Douglas went over the railing no one saw anything, and now there's been a murder, it'll be "what are you doing about it" but still "we saw nothing". I don't know what they expect us to do. We could be a lot quicker if someone actually *had been* looking out for some of the neighbours.' She shook her head. 'Poor Mary. She seemed a lovely lady, even though a bit of a busybody. And where would we be without people like her?' Grace could think of several cases where neighbours had given key pieces of evidence to connect the links to the killers.

'I'm going to talk to the man who found her,' Perry said. 'Want to come?'

'I think I'll go and find Frankie.'

Grace went back downstairs, to be met with lots of people laying flowers. Already there seemed to be half a florists outside the main entrance door. It was heartbreaking and heart-warming at the same time to see the tributes laid out.

There was a community meeting arranged for tomorrow afternoon. It had been set up to talk more about the safety issue of Tyler going over the railing, but now that there had been a murder, Allie was going to use the opportunity to see if anyone had anything to say about Mary Stanton.

Could this be connected to the Tyler Douglas incident

anyway? Had someone seen Mary watching, told her to keep her mouth shut and then an argument got out of hand?

Had Mary Stanton been pressurised into saying 'I saw nothing' and then found it hard to keep quiet? Had she been singled out because she was a witness to Tyler's case?

2012

It was a long night for Ruby. The police had questioned her again but left her alone for now. They must have got all they needed.

Lily was asleep on the settee beside her. The nurses had brought drinks as she waited for news. Finally, after she'd managed to grab an hour's sleep, the door opened and a man walked in.

'It's Ruby, isn't it?' he said, shaking her hand and then sitting across from her. 'I'm Mr Siminidge. I'm the surgeon looking after Finn.'

'How is he?' she asked, not clear from his demeanour either way.

'He's stable at the moment.'

Tears slid down her cheeks as she listened to him.

'We had to remove his spleen. It was a long operation to take care of all the damage, but he seems to have pulled through quite strongly. He'll stay in intensive care for a day or two while we watch over his vitals. I think a few more hours will tell us more, but for now, he's out of harm's way.'

That's if they don't get him next time.

She pushed the thought out of her head.

'Can I see him?' she asked.

'Yes, for a few minutes. He's a little groggy from the anaesthetic but he's awake. He wants to see you. He keeps repeating your name.'

A nurse sat with Lily while Ruby put on a gown and disinfected her hands. She followed Mr Siminidge through into a ward with six beds. There were so many machines around everyone and even though there was hardly a noise except for the beeps on the machines, the silence was comforting.

She paused when she saw him in the bed, then rushed to his side.

'Finn,' she whispered. 'It's me, Ruby.'

At the sound of her voice, Finn turned his head, opening his eyes slightly before closing them.

'Ruby.'

She clasped her hand around his. Finn opened his eyes again.

'Ruby,' he repeated.

'I'll leave you to it for now,' Mr Siminidge said.

'Thank you for saving his life,' Ruby told him, trying to keep the tremor from her voice.

'You need to keep his spirits up now. His physical wounds may heal in time, but it's the mental ones that might be hard to get over.'

Ruby quietly moved a chair over to the side of the bed and reached for Finn's hand again.

'Did you tell—?'

'Don't say his name.' His whisper was loud, his voice hoarse from the operation. 'If we don't tell anyone who did this, then this should be my payback. This'll be the end of it.'

'I can't see that happening.' Ruby shook her head. 'But I've been thinking. I can book train tickets and pack up our stuff ready for when you're able to leave the hospital.'

'It's not an option now.'

'But he's nearly killed you! What if he wants to finish off the job?'

'He won't. It's a test.'

'A *test*?'

'If we keep quiet, he'll leave us alone. What did you say to the police?'

'I said I didn't know who it was.' She paused. 'Can't they help you? Put you under that thing – witness protection, is it?'

He laughed, and it turned into a cough. He settled down again, putting a reassuring hand up to stop a nurse from coming over.

'They won't help me. Not unless I grass on him.'

'So do that. Put him behind bars and we don't have to worry.'

'But don't you see – if I do that, he'll find someone else to get to me. Even in prison, he has men to do his bidding for him. He'll always come after me for putting him there. This way he gave me a warning. He didn't mean to kill me but he'll want me to stay around here so that he can see what effect it's having on me. I've seen him do it to others. If I leave, he'll hunt me down. That's his thing, it's what he likes doing.'

Ruby let him sleep then, leaving a few minutes later. As she walked to collect Lily, she realised she had to become stronger. If she loved Finn enough to stick with him, then she had to do something to get them away. It was the best she could think of.

She couldn't go on living like this. Come hell or high water, she would persuade him to leave. This wasn't the way to bring up Lily.

She was going to fight for her family.

THIRTY-SEVEN

Standing on the walkway, Grace took a breather as she surveyed what was happening around her. It was nearing eight p.m. that evening. Still there were neighbours everywhere, but this time there was a subdued atmosphere. The animosity would happen if they didn't find the killer in a day or two, but for now, thankfully, the people of Harrison House were giving Mary Stanton the dignity she warranted. No one deserved to die in such a brutal way. Obviously, the general public didn't know all the details. As far as they were concerned, until Mary's next of kin had been informed and they had more forensic evidence, this was another accident but this time with a fatal outcome.

She went to find Frankie. When she pushed open the door to the communal staircase, the chilly air hit her again. It must be minus two and she could hardly feel her fingers. She pulled in the collar of her coat, taking care not to slip on the icy tarmac.

Behind the police cordon, she saw Simon. He wouldn't know Mary's death was suspicious yet, but it was his job to report the news regardless. He had his back to her and was talking to an old couple, the woman clearly distressed at the news. She wanted to run up behind him, wrap her arms around him and feel his warmth, his life. Mary's death was taking its toll. She couldn't stop seeing the older woman lying there, the bruising appearing around her mouth.

'Hey,' she touched Simon on the arm.

Simon thanked the couple for their details and they moved away from the crowd.

'How are you holding up?' he asked.

'I'm okay.' She gave him a faint smile. 'It's a woman, I can tell you that much.'

'Do you know how she died?'

'Not at liberty to say yet and it's too soon anyway. It's mere speculation at this point.'

'Do you have an age?'

'Sorry, no.' Grace's eyes burnt with tears and she looked away for a moment. 'I only spoke to her yesterday and she gave me vital information.'

'Oh?'

'You know I can't tell you that.'

'You're a hard one to crack, Ms Allendale,' he muttered playfully.

She laughed inwardly. So much for him caring only for her.

'There's a neighbour that might speak to you tomorrow,' she said. 'He found our victim. Mr Johnson, flat 105. I think he could do with someone to talk to about it. He seemed traumatised just now.'

'Thanks, I'll speak to him in the morning. I take it you're here for the night?'

She pulled her coat closer to her body to keep out the biting wind, trying not to look at the stairwell where Mary Stanton's body lay behind the white sheet being held up by two officers.

'Yes, are you staying around too?'

'I might as well. It's lonely without you in the house.'

She took hold of his hand and gave it a squeeze.

'Love you, Allendale,' he whispered before she let go and walked away.

Grace smiled then, but she didn't turn back. She had work to do.

THURSDAY

THIRTY-EIGHT

It was with a heavy heart that Grace joined the morning team briefing at eight thirty. Everyone was going to be hit hard by what was about to come out.

Allie was sitting at the head of the table, all available staff standing around the room if they hadn't bagged a chair. Her mood was sombre.

'Good morning, everyone. Not a great start to the day but welcome to Operation Spode. As most of you are aware, last night a woman was murdered at Harrison House. She lived in flat 108, almost directly opposite Tyler Douglas's home, the ongoing case that Grace and Frankie are dealing with. Perry, would you like to tell everyone what we've found out so far, and then Grace can follow if necessary?'

Perry stood up, moved to the front of the room and updated them. 'It was made to look like our victim had fallen down a flight of steps,' he added. 'But after an initial observation by Dave Barnett, he said the injuries were from her being attacked. Someone also put a hand over her mouth and nose to smother her.'

Murmurs went around the room.

'I'm open to suggestions for motive.' Allie pointed to the woman's photo on the whiteboard, taken when she was found. Bruising was visible on her face. 'Grace, do you want to add anything?'

'Yes. You all know we've been looking into the incident of Tyler Douglas. Mary Stanton alleges she saw what happened from her window. What she told me was contradictory in itself, but she did suggest it could have been Seth Forrester who held Tyler over the railing. Our fourteen-year-old witness also alleges it was Forrester. We have no evidence to back up these claims yet. Ruby Brassington has also thrown into the mix that she knew the man on the walkway and that he is Finn Ridley, someone who gave her trouble years ago.' She updated them on the details and looked around the room at everyone. 'It's possible this case has nothing to do with Tyler Douglas's but, for now, I want to concentrate on finding out if they're connected. We'll be going house-to-house again, or door-to-door, in this instance. It won't be a good experience as the tenants have only just had us doing it a couple of days ago. But it has to be done. Everyone needs accounting for as far as possible.'

'Thanks.' Allie turned back to the team. 'We have the basics so, like Grace said, let's focus on establishing *if* this has anything to do with the Tyler Douglas incident. Grace, can you update Ruby and Luke once I've confirmed ID with the victim's family this morning? One of Mary's sons drove down last night so my first job is a visit to the mortuary, and then there will be a press conference. There's going to be speculation from people, I guess. There'll be more once people are made aware foul play is involved as, for now, it only appears to be an accident. I think it will be better coming from us rather than via a TV clip.'

Grace nodded in agreement. It seemed fair, even though she

240

didn't want to burden Ruby and Luke any more, but they may be able to establish a link between the two cases.

As soon as the phone call from Allie confirming the formal identification of Mary Stanton came in, Grace went to see Ruby and Luke. The press conference was going ahead at eleven a.m. which gave her a little time to tell them first before it was common knowledge.

It was sad but the case was bringing back terrible memories for her. She was having her nightmares again. Only last night she'd woken up crying out loud. Luckily, Simon had still been asleep so she'd gone to sit downstairs until the melancholy had passed.

Grace knew better than most people the damage abuse could do, yet she could never understand how her mum had dealt with her father all those years ago. George Steele had been so violent. She could recall incidences that would still turn her stomach. He would hit Martha where people wouldn't see it until she was black and blue, and even then she lost count of the number of black eyes she'd had.

She hadn't talked much to her friends or colleagues about what had gone on before she and her mother had fled that night. It was difficult even now to vocalise what had happened. Having experienced it herself, it made her more empathetic to Ruby. She wanted her to be safe.

'You just caught us in time,' Ruby said when she answered the door. 'Luke took Lily to school and we're off to the hospital in a moment. They might discharge Tyler today.'

'Oh, that is good news.' Grace went inside and sat down opposite them both. Ruby's eyes were red and swollen, her face blotchy. A tissue was balled up in her hand. Luke was the worse for wear, the stench of alcohol heavy in the room. His face was a riot of bruising; a split, swollen lip and a black eye.

'What happened to your face?' she asked Luke.

'I tripped and fell on my way home from the pub last night. I sunk a few beers. I had to get out, too claustrophobic here after what happened.'

'You should have stayed at home,' Ruby said. 'I needed you.'

Grace watched the interaction between Luke and Ruby, noticing the frosty look that passed between them. It was clear that Ruby wasn't in his good books.

Luke ignored Ruby and turned to Grace. 'What's happening across the way? I saw flowers being laid downstairs. There're more police here today. Is it something to do with us?'

'That's what I wanted to talk to you about. One of your neighbours was found deceased yesterday around five p.m. Mary Stanton, flat 108.'

'That's terrible.' Ruby's hand covered her mouth. 'How did it happen?'

'We're not at liberty to say yet, as we're still waiting on forensics and gathering evidence.'

'Wait. You don't think we had anything to do with it?' Luke asked with alarm. 'You're going to blame us for everything now, aren't you?'

'No, that's not why I'm here,' Grace said pointedly. 'There will be a press conference about it later today. We can't give out many details at the moment but I wanted to let you both know. We'll do our best to see off the media, but with a case like this, there will be national interest. They might focus on you as well because this is the second incident here this week, so I'd highly recommend you speak to no one.'

'A case like this?' Luke snapped.

'Why are you so defensive, Mr Douglas? I was talking about the incident last night. You make me feel you have something to hide.'

'*You* make me feel as if I'm guilty of something – and I'm

not.' He pointed at her. 'You should leave us alone. We've been through enough.'

'Luke,' Ruby soothed. 'They're doing their best.'

'Well, it isn't good enough.'

'It never is, Mr Douglas,' Grace replied. 'But we can only work with the truth, and lately there doesn't seem to have been too much of that. So, please calm down, let me do my job and I will get to the bottom of your matter too. We're looking into the whereabouts of Finn Ridley as we speak. Unless there is anything else you'd like to tell us?'

When they remained quiet, she stood up. 'I want to help you both,' she said. 'But you have to start being straight with me and telling me everything. If he gets in touch again, we need to know. Okay?'

Two nods this time.

Grace made her way back outside to the team, hoping the couple had been pacified for now. She looked around, seeing lots of familiar faces.

Was Mary's killer among them?

Was the man who'd dropped Tyler Douglas there watching them?

Was it the same person who had committed both crimes?

Questions, questions, questions. What they needed were some answers.

THIRTY-NINE

Shelley was at her wits' end. After finding the envelope, she couldn't stop thinking about Seth. That money had been for something, but what?

So hearing of Mary's death on the Harrison House grapevine had shocked her. The radio bulletin confirmed that police were yet to rule out a suspicious death. Mary wasn't a bad old sort. She'd often see her as she was going across to the shops, sometimes being shouted back to run an errand for her. She hadn't objected; Mary had reminded her of her gran before she died. She was a sweet old soul. Why would someone want to harm her?

She cursed inwardly. She'd been meaning to go and see Mary that morning. Have a word with her and see if there was anything she could find out. She hated herself for it but information was everything at a price.

But now she had been found dead, well, she wasn't sure what to think. Why had Seth given her all of that money? What had she on him that meant he was trying to pay her off? Had she seen something she shouldn't have? What game wouldn't she play?

And was it a coincidence that she was dead shortly after bringing it back? Seth couldn't know about the money unless Mary had told him. And if she had, then Shelley would be in danger too as he'd want to know why she hadn't given it to him straight away.

No, she shook her head. He couldn't know about it. So she'd hide it. If no one knew about it, then why shouldn't she? It was payback time for suffering Seth. She'd keep it for a while and if nothing was said, she would have it.

She shuddered involuntarily. Was she living with a murderer? He was hard, but was he that dangerous?

If it *was* Seth, she wouldn't stay with him. She wanted out.

She sent a text message to Eddie saying she needed to talk to him. Although she still had work to do for him before her debt was paid in full, she didn't feel comfortable doing it now.

Then she went to see if she could find out anything else from Ruby. She had a plan brewing.

The knock on the door had Ruby jumping in her seat. She went to look through the spy hole, sighing with relief when she saw it was Shelley.

'Hiya!' Shelley cried. 'I've just been to the shop for some ciggies so I thought I'd come and see how things are.'

It was good to see a welcome face, especially one with a smile. Ruby was about to tell her what had happened with the police when Shelley spoke again.

'Actually I was after some advice. Do you have a few minutes?'

Ruby let her in. 'Yes, but Luke will be back soon and then we're going to pick Tyler up from the hospital.'

'Oh, he's coming home?'

'We think so.'

Shelley gave her a hug. 'That's great news. Terrible about that old woman across the way, though, isn't it?'

245

'I've just heard it on the news,' Ruby fibbed. 'I didn't know her well, did you?'

'Not really, but I've said hello whenever we met.' Shelley sighed. 'And now we have the police all over us again while they investigate what happened.'

Ruby made coffee and they sat down together. She could sense Shelley wanted to say something but was reluctant to.

'You said you wanted some advice?' Ruby was intrigued enough to ask.

Shelley took a sip from her drink. 'I've found something out about Seth. I think he's making money on the side and keeping it from Leon Steele.'

'I don't understand. Is that wrong?'

Shelley raised her eyebrows. 'It's dangerous. It's like robbing from the hand that feeds you.'

'Oh.' Ruby nodded. 'How did you find out?'

'I found a box under the bed with a few thousand in it.' Shelley pulled her handbag nearer and took out the envelope. She showed Ruby the money inside.

Ruby's eyes widened. 'Have you asked him about it?'

'No, I . . . well, I thought I might leave and take it with me. Severance pay for putting up with the bastard.'

'But won't Seth come after you?'

'Oh, I'll be long gone by then. I've had enough of his controlling ways. He's a bully and I can't take it any more.'

'Where will you go?'

'That's just it. I don't have anywhere.'

'Can't you go back to your parents?'

'They disowned me a long time ago.'

'But stealing money from Seth isn't the answer.'

'I know, but I need it.' Shelley bit at her bottom lip before speaking again. 'Could you look after it for me?'

'No.' Ruby put down her mug and shook her head.

'It wouldn't be for long, I promise.'

Ruby stood up. 'I can't believe you'd ask me to do anything like that. I've had the police all over the flat for the past few days. I've had my son in hospital and my life on hold.'

'Sorry. I guess I'll have to hide it myself and hope he doesn't find it before I leave.'

'You mustn't do that either,' Ruby objected. 'You'll end up living your life on the run. You'll be looking over your shoulder, wondering if Seth has found you and what he'll do to you. Because he will come after you, he won't just forget about it and move on. Men like him don't. You'll be in danger and—'

'Is that what happened to you?' Shelley interrupted. 'That man who dropped your Tyler over the side, is he after you?'

'I . . . I . . .' Ruby looked away. Should she tell Shelley what had gone on in her life before she came to Stoke? She had never trusted anyone with her secret, not even Luke. She decided it was too risky.

Shelley put down her mug too. 'If you can't help me, then that's fine. I'll do it myself. But you need to sort out this man. I know Seth would help if you wanted me to ask him.'

'We don't *need* anyone's help.'

'Are you sure? You only have to say the word and you can feel safe forever.'

'Like you do?'

Shelley's laugh was awkward.

Her story didn't add up to Ruby. What was she playing at? She checked her watch and picked up the two mugs.

'Time I was getting ready to go to the hospital,' she said. 'I'm so excited about bringing Tyler home.'

Shelley stood up and placed a hand on Ruby's arm. 'If you need a loan, let me know. There's more than enough for the two of us to get as far away from Stoke as possible.'

Ruby said nothing.

When Shelley had gone and Ruby had locked the door behind her, she sank to the floor and burst into tears. She hadn't got a single friend she could rely on. It was clear to her that Seth had sent Shelley round to dangle the carrot about the money she wanted Ruby to 'keep safe'. Maybe he thought they would steal it, use it to pay their debt, therefore putting themselves more in it.

Or he was after lending extra money to them. Seth would add it to the five thousand Luke already owed and then he'd put interest on it and before they knew it, it would be ten thousand and they would be running from two sets of people then if they left.

She wiped at her eyes. It was time to get serious about things.

2012

Finn was in hospital for over a week. His wounds on the outside were healing well, but he became more paranoid as the days passed, wondering who might be waiting for him when he was discharged.

Ruby had changed his mind about leaving eventually. During her visits, they had planned for his release. She had packed as much as she could into three suitcases and tomorrow they were going to take a train to Wales. They had a bit of money to tide them over. They would go somewhere a little remote where they might not be found. Ruby didn't mind moving. She was willing to do it for Finn and Lily's safety. She could get a job, they both could, and start again.

On the morning Finn was due to be released, Ruby almost bounced along the corridor towards the ward as she pushed Lily in her pram, asleep for now. She panicked when she found an empty bed, then smiled. He must be in the day room. They would obviously need his bed.

But he wasn't there when she looked.

'Do you know where Finn Ridley is?' she asked one of the nurses sitting at the ward desk.

'He's gone, love.' The woman frowned. 'He discharged himself last night. Just after you'd been to visit. I thought you knew.'

Ruby shook her head. 'He told me it was today. Were you here when he left?'

'I was. A man came to collect him.'

'Did he say his name?'

'I don't think so. He was burly, I'll give him that. Quite scary looking actually.' She put a hand to her mouth. 'Oh, sorry. Is he a friend of yours?'

'What did he look like?'

'Tall, heavy built; too many tattoos for me if you don't think I'm being rude. That thing on his neck.' She screwed up her face.

Feeling the blood rush to her head, Ruby held on to the desk for support.

'Are you okay?' the woman asked, resting a hand on hers. 'You've gone so pale.'

'Yes, I'll be fine. It's just very hot in here.'

'It's *always* hot in here.' She smiled. 'Would you like me to see if he left any details?'

Ruby nodded and waited. But there was nothing.

Where was he? Had Dane got hold of him again?

She raced back to the flat with Lily but he wasn't there. She tried him several times on his phone over the course of the day but there was never any reply. In the end, she left a message.

'Finn, ring me. What's going on? I need to know you're safe!'

It was two days later before he called. During this time, Ruby had been going out of her mind. Wondering if he was coming back or if he had gone for good.

'Where are you?' she cried, so glad to hear his voice at last.

'I can't tell you, Rube.'

'Why not?'

'It's best that you don't know.'

'But I want to see you. Are you coming home soon?'

'I don't know.'

'Don't do this to me! I want to be with you.'

'You can be – soon, but not yet.'

'When?'

'I'll keep in touch. I'll let you know once it's safe.'

'But how long will that be?'

'I'm not sure.'

'No, Finn, please. Don't leave me here. I want to be with you.'

'And I want to be with you, but it's not safe yet.'

'What do you mean? Has Dane threatened you again?'

There was a pause down the line. 'I love you, Ruby. So, so much. I love Lily too. But don't you see, that's why I can't come back yet. If I do, he'll hurt you next.'

'We were going to Wales.'

'We can still go.'

'When?'

'In a few weeks maybe. When I've given Dane time to think I've done a runner without you.'

'But the nurse said he came to see you.'

'He did, which is why I had to leave without you. I wasn't waiting around for him to return.'

'You're sure I can be with you soon?'

'Yes, just hang on for a little while. Six weeks at the most and I'll find a way to get you out of there. You can meet me somewhere. Can you do that? Can you wait for me?'

'Promise me you'll be in touch soon?'

'I promise. You look after yourself until we're together again.'

Tears were pouring down her face now, her voice breaking

as much as his. In frustration, she disconnected the call. She tried to retrieve his number but he had withheld it. It would most probably be a burner phone. Finn wasn't stupid.

They would both lay low for a few weeks. Six at the most, he had said. She could do that. She could wait for him. And then they would be together again.

FORTY

Shelley let herself into the flat to find Seth coming out of the bathroom and heading towards the bedroom. She'd hated lying to Ruby and setting her up. But she needed to get out of this mess now that she didn't trust Seth, and the only way to do it was to provide the proof of what he was up to.

'I've just been to see Ruby, plant the seeds like you told me to about her borrowing money,' she said, all bright and breezy when she felt nothing of the sort.

'Did she take the bait?' Seth towel dried his hair.

'I'm not sure. But I have a feeling they're so scared that they're ready to do a flit.'

'Not until I get my money back. When are they going? Not today?'

'I doubt it. She was getting ready to go to the hospital to collect Tyler. She didn't tell me anything else. I reckon it will be the weekend, though. She needs to know that Tyler is okay first.'

'You're a clever woman.' Seth pulled her into his arms and kissed her passionately. She hoped he didn't want to take things further. She couldn't stomach him at the moment.

But then his demeanour changed.

'What's that?' He pointed to her bag.

She glanced down and gulped. In her haste to check to see if her text message to Eddie had been answered, she'd forgotten to zip up her bag. The envelope containing the money was visible.

'Oh, it came today – I was going to tell you about it now. It's an envelope full of money and a strange message written on it.' She pulled it out and handed it to him. '"I will not play your game,"' she added. 'What does that mean?'

Seth grabbed her around the throat and pushed her up against the wall. 'Have you any idea how worried I've been since the old woman copped it? You should have given this to me straight away.'

Shelley scrabbled at his hands. 'Seth, let me go. You're hurting me.'

But he squeezed harder, his eyes darting back and forth across her own. 'When did you get this?'

'This morning. I—'

'Liar! You couldn't have got it today because the person it was last with was dead last night.'

Shelley cursed herself for slipping up. She still tried to pull his hands away.

'Think about it, you stupid bitch. I gave her some money to keep her mouth shut and her nose out of my business after I beat up Milo Benton. She saw it all, along with everything else she was always going on about. I gave it her so that she would owe me. But now, she's dead and I thought she had the money in her flat and it would lead the cops to me and—'

Shelley tried so hard to keep a poker face. Was Seth actually saying that he *had* been involved with Mary's death? She'd thought he was a little over the top at times, hurting her more than necessary on occasions, and his temper snapping at the smallest of things. But murder?

She wrestled herself free as she felt his grip lessen slightly, and went to walk away.

'Where are you going?' he demanded, grabbing her arm and pulling her back. He sliced his hand across her mouth.

She cried out as her head cracked to the side with the force. Fear gripped her as she realised he was coming at her again. When Seth was in a mood like this, he was capable of hurting her in a bad way, the red mist descending. She'd seen it with him before, several times, when he'd attacked one of the boys for not delivering a package on time, or if they had come up with some excuse as to why they hadn't done as he'd told them. She put her hands up to protect herself as much as possible.

'Actually, I don't want you here.' Seth dragged her towards the front door, fumbled with the lock and at last opened it. Then he pushed her out so hard that she fell to her knees on the ground.

'Stay out of my fucking flat, you piece of lowlife,' he seethed.

Without looking back, Shelley picked herself up and ran along the walkway, trying not to cry out and bring attention to herself.

Seth slammed the front door. His hands curled up into fists and he knew if Shelley knocked to come back in, he would smash her in the face. He'd worried about that money since last night and all along the stupid bitch had hid it in her handbag.

Then he stopped. If he had the money back, then the police wouldn't have any clues to go on as to who murdered Mary. He smiled as everything sank in. He took the money from the envelope and hid it in with the rest of his cash in the bedroom.

He went through to the kitchen and took out his lighter. He flicked it on, stood over the sink and put the flame to the envelope. There was no trace of Mary Stanton here now. No trace at all.

FORTY-ONE

The planned community meeting about Tyler Douglas's fall was still going ahead that afternoon, even though there had been no safety issues as was first thought. Now that the official press conference to say that Mary Stanton's death was being treated as suspicious had happened, it would be easier to talk to people in one large group as well as going door-to-door.

Grace followed Allie into the main hall of the local church, their job to appease the tenants of Harrison House. There were rows of chairs set out and two rectangular tables together at the top of the room. Apprehension began to set in when she saw how many people were sitting in the seats. At a quick guess there must have been at least fifty. Were they coming to help or hinder? Were they thinking of Mary or was Tyler Douglas's accident playing on everyone's mind too?

By her side, she could see Frankie's knee bouncing up and down.

'What's up?' she asked him.

'I'm nervous about this,' he replied.

'About talking to the public?'

'No, just the meeting. There seems to be a bad vibe.'

'Someone has been murdered. There's nothing good about that.'

The room was noisy, people milling around. But as Allie stood up, a call for quiet went around.

'Okay, everyone,' she said. 'Thank you.'

Grace settled into her seat, Perry on the other side of her. It seemed everyone's eyes were on them.

'As you may know, we have now officially confirmed that the woman who died yesterday was Mary Stanton,' Allie began. 'She was sixty-nine years of age and had lived in Harrison House for five years.'

'Two falls in one week can't be a coincidence,' a man shouted up from the back.

Allie held up a hand for quiet but someone else chipped in.

'Disgusting, if you ask me,' a woman on the front row said, folding her arms and nodding her head for all to see.

Everyone began to speak at once then.

'We don't feel safe now.'

'First the boy was dropped and now a woman has fallen to her death. Something's going on.'

'We daren't come out of our own homes.'

'Someone's out to get the residents of Harrison House, aren't they?'

Frustration tore through Grace as they went off on a tangent. The meeting should have been about the investigations, and not about the residents, but she could understand their annoyance. She was thankful when Allie raised her hand again and asked for quiet.

'I get that everyone is upset and feeling vulnerable,' she humoured. 'But we don't want second guesses. We don't need rumours. We want to know if anyone saw anything that can help us to establish what happened.'

'I saw nothing,' a teenager from near to the back smirked.

'Yeah, me too,' his friend sitting next to him added.

'I know you all feel intimidated,' she went on. 'I'm sure coming forward is something that doesn't sit well with you, but this is the death of an elderly woman who you all must have seen on a regular basis.' Allie paused. 'This meeting was set up after Tyler Douglas's accident but, while we have you all in one place, we want to ask – did anyone see anything they feel they want to tell us about either episode?'

The room dropped into silence.

'It doesn't matter how small.'

'You have enough CCTV to go at,' someone shouted. 'Why do you need us to do your job for you?'

'Because the cameras don't cover everything. We rely on the eyes and ears of the public—'

'Doing your jobs for you.' A man near the aisle shook his head. 'If you ask me, you don't have a clue what went on.'

'Yeah, you're pissing in the wind,' a woman shouted.

The meeting wound up shortly afterwards. A lot of the crowd left as soon as they had finished speaking. Most of the outspoken tenants had gone too.

'Why is it that everyone thinks we don't want to find out what happened?' Grace said as she helped Allie stack up the chairs. 'It's in everyone's interests.'

'We're doing our job to the best of our abilities but obviously people in Harrison House "never saw anything". I hope they remember that the next time one of them needs our help.'

Grace stacked the last chair on the pile. 'It's just so exasperating at times. The public should want to help us. I wish they could see that we're not the enemy.'

'Some people are extremely helpful – others are not at all. But we police them all the same and eventually we find that piece of information, the golden nugget that helps us solve the case.' Allie leaned closer to Grace. 'And then the lot of them can go to hell. But don't tell them I said that.'

Grace stifled a chuckle. 'I think it's time for a chocolate break, don't you? I haven't had time to grab much today.'

Shelley ran across the car park and down Rose Avenue, the road that ran along the side of Harrison House. She stopped at Eddie's vehicle, climbing into the passenger seat.

'What's so important?' he asked, the look on his face clearly showing he was annoyed that she'd bothered him.

Shelley hadn't intended to but she burst into tears and pointed to her face.

'Seth has just tried to strangle me and then he hit me. I think he murdered the old woman across the way and he went mad at me and threatened to kill me too if I said anything.' She knew it wouldn't do any harm to exaggerate Seth's threats as she had thought them real at the time.

'What old woman?' Eddie's eyes flicked to meet hers.

'One of the tenants has been found dead. I think it was Seth. He's been acting strange and—'

'What did you call me for?'

'About this! He must have been bullying the woman, and he gave her some money in an envelope. She posted it back through our door with "I will not play your games" written on it. I kept it to give it to him later and then I found out the woman had died. When he realised I had the money, he went ballistic. He was worried it was still in her flat and the police would find his fingerprints on it.'

'That wouldn't be enough to prove he was involved. How did she die?'

'The police aren't saying yet, but I know he had something to do with it. I . . . I didn't think he was that dangerous.'

'He thinks he's beyond the law.'

She latched on to his words. 'Which means I'm in danger if I go back to him. That's why I rung you. I had my suspicions before he assaulted me that it was him.'

'You mean before you thieved the money.'

'What?' She shook her head. 'No! I never. I just kept it for him.'

'How much is there?'

'Nearly three thousand pounds.'

There was a long silence. Shelley knew better than to break it. She waited for Eddie to speak, umpteen things running through her mind. Then he turned back to her.

'Don't ring me, don't call me. This is your mess; you sort it out.'

'But he's dangerous!' she moaned. 'You know what he's capable of.'

'Where is the money?'

'Seth has it. I was going to give it to you.'

'No, you weren't.'

'I was. I just—' Shelley stopped as he raised his hand in the air. She'd had one slap today; she didn't want another. But Eddie wasn't after hitting her; he was telling her to stop talking.

'I suggest you go back to him,' he said, 'apologise and then find out everything you can about his involvement with this woman's death.'

'But—'

'If you do that, it will be the last thing you'll have to do. I have enough information on him now, not that you've given me much. But you'll have served your purpose after you do this one thing. Unless you want to go back to the parties?'

Shelley shook her head vehemently. When she'd first been unable to pay back the money he had loaned, she'd been told to be an escort at a party for Leon. It had been full of older guys, businessmen who couldn't keep their hands to themselves.

She'd heard rumours of things going on and was glad to get out of it when Eddie had said she had to be his mole.

Yet did she trust him not to go back on his word if she got the information he was after? She wasn't sure, but she didn't really have a choice.

'Okay,' she said eventually.

'Good girl.'

Shelley got out of the car and watched as he drove away. Once Eddie was out of sight, she crossed the road, ran down the side path and disappeared into the Bennett estate. She would stay with her friend Mandy tonight. She wasn't going back to the flat until the morning, not until Seth had calmed down.

She needed time to change her plan.

Grace was sitting in her car ready to go back to the station when she spotted Shelley getting out of a black Land Rover. She watched as the young woman ran across the road, along the path into the bowels of the estate.

She paused for a moment before starting the engine. What would Shelley be doing getting out of Eddie Steele's car?

2012

Ruby was in the kitchen when there was a knock on the front door. Finn had left the hospital over a week ago now and apart from that one phone call, she hadn't heard anything else from him. She went to answer it, hoping it might be him, coming to take them to safety.

She opened the door. It was thrust towards her and she was slammed up against the wall. Her shoulder took the brunt of it but she didn't groan or shout out. She didn't dare.

'Well, look who we have here.' Dane squeezed her chin. 'We meet again, oh pretty one. Have you seen him?'

When she said nothing, he squeezed her chin harder. 'Answer me!'

'I haven't seen him since he left the hospital.' The words came out in a squeak.

He relaxed his grip but laughed in her face. 'Now he's gone, you'll have to pay instead.'

A tear fell down Ruby's cheek. 'I didn't know he owed you any money.'

Dane sniggered. 'His disloyalty is going to mean a lot of paying back. You can start by doing an old man a favour.' He put his hands on her shoulders and forced her to her knees. Then he unzipped his jeans.

Ruby's eyes widened at his actions. 'No, please!'

'You don't have any say in the matter right now. Do it.'

'No, stop.'

But he didn't. He wasn't the cleanest of people. But at least it was over and done with quickly. Afterwards, he zipped himself up again and pulled her up from her knees by her hair. She screwed up her face at the pain.

'Okay, now listen here. This is how it's going to work. You can do whatever you want before midday but I may call from any time after that until midnight on any day. I want you looking nice, fresh and clean during those hours so you're ready for me. Do you understand?'

She nodded. She couldn't leave for another month because she was expecting to hear from Finn, but she was going as soon as he got in touch.

'I want you to stay here for the time being. Go and see the social. You're a single mum now; they can pay the rent. Once the kid is older, you can come and work for me.' He patted her on the head like a puppy.

She squeezed her eyes shut for a moment, so tight they stung. This couldn't be happening. It was like a dream. No, a nightmare. But when she opened them, he was still there.

'No running away now.' He jabbed a finger at her face. 'And you tell a soul about our little arrangement and I swear I will rip you into little pieces. Do you hear?'

She started to sob.

'Shut up.' He clamped a hand over her mouth. 'You don't want anyone snooping around here if they think something is wrong, do you?'

His eyes were dark and menacing, and there was nothing but disgust in them.

'It's going to be just you and me from now on. If that loser comes back you tell him to keep away from you and to come and see me if he knows what's best for him. The more trouble he causes the more I will hurt you.'

Once he'd gone, Ruby rushed into the bathroom and threw up. She scrambled into the corner and wrapped her arms around her knees. Then she cried. Lily cried too, but she couldn't even go to her aid. She was so frightened.

She was trapped here, for up to four weeks until she could go to Finn. If she left, Dane would find her. He'd probably beat her up and drag her back. And what would happen if he went too far and killed her? He was a beast of a man, a powerhouse. What would happen to Lily?

Eventually she pulled herself up from the floor to get her phone and rang Finn's number. But there was no reply. It was switched on, yet no one picked up – just like all the other times she'd tried to call him. She left him a voicemail.

'Finn, I need to come to you now,' she sobbed. 'I've just had a visit from Dane and he – he made me do things. He says you owe him because you left. Please call me back. I need you. Please, Finn. Don't leave me to deal with him on my own. I can't do this.'

FORTY-TWO

It was half past four by the time Grace got back to the station. She caught up with Sam who'd found out some new information.

'We've had a call from a member of the public, Daniel Strong, who works as a security guard. He monitors several properties in Century Street and has reported seeing an abandoned Ford Focus in the rear car park of the empty Bathrooms Warehouse building. Says it's been there a few days. Uniform went to check it out. The car was reported stolen in Stoke on Monday evening and it looks as if someone has been sleeping rough in it. We've cordoned it off and forensics are checking for prints. I'm also trawling through cameras and CCTV close by to see who's been using it.'

Grace high-fived her colleague. 'Did you find anything on Seth Forrester's BMW? We still need evidence to link him to the hit and run with Caleb Campbell.'

'I can't find anything on Hanley Road but I'm looking on Leek New Road. Hopefully I can find an image with a regis- tration plate that puts him in the area. Do you realise how many black BMWs are on the road, though?'

Grace grimaced and went back to her desk, updating Frankie

with what she'd learned. Adrenaline rushed through her as she realised there were a few things that might finally be coming together.

Fetching Tyler home from hospital was a bittersweet moment. They'd had to wait hours for the consultant to do a final visit but Tyler had been discharged. Then they'd collected Lily from school and treated both children to a burger and chips. So it was nearing five o'clock when they arrived home. Already the cars were frosting over, the grass gleaming white as the sky was almost dark.

Ruby bustled them into the flat. At least they were all together now, and plans could be made.

'Be careful,' she said to Tyler as he squealed when he saw his toy box. 'I don't want you getting too excited. And watch out for that cast on your ankle or else you'll give someone an injury. Go on, sit down and spend some time with your dad.'

'Yep, Tiger.' Luke crouched down next to him. 'I've missed playing games with you.'

Ruby gave a weak smile. She knew she'd feel like wrapping Tyler up in cotton wool for a while but it was to be expected. She was glad to be home, her family in one place again.

Luke picked Tyler up and placed him on the settee. Ruby could sense her son was nervous. She hoped his subdued mood wasn't because he was home and reliving the nightmare. They'd been very lucky to come away with him unscathed except for his ankle. She was praying that in time he might forget what had happened on Monday evening.

Above the sound of the TV, she heard the letterbox go. It was late: she frowned. It was probably a circular at this time of the day. She started to prepare their tea and thought nothing more of it until a few minutes later when Lily joined her. She held out a pink envelope.

'This was on the door mat,' she said. 'It has your name on it.'

'It's probably from one of the neighbours.' She'd had several get-well cards for Tyler from them and had found it quite comforting.

She opened the envelope. The picture had a mother bear looking after her cub, 'Get Well Soon' emblazoned across the top in lime green. She opened it, and then held on to the wall for support.

I am this close to you. Don't ever forget that. I can get to you or your family any time.

Meet me this evening at 5.30. I'll be behind the bushes after the third lamppost along the path. If you don't show, I will come to you again.

'What's the matter, Mum?' Lily asked.

'Oh, nothing.' Ruby added a fake smile to her face. 'Would you like a drink of hot chocolate?'

Lily nodded and they went into the kitchen. Ruby hid the card inside the drawer but not before reading the words again. She held in her tears, her fear. He wasn't giving her any choice but to go to him.

Yet she couldn't.

She hadn't seen him for so many years although he had lived in her head all that time.

She opened the kitchen drawer, and stared at the knives. Then she slammed it shut. She wasn't that kind of person. Then again, maybe she needed to be stronger. She opened the drawer again and slid one into her handbag. At least she had it there.

She thought back to the first time he had caught up with

her. She had only been gone about six months and was living on her own with Lily. He'd taunted her for weeks. He'd stolen post, he'd taken Lily's push-along bike, there had been a dead bird on the doorstep. The usual nuisance stuff.

At first she'd put it down to kids mucking around – opportunist thieves with the bike that had never been found – until she'd got back from work one afternoon to find her flat had been broken into. The place had been ransacked, nothing taken but it was someone looking for something. On the wallpaper in the living room, written in one of her pink lipsticks, were the words 'I want what's mine.'

She'd upped and left soon after. When he found her for a second time, she'd started to realise that it was a game to him and he liked the chase.

What she had of his was important but wasn't the end result. She knew even if she handed it in to the police, she still wouldn't be safe. He would send someone else for revenge. She didn't know why she'd kept it for so long in the first instance but somehow she'd felt compelled to.

Now she felt like she was back to square one. Had he got straight out of prison and come for her, waiting until he could come and get her himself? Why did he have to search her out again? Hadn't she lived enough of a punishment for the past eight years?

There was only one thing she could do. She had to talk to him, ensure that it wasn't his intention to harm her before she gave him what he was after.

And then she would talk to Luke, explain everything to him and hope that the two of them could get through this. He upset her at times with his gambling, but she loved him. Apart from that, he was strong, dependable, stable and good for the kids. Maybe they could get away and start again, with no secrets this time.

But whether or not he came with her, Ruby wasn't waiting around any longer. She would have preferred to go straight away, yet knew they'd have to be careful with Tyler just coming out of hospital. Once he was rested overnight, they could leave first thing in the morning. Maybe even this evening. He'd miss his outpatients appointment and he'd need to have his cast removed in six weeks but they could go to the nearest hospital for that. It wasn't ideal, but it would have to do.

As the clock started to tick down to half past five, realisation flooded through her. If she told the police, he would harm her and her family, and she would be on the run for ever more. No one could stop him; he didn't care who he hurt. He was mad. She'd seen first-hand what he was capable of.

She had to stop this.

She had to face her fears and go to see him.

FORTY-THREE

In the kitchen, Ruby poured milk down the sink and washed it away. Then she left the empty container on the worktop and went in to Luke.

'We've run out of milk,' she said, reaching for her bag. 'I'm just popping to the shop. Do you want anything?'

'Don't think so.' He shook his head and turned back to the TV. He and Tyler had been playing a game since he'd returned. Lily was sitting next to them, feet curled up at her side, her nose in a book.

Ruby's heart almost burst with pride, with love. That was her family, right there. She had to protect them, whatever the cost. She had to keep them safe.

But maybe he would kill her. She'd known what he was after and yet she'd been unable to tell anyone about it, even when Tyler was hurt. He wasn't going to stop until he got what he wanted.

It seemed like a long time to get from her flat and onto the path but in reality it was only a minute or two. She said hello to the lady from flat 110 as she passed her on the walkway, and then put her head down. She didn't have time to chat. In the car park, people were coming home for the day.

Downstairs there were a few police officers, working on finding out who had murdered Mary Stanton, she suspected. She hadn't heard yet if they had anyone in custody. She supposed it might have taken attention away from them looking for *him*, which could only be a good thing as she didn't want further repercussions. Still, it was understandable, as Mary had been murdered, but Ruby was in danger too.

The communal staircase was still sealed off from the public so she used the fire escape. Ruby could see her breath billowing out in front of her like smoke. How she longed to be in the warmth, sitting next to Lily on the settee.

Protect my family, she repeated to herself over and over. *I have to protect my family.*

She couldn't let him ruin her life any more.

She saw him in front of her and willed her feet to walk towards him; her heart to keep beating.

Had he been watching the area for a while to see how everything worked? Knowing him, he'd picked a spot where he could do anything to her if he wanted to. He would stop at nothing.

'It's about time I caught up with you, don't you think?' Dane came out of the shadows as she drew level.

Every atom in her body willed her to turn away. Every hair stood on end. Her breath began to rasp in her panic at the sound of his voice. If she had to scream, she hoped the police might hear her. It could antagonise him but she would do it if she had to.

Yet she couldn't let him know how much he scared her. How she wanted to turn around and run as far away as possible. How she wondered if she had the nerve to stand her ground.

'I never wanted to see you again,' she said quietly.

'You might have had your way if I hadn't got out of prison early.' Dane sniggered. 'Good behaviour. Kept my head down, served my time. And there wasn't a day that went by without me thinking what I would do to you when I saw you again.'

'Why won't you leave me alone? You know I won't go to the police.'

'I want what's mine.'

Those chilling words again.

'I don't have it with me,' she replied.

He snorted. 'You expect me to believe that?' He took a step closer to her. 'If you do, you're a bigger fool than I thought you were.'

'I'm made of strong stuff to have stayed with you as long as I did.'

He laughed. She looked around to see if anyone could hear them. But there was no one near. Vehicles drove past on Ford Green Road, rush-hour building up. It was a cold night, everyone on their way home to get out of it. To be safe; unlike her.

'I want what's mine,' he repeated.

'You said Monday.'

'Well, I've changed my mind.'

'I can't get it that quickly. Not with all the police around.'

Footsteps and voices approached on the path. Dane grabbed her roughly by the wrist, swivelled her round, pulled her into his chest and put a hand across her mouth before she had time to react.

She could smell him, flashbacks of memories coming back at her. The times he'd thrown the dinner she'd prepared up against the wall.

The times he'd thrown *her* up against the wall.

The times she'd mopped up her own blood and got herself sorted afterwards rather than go to the hospital and face questioning.

She had never understood why he was so obsessed with her. Maybe it was control, a game. It certainly wasn't passion.

She gazed up at the flats, knowing her children and Luke were so close, yet so far away. Tears burnt her eyes at the thought of never seeing any of them again.

As the footsteps began to fade in the distance, she felt his grip loosen. His arm dropped and she stepped away from him quickly.

'You wouldn't have cared if my little boy had died, would you?' she said.

'Collateral damage is part of the game.'

'This isn't a game! This is my life.'

'Mine too. So get it for me and I'll be on my way.'

'You expect me to believe that?' She repeated his words.

'Well, I won't harm you yet. But if you don't bring it to me, I will hurt your family first. And then I will come after you.'

A sob caught in her throat. She swallowed it down. 'I . . . I need more time,' she pleaded.

He stepped towards her, and she saw the glint of a knife in the street lamp.

'I could finish you off right now. But what would be the fun in that?' His laugh was taunting, cruel. 'I will be back on Monday.'

He disappeared into the bushes and left her standing there.

She bent over, the bile in her throat forcing its way into her mouth. Stood there gasping for air as her body was wracked with the pain of seeing him again. Knowing he was close; hearing what he was planning.

Once her breathing had returned to normal, she turned and ran to the shop. It was on her way back that she made up her mind what to do.

Grace was at her desk. Allie was sitting opposite her while Perry was gathering mugs.

'Cup of tea, Ma'am?' Perry asked with a slight snigger.

Allie nodded. 'Stop calling me that. It makes me feel as old as the Queen. Boss will do,' she grinned. 'Like old times.'

'Yes, boss.'

'Hey.' Sam raised a hand for attention. 'Gather round and help me out with this.'

They all went to stand behind Sam's monitor.

'I've been sent footage on Century Street, which is covered by city centre CCTV. This is Tuesday evening.' Sam pressed a button. A road scene came into view and a man walked along the pavement to the old Bathrooms Warehouse building and went around the back.

'How long does he stay there?' Allie asked.

'I fast-forwarded through to the next morning and he leaves at nine twenty-seven a.m. He comes back that night at eleven.'

'He's there overnight?'

'Yes, and again on Wednesday.' Sam pressed a few more buttons and pulled up another image. 'This is another view.'

They all leaned forward to get a better look.

'It's definitely not Forrester, is it?' Grace asked.

Perry peered a little closer. 'It does look similar to him.'

'It really does, but it isn't him.' Sam pointed to the image. 'Seth is taller than this guy.'

Grace sighed. 'Well, at least we have one suspect ruled out.'

'That would be great if we had any more.'

'We don't have all the forensics back yet,' Allie soothed. 'Let's keep at it.'

'But this could be Finn Ridley.' Grace turned to Frankie. 'What do we know about him?'

'He's known on the system but not coming up anywhere since 2010. I'm waiting on DC Hope from the Met to get back to me with some intel.'

'Which means it could be him,' Grace said. 'So no images?'

'Nothing since then,' Frankie replied.

Grace pointed to the screen. 'So who the hell is this, then?'

2014

Time had gone by without any further contact from Finn and as the weeks turned into months, Ruby had hated him for leaving her and Lily to face Dane. She had suffered abuse, all the while wondering where he was, what he was doing; why he hadn't come back for them.

Now two years later, she could understand why. Dane controlled her like he must have done Finn. He had her at his beck and call, too scared to run, too scared to answer back. Too frightened to do anything. He'd taken to staying over whenever he fancied, often turning up in the early hours. She was stuck in a mess that she didn't know how to get out of.

Dane often sent his men around if he didn't want to see her. None of them were nice either, always taunting her about Finn running out on her because she wasn't good enough. She'd been passed along from one to another like a playmate. Dane had his people everywhere too, which is why she could never leave. She'd hated herself for a long time, for being weak. But he had worn her down. He took what little money she had, gave her even less to get by on and saw to it that he made her life miserable at every turn. She didn't know why he treated her so cruelly.

She liked to convince herself that a part of her stayed behind because she hadn't given up on Finn. It was nothing of the sort really. He would never be coming back. Two years was a long time to be away from her and Lily so there had to be a reason for it. This was her life until Dane let her go. If he ever did.

She hadn't seen her dad in all that time either. Ruby hadn't even told him about Finn leaving, nor what Dane made her do.

That morning, she sat in the chemist, her foot tapping up and down as she waited. The clock said half past eleven and she was going to be late home. But Lily had been up for most of the night; she hadn't stopped crying. Luckily Dane hadn't stayed over or else he no doubt would have told her to shut her up.

Lily had been coughing so bad that morning she could hardly get her breath. Ruby had rung the doctors and got an emergency appointment but there was only a slot at the end of the morning's surgery. She knew as she was waiting to see her that she wouldn't be home for midday.

Luckily, Lily was given a good bill of health apart from the cold virus, which at least made Ruby feel better. She prayed she wouldn't catch it too, but at least if she did she could cope with it, keep it at bay long enough for Dane not to get too mad at her looking a mess.

The prescription ready at last, Ruby almost ran home with the pushchair. The final ten minutes was all uphill. She was exhausted, sweaty and red-faced when she finally saw the flats. And then she groaned when she spotted Dane's car.

The lift wasn't working so she banged Lily's pushchair up two flights of stairs, trying to ignore her little girl's cries. She needed to get the medicine into her, try to get her to sleep.

Dane was sitting in the living room when she pushed open the front door.

'I'm sorry.' She rushed in. 'Lily has been poorly and—'

She felt a sharp pain in her head as he wrenched her into the kitchen by the hair.

'Where the fuck have you been until now?' he demanded.

'I took her to the doctors. I couldn't get an earlier appointment. I had to wait at the chemist for a—'

'You disobeyed my order.'

'For the first time, Dane. I'm sorry but Lily—'

'You put the kid before me?'

She said nothing. She would always put her child before him, even if she didn't want him to know that.

'You should have been back ten minutes ago. Look at you. You're a mess. And will you stop that child from screaming before I do something I regret?'

Ruby raced over to Lily as he lessened his grip. Her daughter was red in the face, tears in her eyes as she scrunched up in pain, coughing. Quickly she got out the medicine, gave it to her before taking her from the pushchair, hoping to soothe her in her arms.

It worked and ten minutes later, she put a sleeping Lily down in her cot. Then she hurried back into the living room. Dane hadn't moved; he was watching the TV. He glared at her as she stood in the doorway.

'I can't be bothered waiting for you to take a shower.' He curled his finger beckoning her over. 'Come here.'

She went to him. At least he didn't seem that mad. Maybe she could satisfy him and he would leave. But as she reached his side, he stood up, raised his hand in the air and punched her in the mouth. The force of it made her fall into the wall. She groaned as her cheekbone hit the plaster.

'Don't ever fucking defy me.' He bent down close to her face. 'Do you hear?'

She nodded quickly, knowing not to say anything. It would

only make things worse if she fought back. She'd learned that the hard way.

Once he was gone, she let her tears drop. One day she would get away from here. She wasn't strong enough yet but she couldn't live her life like this any more.

FORTY-FOUR

Not wanting to draw attention to herself, Ruby tried to stay calm and walked rather than ran to the safety of Harrison House. Once she was on the walkway and a few metres from her home, she stopped. It was bitterly cold, her fingers frozen, her feet cold from standing on the grass. But she gulped in the fresh air anyway, to stop herself from throwing up.

Dane had given her breathing space and she was going to take it. It wasn't going to be pleasant but she had to tell Luke what was going on, and hope that he'd trust her afterwards. She couldn't bear to lose him.

She went inside, put the milk in the fridge.

'Kids, I've bought you a treat. It's in the kitchen,' she shouted through to them. 'Lily, can you help your brother?'

'Chocolate marshmallows!' Tyler cried when she saw him in his sister's arms. 'Can I have two?'

Ruby laughed. 'No, you can't, greedy guts. Lily, can you plate them up and sit in here to eat them? Mum needs a word with Luke.'

She left them to it and went into the living room, sitting

down next to him. Swallowing her nerves, she took one of his hands in her own.

'We need to talk,' she said. 'Later, when the kids are asleep.'

He sat forwards, a look of frustration clear. 'Don't say there's something else you haven't told me? I thought there weren't any more secrets?'

'Have *you* told me everything?' she challenged, her defences up.

He looked away for a moment. She turned his face towards hers again.

'Do you trust me?'

'What do you mean?' He pulled away from her. 'Is this about this Ridley man?'

She paused, knowing everything was on the line once she replied. Would he stand by her? Would he leave straight away? Would he listen to her reasons why before passing judgment? Either way, it was time to tell him the truth.

'There's more isn't there?'

She nodded.

He pulled her into his arms, his eyes filled with resignation. Then he cupped her face with his hands. He kissed a tear that had fallen.

'Whatever it is we can get through this,' he said.

She gave a faint smile, hoping that they could.

It wasn't an easy night, knowing something was hanging over them, but once both children were asleep, Ruby sat down next to him on the settee again and took a deep breath.

'The man after me isn't Finn Ridley,' she told him. 'It's someone much worse, and he wants to punish me.'

Luke shook his head. 'Why all the lies, Ruby?'

'Just hear me out, okay! When Finn left me, I had a visit from a man named Dane. Finn was in a lot of trouble because he was with me. He was a member of a gang. They committed a lot of crimes and once he met me he wanted out. He tried to leave but they wouldn't let him. The gang leader, Dane, didn't like his disloyalty and he got into a lot of trouble for it.'

'What a bastard.'

Ruby's voice caught in her throat. 'They attacked him because of it. I . . . I saw it. I was hiding and they didn't know I was there. They left him for dead. At the hospital he went straight into surgery. He lost his spleen and was very ill for a few days. But on the day he was discharged, I went to meet him and he'd already gone. The nurse said he'd had a visitor; I think it was Dane and he was running scared. He didn't even dare to go to the police for protection.'

Luke sat quiet for a moment, as if he was taking it all in.

'Did you ever hear from him again?' he asked.

'I had one phone call. He said he'd come and get me when things were safer for him. They knew he loved me, and Lily, so I think they took that away from him. It was his punishment.'

Luke shook his head. 'I don't buy that. I couldn't leave you and the kids behind. No way.'

'Not even after Seth attacked you?'

Luke pulled a face. 'I guess it's easier said than done.'

'I think he stayed away because he thought they would hurt me, but in the end, they did that anyway. I'm sure Dane knew where Finn had gone, but he told me he didn't.'

Luke's shoulders drooped. 'Shit, you didn't have to . . .'

Tears rolled down Ruby's cheeks. 'I shut it out as much as I could. Sometimes it helped; other times it didn't.' She couldn't bear to see his look of anguish. 'He told me if I didn't do as he said, things would get much worse, and I couldn't have that.'

'Why didn't you go to the police?'

'You saw how dangerous he is on Monday. He came every

281

few days to see me for his . . . payment. I was so scared, and naive at the time. In the end, I just put up with it. But when he was sent down for six months, I made my escape. Lily was two.'

'So why has he kept away for so long? That was years ago.'

'He was sent to prison again shortly afterwards, for armed robbery. He's served half of his sentence and now he's out.'

'And he came after you straight away?' Luke stood up and paced the room. 'Have you any idea why?'

'No.' She lowered her eyes for a moment, afraid she would give herself away. 'Just before I left, it got to the point that my life revolved around making him happy. I showed him only what he wanted to see. I didn't lip back even when I wanted to. When he wasn't there I was on edge all the time, watching my phone in case he rang and I missed it. He would call at least five times a day by then. It was a game, all control. And I couldn't get out of it, because he said he would kill me. I'd seen what he'd done to Finn in only a few minutes, so I knew that he meant it.'

Luke shook his head in disbelief as she continued.

'I tried to leave once before I managed to get away for good. I was packing mine and Lily's things when he turned up. That's the thing, I never knew when he was coming, and he had a key to let himself in. I got a backhander and a punch in the stomach for that one.' She looked at him through watery eyes. 'He almost broke my arm one night when he pushed me up against the wall and thrust it up my back. I couldn't use it for a week afterwards. Now he's come after me again and I'm scared of what he'll do.'

She burst into tears, unable to contain her emotions and he pulled her into his arms. As he held her, she wished they could stay like that forever, with the kids tucked safely in their beds. The door shut to the world and all its horror.

But when is life ever that easy? She pulled away to look up at him.

'You have to trust me as much as I trust you. I need to leave. I . . . I want you to come with me, but I'll understand if you don't.' Tears flowed freely now. 'I know I've kept things from you and I've hurt you. You might not ever trust me again but I still have to go.'

'Wait, slow down. I don't understand.'

'If you are coming, we have to go tomorrow, first thing in the morning before too many police officers arrive,' she went on, not stopping to explain. 'We need to pack as much as we can in the car while the kids are asleep. We should really go now, but Tyler is only just home and—'

'But—'

'Please! I've always stood by you, even though you've lied to me.'

Ruby collapsed in his arms again. She cried hard, letting out all of her anger, grief, fear. For the past two days she had hated herself for saying all those things about Finn, when all he had done was fall in love with her and want to stop his life of crime. But it was easier to blame Finn and try to stop the police finding out about Dane, and then to move on again. If she grassed on Dane, she would be in even more trouble. He might be dangerous alone, but he had a team of heavies behind him who would do anything for him. And Finn had betrayed not only Dane, but the other gang members too.

'I don't know how you got through that,' Luke said eventually. 'I really should be angry with you for not telling me in the first place but I'm worn down with all this. I'm actually quite proud that you made a go of things on your own after what happened.'

'I had no choice.'

'But you were strong and you survived. That mustn't have been easy. I can't wait to get out of here now, but I'm not sure

283

what to do about Seth. What about the money I owe him? Will he come after me like Dane has come after you?'

'It's a chance we'll have to take. We can't pay him back.'

His face was riddled with guilt. 'I'm so sorry about the gambling. After this, I don't think I'll ever do it again. Life is too short.'

Ruby gave him a half-smile. She only hoped he'd stick to his word. It was high time they got out of the hole they'd landed themselves in.

She feared she would have to tell the police soon just exactly who Dane was if they didn't manage to get away. But she knew he would harm her if she did. She'd thought it was too good to be true when she hadn't seen him for so long.

Running from Dane in 2014 had been one of the scariest days of her life. Being threatened by him again meant the nightmare of being chased was never going to end. She wasn't strong enough to stand up to him, to ensure this was over.

Which meant one of them needed to disappear.

FORTY-FIVE

Dane downed a pint as he tucked in to steak and chips from the pub on Ford Green Road and then bought himself a few cans from the off-licence.

Finding another vehicle hadn't taken long. It was easy to steal something around here. Rows and rows of cars in front of terraced houses, and even though he was frozen, the cold weather snap was on his side. The car he'd chosen probably wouldn't be missed until the morning. He'd watched the owner lock it up and then rush briskly to his door, several metres away, closing the cold out. It had taken him seconds before he was out of the street and away.

Hunkering down in it now, he waited. He knew time was running out now they'd probably have his fingerprints on the first car he'd stolen. But Ruby wasn't going to get away with what she'd done, no matter what.

He wondered if he'd fooled the police by not going back to Century Street. He'd known it was risky that he'd be spotted but after seeing that guy snooping around this morning before he left, he knew he'd overstayed his welcome. He wasn't taking any chances. They might have someone waiting for him if he went back. He'd be better off being cautious rather than getting caught at the last hurdle.

Because he was looking forward to tomorrow so much and no one was taking that away from him. He wasn't going to wait until Monday. He'd earned his right over the past years to have some fun.

Dane still couldn't believe she'd had the guts to do what she did. Ruby had been a teenager at the time and he didn't think she had it in her to hold him over a barrel. Seeing her earlier had reignited all the hatred he felt for her. He couldn't wait to cause her pain.

He'd go and search her out first thing and then he could be on his way before anyone in that block had woken up.

All the years he'd spent in prison, now it was payback time. If he hadn't been locked up for so long, he would have come after her sooner. Instead, he'd lain on his bed in his cell, planning, scheming, plotting for this very day.

He had waited this long to get what was his, and nothing was going to spoil it for him. Nothing, or no one.

And when he had got what he'd come for, then he would take his revenge.

But the boy. It was messing with his head. He banged a clenched fist on the steering wheel over and over. It wasn't meant to turn out that way. He would never harm a child. It had been pure reflex to hold the lad over the edge. He had come at him as if he was a friend, and when he saw the look on her face, he knew he'd found his bargaining tool.

It was meant as a scare tactic but the little bastard hadn't stopped wriggling. And when she'd hurled herself up against him, he'd lost his grip and then watched in horror as the boy fell.

He could still recall the thud of the body hitting the ground, the screams behind him as they ran one way and he climbed over the railing and lowered himself down to the ground. There was no time for them to react to what he'd done, even if they'd dared.

He'd run along Rose Avenue, got in the stolen car and driven off slowly, not wanting to bring any attention to himself. And then he'd watched from a distance over the past few days, figuring out what to do next. It was easier owing to the weather. Everyone was wrapped up, not much visible, and it went dark quite early.

One thing was certain – he wouldn't be getting caught. He wasn't ever going back to prison.

2014

Ruby reached for her mug of coffee and took a sip. Dane was still in bed, having turned up last night near on three a.m. He'd taken to arriving whenever it suited him now. Lily was playing at her feet, the sun shining in through the window making her blonde hair seem even brighter.

Eight thirty. It was the time of day that she cherished as much as the first coffee of the morning. It meant she could live without fear for a whole hour at least. If he stayed over, Dane never usually got up before ten every morning. She could sit and relax, knowing he wouldn't pounce on her or say something nasty just to upset her.

She was thinking about Naomi. She'd often wondered how her life would have been if Finn hadn't gone to Naomi's party. She would have been at college, maybe had a career. She might have met a nice man, got married and been happy. But then that meant not having Lily and she wouldn't want that.

She hadn't seen her dad in a good while. She had been so embarrassed about the mess she'd got herself in. So hurt that Finn had dumped her and left her to deal with his cronies. So angry that she let Dane do the things he did to her because she feared for her life.

She wished she had the courage to go and see him again. She knew he would welcome her back into the fold, no questions asked. He would make things right, she was certain. But she didn't dare risk it. Dane had told her he would find her if she ever tried to leave. She had a child to look after. And she had got herself into this mess; she would have to suffer the consequences.

Part of her still wanted to stay in the flat in case Finn ever came back for her.

Part of her knew he would never be coming home.

She tried not to think about how the man she had loved with all of her heart had let her and his daughter down. Although she often wondered if Finn had met someone new, got married and had other children. Would he ever think about her? About how he had let her rot?

She wished she wasn't so weak. In a way she was tough to put up with what she did. But a stronger person would leave, not accept Dane's physical and mental abuse.

Who was she kidding? No one knew what she was going through, how scared she was to be at his beck and call. How terrible it was to live in a constant state of fear. How awful it was for Lily to be on edge all the time, in case she made too much noise, or a mess he'd hit out because of.

As soon as she was able she was going to get out of there. But for now, she couldn't stand on her own two feet long enough.

So bit by bit she'd start to save a little from the money he sometimes threw at her when he'd beaten her. She would save it all and when she had enough, she would leave. No matter how long it took. Surely this couldn't be her life, now that Finn had gone.

FORTY-SIX

Shelley hadn't managed to stay away from Seth's flat as planned. She'd visited Mandy's house for a couple of hours, until she was certain he would be at work, and then she'd hot-footed it back to Harrison House. There she'd walked quickly along the walkway.

She knew she had to be careful. If he was still in, she would be done for. But she couldn't see his car in the car park, so she had to take the chance.

She put her key in the lock and opened the door, thankful that silence greeted her.

'Seth?' She waited, but nothing. She stepped inside, leaving the door ajar in case she needed to make a quick escape.

After checking every room she breathed a sigh of relief. She was alone. But she wouldn't feel safe until she was out of there. She would work quickly and methodically and see how much money she could find. Then she would take every last penny and get herself out of there.

She went room by room, making sure to put everything back as she had found it. There was nothing in the kitchen she could see. Of course she understood Seth would have hiding places everywhere. She herself had rolled her money up and hidden it inside an old bra, tucked away at the bottom of a drawer. There wasn't time to look closely, tear things apart. She had to be vigilant and on guard.

There was nothing in the living room but she found two hundred pounds in the bathroom, rolled up and shoved inside the cistern in a plastic bag. In the bedroom, she sat on the bed with a sigh. She had been stupid to look and risk another beating if that was all she could find. He wouldn't hide the bulk of his money here in the flat, would he? But then again, where else would he keep it?

A loud bang made her jump off the bed. She froze, waiting to hear what it had been. She listened more, ascertaining that it must have come from outside. Still, she'd better hurry.

Quickly, she opened the holdall she had brought with her. Knowing she wasn't coming back, she shoved clothes, make-up, perfume and anything else that could fit into it.

Another bang outside, which she realised was a door slamming, and her nerves couldn't handle much more. Taking one last look under the bed to see if she'd missed anything, she lifted up the valance sheet and tilted her head. There was nothing of hers but she spotted something in a plastic bag shoved underneath the mattress in the slats. She pulled at it and looked inside.

It was a T-shirt. She recognised it as one of Seth's but she wasn't going to pull it out to check because it was splattered in blood. She wondered who it belonged to – could it be Mary Stanton's? – but didn't stop to find out. She shoved the bag inside her holdall. She could pass it on to Eddie at the very least.

She took one final check of everything, the drawers by the side of the bed and a last look in the wardrobes. There was nothing else she could carry. She didn't have many clothes and most of it was cheap tat that she wouldn't miss anyway. She had all the personal possessions she needed.

She closed the wardrobe door and then suddenly stopped. She peered down the gap between the two standalone wardrobes. There was something there behind the unit. She slid in her hand and tried to reach it, pressing her body against the corner and stretching her fingers. Finally her hand clasped around it and she pulled it out.

It was a black drawstring bag. She looked inside; it was full of twenty-pound notes, bundled together in five hundred pounds, red money bands around each one. She quickly counted them. There were nine that seemed to be full and one that had a few notes missing.

Nearly five thousand pounds! This was more than the money Mary had posted through their door.

She sat down on the bed again, unable to believe Seth would hide his money there. Or had he put it there for quickness when he'd got Mary's money back? She had swept the place every now and then, to see if she could find his hiding place, but until now she hadn't been lucky. Quickly she pushed that in the holdall too.

Her shoes in a carrier bag in one hand, she hurled the holdall over her shoulder and let herself out. She glanced over the railing. Seth's car still wasn't in the car park. With a quick step, she flew along the walkway, raced down the steps, pushed open the door and went out into the night. She didn't slow down until she was back at Mandy's house.

FORTY-SEVEN

Grace upped the pace on the treadmill and began her thirty-minute session. Running at the end of her shift often cleared her head when it was full of information. It was like going to sleep on a problem and waking up with it solved.

The day had turned out a frustrating one. They had found out lots of things but nothing in particular that they could move forward on. They were still waiting on specific forensics for Operation Spode and nothing had come of the house-to-house calls. Why hadn't anyone seen anything? It was crazy in a block of flats this size.

Bringing in Seth earlier in the week and finding he had nothing to say had been annoying. Something told her that he was involved in the hit and run on Caleb Campbell and the assault on Milo Benton but she had no evidence yet to prove it. There was time though. They would have more forensics over the next few days about Mary Stanton too. Nothing ever happened as quickly as it appeared on the TV cop programmes.

And then there was everything to do with Ruby and Luke and Tyler. So many unanswered questions. Was that something to do with Seth Forrester, even though he'd been ruled out by Ruby's admission to it being Finn Ridley who had dropped Tyler over the railing? Were they wary of him, and what he might do to them if they talked?

Which brought her to the thing that was troubling her most. What had Shelley Machin been doing getting out of Eddie Steele's car? Grace couldn't tell who was driving it because of the blacked-out windows but it was his vehicle. She knew that licence plate off by heart now.

She remembered the last time she had seen the Steele brothers together. They had all been present at the trial when her half-sister, Jade, had been sent to prison for life. It hadn't been a good experience but as it was her job, she'd had to give evidence in the dock.

For three long weeks, she had endured Leon's glare while they sat in the courtroom, his taunts and jeers in the corridors outside, screeching out of the car park at the end of each session – narrowly missing her on one occasion. He wanted her to know she wasn't welcome.

Seeing the young woman getting out of his car meant Eddie would be using her for something, she was sure. But what? Finding out information about Seth perhaps?

In the shower, she banged her hand against the tiles. First someone had hung a child over a balcony. Then someone had knocked a teenager off a bike deliberately. Then a defenceless woman is pushed to her death. It was frustrating not knowing if it was the same person who had done it all. Were these cases linked? They were all tied to Harrison House.

Once downstairs in the kitchen, she waited for Simon who had texted to say he was on his way home. She'd seen him several times during the day as she'd been gathering information on both cases.

'Hey,' she said as he joined her a few minutes later.

She kissed him but squealed when he pushed cold hands underneath her jumper. 'Get off me.'

'I've been frozen all day,' he said. 'I need warming up.'

'Well, you'll have to wait until we've eaten. I'm starving, you?'

'Yeah. What frozen delight have you got for us tonight?'

'Pizza?'

'Can't wait.'

It wasn't a dig at either of them. Often they arrived home and grabbed whatever was available.

Once he'd showered and changed, and their meal had been eaten, Grace flopped down next to him on the settee. He put an arm around her and pulled her close.

'Teagan has been asking after you,' he said, stroking her arm idly. 'Wants to know when she can come around. I told her you were involved in a case.'

'Thanks. Maybe we can catch up at the weekend. If I'm still working on this, I can fit time in for a coffee with her. How is she?'

'Okay. Studying hard for her exams.'

She turned to him. 'She's clever though. I'm not sure how you managed that. She must take after Natalie.' She added a wink.

Natalie was Simon's ex-wife. The couple had divorced a few years ago. Natalie had remarried and Teagan got on as well with Mark, her step-dad, as she did with Grace. It was nice to be a part of their small family unit.

Her thoughts turned back to Mary Stanton. She couldn't stop the image repeating itself on a loop, of the older woman falling down those steps. At least now she wasn't imagining seeing little Tyler dropping to the floor. No matter what she worked on, the last image swapped itself with the new one. She never switched off.

'That poor woman,' Simon said.

'You're thinking of her too?'

'Hmm-mm.'

'Your article was good on it.'

'Thanks. How are you doing with your case?'

'So-so.' She was non-committal, even though her opinion of Ruby Brassington and Luke Douglas had changed somewhat over the past two days.

'So is it all busy there again?'

'Yes. Forensics are due in soon.'

'Nothing you can tell me first?'

'Not yet, sorry.' Grace paused. It was her time to trust him. She needed someone to talk to away from the office. She drew away from him and looked up. 'Can I ask you something?'

'Fire away.'

'It stays between us.'

'Of course!'

'I think I saw Eddie Steele today. He was outside Harrison House, in Rose Avenue. I only spotted him because Shelley Machin got out of his car.'

'Shelley Machin from 116? She gave me a few lines. Said she saw a man running away shortly after Tyler Douglas fell.'

'That's the one.'

'And she was coming out of Eddie's car, you say?' He stroked her arm again, making her shiver a little this time.

'Yes. I don't know what to make of it. We know he likes to use young girls as his informants.'

Grace was referring to her first murder case in the city. Clara Emery used to work in Posh Gloss, the former nail bar inside Steele's Gym. She had gathered information for both Leon and Eddie, but had paid with a short prison sentence when she was found to be helping coordinate sex parties for young girls, which Grace knew were run by Leon. With her team, she had shut the parties down, but they were still unable to catch Leon for his part in things.

'I wonder if Shelley is working for him and is keeping an eye out on Seth,' she added. 'We know Seth works for the Steele brothers. What if she's in danger? I'd hate it if I did nothing about it and she came to some harm.'

'The nature of the game, I'm afraid.'

'That's a little harsh.'

'But true. She knows what she's getting into.'

'Not necessarily. We don't know everything the Steeles are doing, more's the pity.'

'You're after visiting Eddie.' He frowned. 'And you're asking me if it's the right thing to do?'

'Oh, I don't know.' She sighed. 'I doubt it would do any good, anyway. But I worry about young women like Shelley. And Ruby. It's as if—'

Simon placed a finger on her lips. 'Grace, you can't save everyone.'

'I know that.' She grinned. 'But I do like to try.'

They sat in companionable silence, each with their own thoughts. Grace didn't know what to do for the best. Maybe she should chat to Allie about it once things had died down at work again.

A yawn escaped her and she tried to hide it behind her hand.

'Fancy an early night?' Simon suggested.

'It's half past eight, I'm not *that* tired.'

Gently he pushed her to the floor. 'Who said anything about going to bed?'

As he kissed her, Grace felt the troubles of the day melting away. It was hard as a cop to switch off but she had to try. And what better way to wind down.

2014

September

Over the next few days, Ruby packed away her belongings. She chose a few of her own and a few of Lily's every day, hoping that Dane wouldn't notice. Not that she expected him to. Even though he used to come several times a week, sometimes he didn't show up for days at a time. Those were the good times. So she packed a little each morning before midday, before she knew she had to be on her best behaviour for him.

After turning up one night in the early hours, Dane had suddenly gone missing for a week. Finally, she was told by someone in the flat below that he had been remanded in prison for six months. The relief was instant. It was then she made up her mind to leave.

It had taken her another week before she dared to go. Being afraid that one of his cronies would step in to look after her while Dane was gone was the thing that finally spurred her on. She couldn't deal with that, not after what she had been through. She had to get out of there now for her own safety, and Lily's. She had to be somewhere else with her child.

Nearly four years after the first time she had visited Finn's flat, she walked out of it with their daughter, and sped off in a waiting taxi. The first stop was to see her dad. There was something that she had to do while she was there.

Even though she had been embarrassed to face him, and had never visited since Lily had been born, she swallowed her pride. He'd seen Lily a few times when he had bumped into her in town, pleaded to be let back into their lives. She'd always promised she would go and see him, but never did. Dane was evil. He had no morals.

The look of surprise on his face when he answered the door made her burst into tears.

'I've escaped,' she said and flew into his arms, relishing feeling safe in his embrace for a moment.

Without a word, he took her bags from her, but when he turned to go upstairs with them, she put a hand on his arm.

'I can't stay here.'

'Why not?'

'Because he will hurt you to find me.'

Ruby would never forget the look of distress in his eyes as he nodded.

'You have time for a cup of tea though while I get to hold my granddaughter? She's so much like you were at that age.'

'Just about.'

He sighed in resignation. Ruby knew he'd want to change her mind while they drank it so she came clean. But at least it gave her the chance to explain everything.

'You remember when you met Finn and you weren't too sure about him?' she began.

'He wasn't good enough for you. I've always said that. But you loved him.'

'I did, Dad. I loved him with all my heart and he loved me too. But it went so wrong.' She told him about Finn, how wonderful her life was with him. About his past and how he tried desperately to get away from it. How it all changed the night he was attacked.

She told him how he had gone missing. And then she told him all about Dane taking over her life.

Her father looked on in shock.

'And you never heard from Finn again?'

She shook her head.

'You should have told me. We could have gone to the police.'

'Dane's known to them,' Ruby explained. 'He's a gang member, a criminal at the top of the ladder. Finn was only small fry, and when he wanted to leave, the gang became violent. They threatened me, they threatened Lily and I know they would have got to you if I hadn't kept away. That's why I didn't visit. We were getting ready to leave once but someone must have told him. That was when Finn got stabbed. I . . . I was there.'

'Oh, Ruby.'

'Dane kicked down the front door. We'd talked about what to do if it ever happened. I would hide behind the armchair which was in the corner of the room. Whenever I made a drink or had something to eat, I'd clear up straight away. I'd hide my handbag, so it looked as if I wasn't home. Things like that. That's why I managed not to be seen, but I heard it all. It was so awful. When Dane left, I thought Finn was dead.'

She could see her dad wrestling with his thoughts, his anger.

'Let me help you,' he said. 'I'll find you somewhere to stay, then I'll sell up here and move to anywhere you like.'

'He'll find us, Dad.'

'So you go on your own? It's better if you're with me. I can protect you.'

'I won't put you in danger. I have to go.'

'What about Lily?' He glanced at the little girl who was now sitting on his knee chewing a biscuit.

300

'I'm thinking of her. I don't know what else to do.'

He stroked his granddaughter's hair. 'How long is it before you have to leave?'

She checked her watch. 'Not long. I wanted to see you though before I go.'

'That fucking monster.'

Ruby had never heard her father swear before.

He handed Lily back to her, jumped to his feet and grabbed his car keys. 'There's a larger suitcase upstairs on top of the wardrobe. Put those bags inside it, it will be easier to carry them, and I'll go to the bank and get you as much cash as I can.'

'You don't have to—'

'You won't let me call the police. It's the only thing my conscience will allow me to do without ringing for help.'

Ruby followed him upstairs, Lily still in her arms. She went into her old room. It was almost as she'd left it, except for the posters that had been removed. Freshened-up walls and a more mature duvet cover to match the curtains. But all her teddies were there. She handed her favourite one to Lily, tears welling in her eyes. She would ask her dad to save everything for her. It would give him some hope that one day she would return.

How her life had changed since she'd left home. She sat down on her bed, popping Lily onto the floor, and was instantly transported to a time where she would be putting on a little make-up, the rest in her bag, before she would go off to meet Naomi. She remembered how they had squashed together when Naomi had slept over, whispering to each other long into the early hours. They'd had their best conversations during those nights. Sadness tore through her at the loss of her innocence. At nineteen, she should be starting life, not feeling like it was already over.

She wondered what had become of Naomi now. She hadn't heard anything from her since she had left to go to university.

She hadn't even been around to see Lily. But that was through mutual choice. Ruby had chosen Finn over Naomi, even though she wished she could have had both.

Naomi would no doubt get married to a gorgeous husband and have irresistibly adorable children. She'd live in a large and beautiful home, maybe have a career if she wanted one. She had always landed on her feet.

That wasn't fair, she chided. Naomi hadn't fallen in love with Finn. She had.

By the time her dad got back, she had done what she'd come to do and the case was packed. She popped Lily down on the settee in the living room, wiping her face clear of crumbs.

'Mummy's little angel.' Ruby smiled at her. 'What would I do without you?'

'Mummy's angel,' Lily repeated and giggled.

'There will always be a room here for you.' Dad was standing in the doorway. 'I said I'd never change anything.'

'Thanks, Dad.' She only hoped he meant it.

'Can I drive you somewhere?'

'I need to get to the bus station.'

'I meant further afield than that. I can take you anywhere you want to go.'

'The station is fine, thanks.' She didn't want anyone to see her with him. The sooner she was away, the less danger he would be in. Because Dane might send someone there, hurt him to get to her. Try to make her come back.

'Where are you going?' he asked, once he'd given them a lift.

'I don't know,' she said. 'And it's best you don't find out. I'll call you as soon as I can. I promise.'

'Are you sure we can't go to the police?'

'Maybe later, but not yet.'

'I can't just let you go like this!'

'You have to. I just want to feel safe for a while. I love you, Dad.'

'I'm so sorry I wasn't around for you after your mum died.'

'Don't be. It was hard for both of us.'

They hugged as if they didn't want to let each other go. But she'd had enough of her life as it was and it was time to leave.

'I love you, poppet, and this little one.' He gave Lily a kiss. 'Stay safe.'

Ruby walked away, knowing she had done the right thing. She had the security she needed now, hidden safely away. Dane might come after her, but it was the chance she would take to keep herself and her child safe. And to have a life somewhere without living in fear.

She would always look over her shoulder, but if she moved around, she might stay under his radar. He was a thug but he wasn't that clever.

Was he?

FRIDAY

FORTY-EIGHT

Ruby and Luke had spent most of the evening packing things and taking them to the car.

Now it was half past seven that morning. Ruby was making sure that every scrap of evidence was gone, so that nothing would give Dane information about their plans if he broke into the flat once he found out they had left.

It was so hard to think they would have to move somewhere else. Leaving all the furniture behind and having to start again with nothing was unpleasant but a necessity. And knowing that wherever she went Dane could still find her would always be at the back of her mind. But she wasn't going to give him the satisfaction of hurting anyone else that she loved.

And she still had what was his.

She'd often wondered what would happen if she'd given it back to him. It wasn't as if she was safe either way, with it or without it. If he got it, he would still hurt her. And if he didn't get it, he would come after her until he had. It was a lose-lose situation but she felt better keeping it for insurance.

The car was packed so they told the children they were going on an adventure. Tyler was all excited but Ruby could sense that Lily knew this game from old.

'Is someone after us, Mum?' she asked as she dressed.

'Not at the moment, but I'm not sure.' Ruby felt it best to be honest with her. 'We just need to go as quickly and as quietly as possible. Will you help me to do that?'

Lily nodded.

Ruby smiled her thanks. But inside she was breaking. How could her child accept that they had to leave and not question if they would be coming back? She'd lose all her school friends again, her sense of belonging. It was so tragic. Lily had lost her childhood because of her. Ruby had to put things right if she could.

'Tyler's in the living room,' Ruby told Luke when he came back from the car park. 'Can you go and get him and also fetch his favourite teddy bear? I've left it on his bed.'

She ushered Lily into the kitchen. She grabbed the bags that she'd packed for the car journey.

'Here, take this.' She gave one to her.

'Where are we going, Mum?'

'To visit Luke's parents.'

It was the only place they could think of going at short notice. Once they were away from here, she could register them as homeless and get temporary accommodation.

She pushed back tears, wondering how many times she would have to do this. Drop everything, leave all their possessions behind, move on, start Lily at a new school. It was exhausting and heartbreaking.

She looked at Tyler, now in his dad's arms, and smiled. 'Let's get your coat, little man.'

Luke reached it from the hook in the hall and she helped him to put it on.

'We're going to play a game,' she told him. 'We're going to

leave the flat as quietly as we can, like mice, and get into the car. Can you do that for me and Daddy?'

Tyler nodded his head, and put his finger on his lips. 'Shush.'

'That's right, Tyler.' Ruby turned to Lily. 'I need you to do something for me, too. I want you to watch your brother when we get into the car. If anything happens, you must stay with him.'

When Lily nodded, Ruby spoke to Tyler again. 'Do as Lily tells you when you're in the car. Can you do that?'

He gave a slight nod.

Ruby glanced at Luke.

'Ready?' he asked.

'As I'll ever be.'

Luke opened the door, had a quick look outside and beckoned them forwards. Quickly, she bundled her children out of the flat, in the opposite direction to Seth. Every part of her body was on full alert for Dane, her eyes scanning the darkness for a shadow, a sign that he was there. She spotted Lily's anxious face, so she tried to put her at ease.

'Let's pretend we're invisible until we get to the car,' Ruby whispered loudly, hoping to inject enthusiasm into her words. But only Tyler picked up on them, closing his eyes as if this helped. It would have been comical if it were under different circumstances.

Ruby raced along behind Luke, thankful that he was with her. Faster and faster as they rushed, her eyes were on alert for any sudden movements. All she could see beyond the walkway was the morning waking up. She hoped no one was out there, watching her, waiting for them to make a move.

At the communal doorway, Luke pushed out into the car park and she hurried on behind, Lily in between them. Ruby looked around, continually watching out.

As they got to the car, she almost cried with relief.

*   *   *

Seth had just finished an all-night shift. He was full of life, having taken an upper to get him through the long dark hours. He'd been overseeing a poker game at Flynn's. Normally he'd join in but he'd been too jittery. Even Eddie had asked him if he was okay, telling him to calm down when he'd got heavy stopping a group of men coming into the club earlier on. What the fuck gave him the right to do that?

He parked at Harrison House. There weren't many lights on in the flats. He laughed loudly. Idle bastards – he should start shouting to wake them up.

But then again he wanted to keep his cool, not alert Shelley that he was home. She was in for it when he got his hands on her, if she'd dared come back at all. And if she wasn't there, he was going on the hunt for her. The first place he'd look was her dippy friend, Mandy. He knew she wouldn't go back home.

He got out of the car and locked it up. As he turned to leave, he saw Luke Douglas and his family coming around the corner. He bobbed down out of sight, watching as they rushed to their car, with bags and a large suitcase. He peered around the side of the boot. It looked as if they were about to do a runner.

Over his dead body.

FORTY-NINE

Eight a.m. The Major Crimes Team briefing wasn't for another half an hour but most officers were at their desks. When Grace saw her DI coming in, she headed for the kettle. A few minutes later, she knocked on Allie's office door, two mugs of steaming coffee in her hand, a packet of biscuits in the crook of her arm.

'I need fresh eyes,' Grace told her. 'Do you have a few minutes?'

'As long as those biscuits are for sharing,' Allie grinned. 'Give.'

Grace put down the mugs, handed the packet over and pulled up a chair.

'What's up?' Allie asked, taking a bite of a chocolate digestive.

'Forensics are in regarding fingerprints found on the stolen car we thought that Finn Ridley was sleeping in. They picked up a partial belonging to a guy called Dane Walker. He was the leader of a gang in Hounslow, London, where Ruby said she first lived with Finn Ridley. Frankie's been doing some digging and according to our records, Ridley was working for them from his early teens but he's been off the radar for

311

years.' She paused. 'Do you think Finn Ridley is really Dane Walker?'

'As in the same person?'

'No, as in two different people. Ruby is telling us it's Ridley and yet it might be Walker.'

'But why?' Allie clicked on her screen and began to type.

Grace sat forward as she turned the screen slightly so she could see it too. A police record came up with a photo of Dane.

'He looks similar to Seth Forrester, doesn't he?' she said. 'So he could have been mistaken for him from a distance.'

'Or he could be the man running along the path after Tyler fell.'

'We can't rule him out of the attack on Milo Benton, either. Milo still won't tell us who it was.'

'Do you think giving us the wrong name might be something to do with Lily?' Allie reached for another biscuit. 'Could she be Walker's daughter? He might have wanted to harm Tyler because he wasn't his son.'

'It's possible.'

Allie clicked again and then pointed to the screen. 'Now we know he's linked to Finn Ridley, Ruby must be able to give us more than she's letting on. Off on a tangent, but do his finger-prints come up anywhere at Mary Stanton's murder?'

Grace shook her head.

Allie paused. 'Well, this is a riddle. According to Ruby, Finn Ridley is missing. Walker has served six years for armed robbery. He's been out for three weeks. And let's face it, Ruby has lied so much. This could be Walker rather than Ridley. Either of them could have come after Ruby.'

'But why did she lie?'

'To protect her family?'

'We could have done that.' Grace rolled her eyes. 'Well, maybe we could have.'

'Whatever the case, we need to speak to her. Do we know where Walker should have been?'

'Bail hostel. He was reported as going AWOL this Sunday.'

'Which would mean if it is him, he went out of his way to harm Tyler Douglas to prove, what, some kind of point?' Allie wiped biscuit crumbs from her trousers. 'Perhaps this man went to see Ruby but somehow Tyler became a bargaining tool.'

'Surely not.' Grace pulled a face. Why was Ruby Brassington still lying to them?

There was a knock on the open door.

'There's been a call-out,' Frankie addressed them both, urgency in his voice. 'Disturbance at Harrison House.'

Grace shot to her feet.

'Go,' Allie waved them off. 'Keep me informed of any further developments.'

'Get Tyler in and strap him up as quickly as possible,' Ruby told Luke.

'I know what to do, Rube,' he scolded.

'Sorry, just playing Mum.' She placed a hand on his forearm and gave him a smile. They were both understandably antsy.

She made her way round to the back of the car. It was quiet outside, the lone figure of a man walking his dog on the green in the distance. She opened the boot and hurled the case inside, along with the two bags she was carrying. Her worldly possessions down to so little yet again.

Pushing down the tailgate, she spotted a shadow out of the corner of her eye. Before she could react, she saw Seth.

'Going somewhere?' he said, his hands clenching into fists. 'I hope you have my money before you do. Because if you haven't, then you must be more stupid than you appear.'

'Quick, Ruby,' Luke demanded, shouting to her over the roof of the car.

She scrambled round to the passenger side. Just as Luke was about to get into the driver's seat, Seth swung a punch that hit the side of his head knocking him to the floor.

Ruby was unsure what to do first. Should she help her children or go to Luke's aid?

FIFTY

Ruby froze as Seth laid into Luke. He hit him in the face, then the stomach and pulled him up as he sank to the floor. As punches rained down on him, Lily began to cry and Tyler started to scream.

Ruby suddenly came to her senses and ran around to help Luke.

'Stop,' she cried.

But Seth wasn't listening. She heard a sickly crunch of bones as he stamped on Luke's hand. Luke had stopped groaning and was trying to protect himself by curling up into a ball. Seth reached for the collar of his coat and pulled him up, punching him again and again.

Ruby opened the rear door of the car on the opposite side to the fight. Reaching over the seat, she quickly undid Lily's seatbelt.

'Run as fast as you can and hide where I showed you. Remember?' She pressed the button on his car seat to release Tyler, who scrambled across to his sister. 'Quickly. Run.'

Lily helped her brother out of the car. Then she ran across the car park with him in her arms.

When Ruby could see them running to safety, she raced around to the other side of the car. Lights were going on in some of the flats as a result of the noise now, but no one had come out yet. Ruby hadn't heard Luke make a murmur in a while. A horrible sense of déjà vu engulfed her, the same thing happening to Luke as it had to Finn.

'Help,' she screamed. 'Someone help us!' She charged at Seth and tried to push him out of the way. 'Leave him alone.'

Seth stood his ground and sliced his hand across her face. Ruby staggered backwards with the impact. It gave him vital seconds to go at Luke again. Realising she wasn't strong enough to make a difference, she said what he wanted to hear.

'Wait. I can get you some money!' She pulled at Seth's arm. 'I don't have it all but we will pay it back, I promise. Just leave him alone.'

Seth turned to her. His eyes were wild, as if he was possessed by something. He didn't seem to care if Luke was alive or dead. But she did.

She really did.

Seth grabbed her by the arm, pinching her skin. She glanced down at his hand, his knuckles covered in Luke's blood.

'How much do you have?'

'A few hundred. And I can get you more from the cash machine.'

'He owes me five grand.' Seth raised his eyebrows. 'That's not enough.' He raised his fist to strike her again.

'But you'll end up in prison if you carry on beating him. If you let us leave, I'll get the rest to you later. Please.'

Seth wouldn't fall for her silly plan but it was the only thing she could think of. Her family were split; she had to get to Lily and Tyler. She looked behind him to see with relief that her children were nowhere in sight. Then she glanced at Luke who was crawling towards the grass, his face a mash of red. She wanted to drop to her knees and see if he was all right.

'Please,' she repeated.

'I'll drive.' He nodded his head towards the car. 'Give me the keys. I don't trust you.'

She tentatively stepped forwards and handed them to him. Seth pushed her towards the car. It was clear he wasn't thinking straight as someone would find Luke and alert the police if they left.

Ruby did as he said and climbed into the passenger seat. Seth fumbled with the keys, but managed to start the engine. He reversed the car out of the space and a sob caught in her throat as she looked at Luke lying on the grass. He wasn't moving at all now.

She wasn't going to leave him. And there was no way she was being separated from her children.

She could tell from Seth's eyes that he was on some kind of drug, so she hoped his senses wouldn't be on full alert. They didn't seem to be as he was putting himself in danger by leaving with her for the small amount of money she could get from a cash machine. But her silly plan seemed to be working.

As they drove towards the exit, Ruby reached across him, grabbed the steering wheel hard with both hands and yanked it down.

'What are—'

The car lurched to the right and drove straight into the wall surrounding Harrison House. There was an almighty bang, metal crunching as the driver's door wrapped itself around a brick column. Ruby shot forward but was saved from harm by her seatbelt.

Seth slammed into the side window, hitting his head on the glass before ricocheting back again. Dazed, he put a hand to his ear and it came away bloody. He groaned.

Ruby opened the passenger door, and was about to get out when he grabbed her arm. She punched out at his hand, screaming with rage, but he wouldn't let go. Instead he gripped her with both hands and forced her to face him. Leaning over her, he pushed her back into the seat as his hands went to her neck.

2014

August

Ruby sat up in bed and looked at the clock. It was half past two and something had woken her. She stayed quiet in the dark listening. Then the door to the bedroom opened. Dane was standing in the doorway blocking out the light.

Through the two years she had known him, she had got used to his temperaments. She knew when she could get away with answering back; when he was on edge and wouldn't lash out if she did. This wasn't one of these times so she feigned sleep.

He disappeared and she sat up when she heard him rooting around. She crept to the door and peeped around the frame. Dane was on his knees, the doors to the sink unit open. She couldn't see what he was doing. Was he looking for something? If so, she had no idea what it could be.

He stood up and she rushed to her bed so that he wouldn't catch her snooping. But he didn't come back to her room. Within seconds he had gone.

She sat up again, not daring to turn on the light in case he saw it when he left the building. Whatever he'd been doing, she'd have to wait until the morning to find out. If he didn't come back before Lily woke her up, then she would look. It would be better for her not to get caught snooping around.

At six a.m., Ruby made breakfast for Lily and popped her into her high chair. Then she stooped down and opened the doors to the sink unit.

It didn't take her long to find out that Dane had left something in there. Pushed into the gap behind the u-bend was a parcel wrapped in a black towel. Inside that was a carrier bag. She pulled the sleeves of her pyjama top down over her hands for fear of contaminating whatever it was with her fingerprints, and looked inside.

She was staring at a hand gun.

What the hell?

What was he doing bringing it to her flat? Wrapped up and put where it was, it must have been used in a crime.

Coming to her senses, she quickly put it back where she had found it. She wasn't sure what it was doing there, nor why Dane was hiding it. And she didn't want any part in it.

Until she heard the news.

A man's body had been found not far from them overnight. The police report said he was shot in the head at point blank range.

Ruby sat down with a thud. Had Dane killed someone? She'd heard from Finn that he was capable of it. Or was he keeping the gun for someone? She shook her head. He wouldn't do that for anyone else.

Then again she had underestimated him before, several times too many. That was why she was still living in this flat, in constant fear for her and her daughter's life.

The gun was still there a week later. The news had died down and there had been no police calling to see her.

There had been no arrests made in connection with the murder. The victim was in his early twenties. He was a security guard who had seen a van pull into the car park of the premises he was patrolling. When he'd gone over to question the occupants, he'd been shot dead.

Dane hadn't called for a few days. The more Ruby thought about the gun, the more she thought that he had something to do with the murder. And the more she thought that, the more she realised that if she could get away with the gun, she would have a hold on him and he wouldn't be able to hurt her again.

She could put it somewhere safe, somewhere he wouldn't find it, and then take off with Lily. It was her way out of things. Finn wasn't coming back, she knew that now.

FIFTY-ONE

Grace drove through the streets of Stoke towards Harrison House, Frankie in the passenger seat. Turning right onto Smallthorne Bank, she couldn't stop thinking about Ruby. Growing up in an abusive household herself, she could understand completely why the young woman wouldn't trust anyone with her past. But she seemed to have put her faith in Luke after taking so much abuse from Dane and being abandoned by Finn. Then again, Grace wasn't the one who was scared to talk, who had lied consistently to protect herself and her family.

'Did the caller say what was happening, other than a fracas?' she asked Frankie.

'Said he'd heard shouting and a woman screaming. He looked over the railing and saw Forrester laying into Douglas. The woman was trying to pull him off.' Frankie held on to the strap above the door as the car flew around a bend. 'Why do you think Ruby keeps lying to us? Do you think it's because she's so scared that she's trying to put us off Walker's scent?'

'Possibly. Or maybe she knows that something has happened to Finn Ridley and she's worried the same will follow for her too. Either way she has some explaining to do.'

Grace slowed to squeeze through traffic as it moved aside at a set of traffic lights. Next left was Rose Avenue, leading on to Harrison House.

At the entrance, she could see a vehicle embedded in the wall.

'That's Luke Douglas's car!' Grace screeched to a halt. They both got out, abandoning their vehicle, and raced to help. Residents from the flats were coming out too.

'Stay back, please,' Grace shouted to them. She called for backup as she ran.

When they reached the car, Seth had his hands around Ruby's neck. Blood was coming from a cut on his forehead but it didn't seem to be calming his temper down.

Ruby's face was red, but she was fighting too, punching out at Seth as she struggled in her seat. The driver's door was all mangled and there was no way he could escape through it.

Grace reached inside for Seth's hands and pulled at them to release his grip.

Frankie jerked open the rear door and climbed inside. 'Let go,' he demanded.

She was about to get out her baton and strike at his arm when, with Frankie's help, they forced Seth to loosen his grip.

Grace pulled Ruby out of the car while Frankie tried to do the same to Seth. But Seth was still fighting. Grace went back to assist and the two of them finally managed to pull him out of the car, get him down to the ground and cuff him. All through, she read him his rights, arresting him for the assault on Ruby.

'He hurt Luke,' Ruby sobbed.

'Where is he?' Grace asked.

Ruby pointed to the car park. 'He's over there, on the grass behind the cars. Please help him.'

'And your children?'

'They're safe.' Ruby ran to Luke, dropping to her knees by his side. 'Luke! Luke, can you hear me?' She cradled his head in her hands, tears pouring down her face. 'Help him!'

Grace was sat astride Seth's back. She looked at Frankie. 'Are you okay with him while I go and see how Luke is? I can still hear you. Shout if you need me to come back.'

'I'm good, boss.'

'You sure?'

Frankie nodded.

Grace ran across and sat down beside Ruby. 'Is he breathing?'

'I don't know.'

She pulled a pair of latex gloves from out of her pocket and flicked them on. She checked his pulse, to find it there but weak. There was blood in his mouth but his airway seemed clear. With memories of what she had done to Tyler earlier in the week, she took off her coat and covered Luke's torso to keep him warm, thankful to hear sirens coming closer.

Luke gave out a groan and Ruby burst into tears. Grace breathed a sigh of relief.

A marked car pulled in beside Frankie. Grace turned to see two uniformed officers rushing to his aid. Another car pulled up and two more officers ran towards her.

'Wait with our victim until the ambulance arrives,' she told one. 'Seal off the road and the entrance and only let emergency vehicles through,' she gave orders to another.

There were more neighbours coming out now but she didn't stop to answer any of their questions. Spotting an ambulance driving in, she raised her hands.

'Over here.' She waved to get the driver's attention. 'I need help.'

Grace let the paramedics do their job, sighing with relief as she caught her breath, knowing Luke was in safe hands. She looked to give Ruby reassurance but she couldn't see her.

'Where's Ruby?' she asked Frankie, who had joined her after putting Seth into a car.

They both scanned around but she was nowhere to be seen.

'Where were her children?' she asked next.

'She didn't say.'

'Maybe she sent them back to the flat. Let's check to see they're okay.' Grace ran across the car park, Frankie hot on her heels.

Now that Ruby knew Luke was getting treatment, she had gone to find Lily and Tyler. Dane was still out there and even though the police were on site, she wouldn't rest until they were back with her. It would be up to her to get them to safety.

She raced around to the back of Harrison House, hoping her children had got to the hiding place she had shown Lily.

She ran to the metal rubbish bins. Pushing them aside, she saw her daughter first, her arms wrapped tightly around her brother. Both of them were crying.

'Mum,' Lily sobbed.

Ruby began to cry too. Her children were safe and in her arms, shaken but not hurt. The police were here and Luke was getting help. It was over.

But someone grabbed her hair from behind.

Forced to stand up, she had to let her children go. Even before twisting around to see who it was, she knew it would be him.

'Quite an eventful morning you're having, aren't you, Ruby?' Dane pushed her forwards.

She tried to stay on her feet but landed on all fours. She scrambled over the hard grass on her hands and knees but he kicked her in the stomach. It winded her but he wasn't done with her yet.

'You think you're going to get away with what you did?' He turned her over onto her back and slapped her face.

'Stay away from me,' she cried.

'Oh, no, no, no. You see it's about time I told you some home truths. I want to tell you about your precious Finn. You think he's still alive, don't you?' He shook his head. 'I took him out, shortly after he left the hospital.'

'What?' Ruby shook her head in denial. She perched on her elbows as he stood over her. 'No, no.'

'Yes, yes!' he taunted. 'He should have died after that first attack. So I went to see him in hospital, got him on side. A few days later, I offered him a solution. I told him that if he moved away, I wouldn't hurt you. I gave him a lift but it wasn't to where he was expecting to go. And then . . . boom!'

'You're lying.' She sat up now.

Dane laughed, pointing to the expression on her face. 'He was a traitor. He deserved what he got.' He held up his hands and fired an imaginary gun. 'And guess what I killed him with? The gun that you stole when I was sent to prison.'

Ruby wanted to close her eyes, rid herself of the images that were crashing to her mind but she couldn't. Finn with a bullet in his stomach, dropping to his knees. Finn with a bullet in his head, leaning back on a settee, eyes wide open. Finn, her first love. The father of her daughter had been murdered in cold blood. How could Dane have done that?

'I've given it to the police,' she told him.

'I doubt that very much after keeping it for all these years.'

Ruby was out of her depth and knew she couldn't get away. She had never known such a vile and evil man. If she could keep him talking, maybe help would arrive. But if she had to sacrifice herself to save her children from a life on the run, then that's what she would do.

No matter what he said, Dane had come here for one reason.

He wasn't after the gun. He wanted to finish her off. She was the thorn in his side, the one that got away. She was the one mistake he'd made; the girl he'd thought was useless.

He was the stupid one thinking that she hadn't changed.

She could see the police in the distance now. As he came at her again, her hand found its way inside her coat pocket. Her fingers clasped around the knife she'd put there that morning. She stood up quickly and, with as much force as she could muster, plunged it into his stomach.

'That's for Finn,' she said. 'For pretending he was alive when you'd killed him. For using me for two years. For being a bastard and making my life hell coming after me.'

The look on his face was almost amusing, as if he didn't believe she had it in her to do what she'd done. She'd said she would look after her family, and this was the only way she could think of how to stop him.

With the knife still in his side, he lunged for her again, pushing her to the ground and straddling her. He punched her in the face. Pain erupted all over it and she turned her head away from him.

He hit her again.

Alerted by children's screams, Grace and Frankie had changed course and headed for the back of the building. Three uniformed officers were behind them.

Grace turned the corner. Someone was coming towards them. Lily was running with Tyler in her arms, the poor boy bobbing up and down as she struggled to carry him.

'Take the children to safety,' she shouted to an officer. Racing forwards she could see Ruby on the grass, Dane on top of her.

'Police! Stop what you're doing!'

Dane didn't even look in her direction. As Grace drew level, she jumped on him, pushing him over to the side. He didn't get up, but rolled over onto his back. It was then she saw the blood staining his jacket, the knife embedded in his stomach.

'Get a paramedic here, right now,' she told Frankie.

She dropped to her knees, while she caught her breath. They had got him.

FIFTY-TWO

Harrison House was a riot of organised chaos. The area had been cordoned off to allow the CSIs to do their work, as well as the police. The smashed-up car had been towed away to the pound. Luke Douglas and Dane Walker had both been shipped off to the Royal Stoke, one under police guard.

People had been hanging around and there were several uniformed officers asking questions yet again. Grace laughed inwardly as she knew some of the residents would be sick of the sight of them. She had been joined by Allie and Perry, who she had then left at the scene.

Three hours later, she and Frankie went into a side room in the hospital. A battered and bruised Ruby had a child under each arm. Both clung on to her as if they didn't want to let her go.

'How's Luke?' Grace asked immediately.

'He's been taken into surgery,' Ruby replied. 'I'm not sure I can go through this again.'

'Again?'

Ruby glanced at her children.

Grace nodded her head to the door. 'Frankie, would you take Lily and Tyler to get a drink of juice?'

Tyler clung to his mum but Lily knew the drill. 'Come on, Ty. I bet we can get some chocolate too.'

'I want to stay here,' Tyler cried.

'I promise I won't move,' Ruby told him. 'No one is going to hurt any of us ever again.'

'Come on, little fella.' Frankie held out his hand. 'We can be back in no time.'

A tentative Tyler paused and then took Frankie's hand. Frankie lifted him into his arms.

'Whoa, that plaster cast on your ankle is heavy.' He staggered around the room. Tyler giggled.

Grace smiled at Ruby. It must be a good sound for her to hear.

Once they were alone, Grace took out her notebook. 'I have to get a first statement from you, and then we'll need an official one from you later. Okay?'

Ruby nodded. 'I stabbed him.'

'Yes, I realise that,' Grace spoke gently. 'If you acted in self-defence then a judge and jury need to know that too.'

After a moment's silence, Ruby told Grace everything that had happened that morning. How they'd bumped into Seth in the car park, and he had attacked Luke. How she had run to get her children, only for Dane to attack her. Grace took notes through it all.

'I have a gun belonging to Dane,' she finished. 'That's what he was after. It was my security.'

Ruby spoke so quietly that Grace had to ask her to repeat what she'd said. But she was none the wiser. She shook her head.

'I don't understand.'

Ruby explained to her what had happened the night she had taken the gun and made a run for her life.

'Why didn't you bring it to the police?' Grace asked.

'Because I realised how much danger I was in. I knew that he would have found me anyway, like he has done now, and he would have got rid of me regardless. Just like he did with Finn.' Her voice broke at the mention of his name. 'Dane was obsessed with getting revenge. I took the gun so that even if he caught up with me, I was one step ahead.'

'But if you hadn't got the gun, he might not have come after you.'

'I couldn't be certain of that. Even if I'd left without it, he could have sent someone else if he couldn't get to me. You don't know him like I do.'

'Where is the gun?'

'It's at my dad's house. I hid it in the loft on the day I ran from Dane.'

Grace smiled, even though it didn't seem appropriate. Here she was thinking Ruby wasn't a strong woman because of the lies she'd told. Yet everything she'd heard about what she'd been through meant she had great strength to come out of this still standing. She was *very* tough, looking out for her family as well as trying to protect her own life. But it could be deemed as concealing evidence if the gun turned out to be linked to other crimes as Ruby had kept it away from them.

'You do understand that charges may be brought against you for withholding this?' Grace explained.

Ruby nodded. 'It was worth it to keep my family safe.'

And then she understood. Ruby was right. Dane would never leave her alone. So she'd done what she could to protect everyone, knowing that either she would be in trouble with the police, or equally she could be dead at Walker's hands.

It was a tough call, but Grace knew she would have done the same in those circumstances.

'Thank you for your help.' Ruby paused. 'I'm sorry I lied to you about . . . everything. I just didn't know what to do for the best.'

The door opened and Lily came running in. Frankie still had Tyler in his arms and he put him down on Ruby's knee.

'Chocolate, Mummy!' He handed her a wrapper with a half-eaten wafer biscuit.

'Is that for me?' she said, mouth wide open in mock surprise.

'We save for Daddy.'

'We will.' Ruby pulled him close. She put an arm around Lily too.

Grace stood up. 'I hope Luke goes on okay.'

'Thanks.' Ruby nodded at them both.

They left her to it then, a family reunited, hopefully soon to be all together as one.

TWO WEEKS LATER

FIFTY-THREE

Grace sat at her desk. She'd enjoyed being back on the estates since Dane Walker had been charged with the assaults on Ruby Brassington and Tyler Douglas two weeks ago. With his previous convictions being taken into consideration and the fact he was on licence, plus the new evidence, he'd most likely get another lengthy sentence.

Grace really wanted him to suffer for what he had done to Ruby and her family, murdering the man that she had loved and hounding her for years. Dane was a sick and twisted individual who she thought belonged in prison.

Ruby would be safe from him for a fair few years now, yet would always know that his release may bring him looking for her again. She would have to continue to live her life looking over her shoulder. A sentence for both of them. And there was nothing anyone could do about that.

The murder of Mary Stanton was still being investigated. Forensic evidence came back linking fibres found around and inside Mary's mouth to a pair of leather gloves located in a search of Seth's flat. Traces of her saliva were on them too. But there was no evidence to say the gloves belonged to him, and

Seth had denied it. There was nothing caught on camera, no witnesses coming forward but they were confident they would get their conviction soon.

Seth had been charged with GBH for the attack on Luke Douglas. There was also a baseball bat found in his flat, with blood from a number of victims on file, including Milo Benton. Milo had finally admitted it had been Seth who attacked him, now that he knew Seth was behind bars.

Seth had also been charged with the minor assault on Ruby Brassington. Also, after hours of searching, Sam had finally come up with footage of his car on the main road on the day Caleb Campbell had been hit. On further investigation, Shelley hadn't backed up his alibi that she had been with him either.

Grace had also been doing some digging into Dane Walker's past, and his associates, and in particular the gun that they had collected from Ruby's childhood home. Ruby had insisted her father knew nothing of it being stored there, and after meeting him to fetch it, she'd had to agree. He wasn't under suspicion of hiding it for her.

She'd arranged to see Ruby at her flat to talk to her about it. When she arrived, she was pleased to see Luke there. The bruising on his face was a faded green-yellow now, his operation a success after repairing a fractured jaw and cheekbone. His mental scars would take a lot longer to fade, if at all, she thought.

After asking how everyone was, they sat down in the living room together. It was going to be a difficult conversation and although Ruby would need Luke afterwards, it would still be hard for him to sit through it. Luckily, the children were next door being looked after by Norma.

Grace was about to speak when Ruby went first.

'I need to tell you what happened after I left Dane,' she started. 'I got on the first bus out of London. It was going to

Manchester. Lily was two then and I bundled her onto the bus, looking over my shoulder convinced that he was going to come running up and stop us before we had time to leave.

'I cried with relief most of the way there. I couldn't believe I'd got away from him. I remember holding on tight to Lily as she slept on my knee, the bus putting miles between me and my old life.' Ruby glanced at Grace. 'Once there, I made my way to the local housing office and declared myself homeless. It was embarrassing and they wanted to know a lot more than I was comfortable sharing, but if it meant me and Lily were safe, then I was fine suffering the humiliation. They put us into a bed and breakfast in a small hotel. It was one room and a bathroom but for the first time in years, I felt safe.'

Grace's eyes brimmed with tears. This young woman's life had been tragic, and it could have been much worse had she not looked after herself.

'It wasn't nice staying there though,' Ruby went on. 'In the harsh light of day, it was worse than I'd thought. The place was full of weird people. Most of them were okay, but as you can imagine there was lots of noise, people taking drugs, breaking into rooms. But I got used to it, and people looked out for me because I had Lily with me.

'Three months later, I was offered a small flat on the fifth floor of a tower block in Salford. It was hard work with the pushchair if the lift wasn't working but I didn't care. I was there for six months, still looking over my shoulder, even though I knew Dane was in prison. We visited my dad twice, and set up a private account on Facebook so that I could send photos and messages about Lily. There were no addresses sent. I could never tell him where we were living.'

'I really don't know how you coped back then,' Grace told her. 'You were so young to have all that weight on your shoulders.'

'Luckily when he first located me, I saw him hanging around the building so I was alerted. He wasn't long in prison that time. I didn't know what to do so I called the housing officer who assisted me to move in. She was so helpful, packing up my belongings and getting me a temporary room in a hostel. She even drove me there, picking me up away from the flat so he wouldn't see me. I don't know how he found out where I was, though.

'I moved, he caught up with me once more, and then he left me alone for a while. It was then I found out he'd been sent to prison again for armed robbery. He got twelve years. I sobbed so hard that night. Twelve years of not looking over my shoulder. I kept an eye on the news myself that time, googling him every now and then to see when he was out on parole. I must have missed his release because he got out earlier than I expected.'

'Yes, he was let out on good behaviour.' Grace harrumphed. 'I really detest the system for that.'

'Even before he was in prison, I felt as if I was the one who'd been given a life sentence,' Ruby went on. 'I lost contact with my friends, had to move away from the place I called home. It didn't seem fair that my life could be so disrupted when I had done nothing wrong. Finn was the one in the gang and he was disloyal because of me. He wanted to be with me and live a normal life, away from the violence and the crime, and they wouldn't let him.' She glanced across at Luke. 'That's why I told no one. That's why it took me a long time to trust anyone again.'

Grace blew out her breath. Ruby's story was hard to hear and not what she was expecting. It made the news she'd come to deliver even more heartbreaking.

'Since you gave the gun to us, we've carried out forensic tests on it and we've been able to link it to a serious crime.'

'That's good, isn't it?' Ruby let out a sigh, which turned into a sob.

338

'There was a body of a man which turned up with gunshot wounds but no identification. Ruby, I'm sorry to say this but there wasn't enough left of the body that we could get prints or dental records from at the time but we now believe, after Dane's taunt when he confessed to you, and evidence from the gun, that victim was Finn.'

'You mean Dane smashed him and cut him up so he couldn't be identified after he was shot?' Ruby gasped at the enormity of her words.

'Yes. I'm so sorry.'

Ruby turned to Luke, who took her in his arms as she began to cry.

Grace looked away for a moment, the emotion becoming too intense. Ruby had lived in hope of Finn being alive for eight years. She would never see Lily's father again but Grace trusted it would bring closure for the young woman. Finn Ridley hadn't left her.

'If I'd given you the gun, he would have been in prison, wouldn't he?' Ruby spoke quietly.

'Not necessarily. It would have been hard to prove Dane was the one who had pulled the trigger.' Grace wouldn't sugar-coat anything. 'But even that wouldn't have kept him inside forever,' she noted. 'And when he does get out of prison again, rest assured that the police will offer you and your family protection from him, given his history of hunting you down.'

'It's better than living in constant fear,' Luke said. 'And at least we're all safe for now.'

'I don't know how you did it.'

'I know some people will question why I didn't leave,' Ruby added. 'It's not as simple as walking out of the door and not looking back. It's what follows you, regardless of whether it's a person or not. He got inside my head. I was so scared of what he might do, even when he wasn't there. He's evil.'

'He is. But he's locked up for now. For a good while.' After a natural lull in the conversation, Grace stood up. 'I'll let myself out,' she told them.

'Thank you for everything,' Ruby said when she got to the door.

Grace nodded. It certainly hadn't been a pleasure but it was job satisfaction at its best.

Stepping out onto the walkway, she breathed in the fresh air, as if it was filling her with the good stuff again rather than the tarnished.

She leaned on the railing where Tyler Douglas had been held over, shutting out the image of him on the ground below.

She looked down to the car park where Milo Benton had been beaten with a baseball bat.

She glanced across the way to where Mary Stanton had lived, and been pushed to her death. So many innocent people had been hurt during one week.

She turned and walked away, for now happy with the results if not the resolution.

FIFTY-FOUR

At Stoke railway station, Shelley sat on a bench on platform two waiting patiently for the train to Manchester Piccadilly. After the events of the past month, she couldn't wait to get out of the city.

In the suitcase and holdall at her feet were all of her worldly possessions. Her clothes, photos she loved, two books she hadn't yet read, her favourite shoes, nearly four thousand pounds deposited into an online savings account and one thousand pounds in cash. She had no friends in Stoke, no family she cared for, or who cared for her. So she was going to start again.

Before she left, she'd gone to square things up with Eddie. She hadn't really been able to tell him any more about Seth but she wanted out. She thought she might have a bargaining tool but wasn't sure what his reaction would be. She was tired of her life with them: first the threat of the sex parties, then having to be Seth's woman to gather information for Eddie, being in danger all the time in case anyone came after him and hurt her instead.

Eddie had been true to his word after the conversation in his car. Now that Seth had been sent down, her job had finished.

Seth wasn't there to encroach on the Steeles' patch any more. She'd half expected him to say she couldn't leave, but she'd begged him and he had seen sense – she'd served her purpose to him now anyway.

Especially when she had given him the T-shirt. She reckoned the blood on it belonged to Milo Benton, the young teenager that Seth had beaten with a baseball bat just before Tyler had been dropped from the balcony. It wasn't much to convict Seth on, not that he wasn't already looking at a long sentence for what he'd done, but Eddie had seemed to like her loyalty.

Seth might come after her later, now that she'd taken his money. She might be on the run for the rest of her life like Ruby. But she was willing to take the chance. She'd stayed at Mandy's house, hiding the stash without her friend knowing. Then she'd waited for the police enquiry to go quiet.

She'd had a restless night as she worried that Eddie would find out about her plan, but he hadn't questioned where Seth's money had gone. Now she was on her way out of Stoke, leaving her troubled past behind her.

The wind blew her hair as it flashed through the open ends of the station, making her feel alive. It was her time to shine now. She had a train booked to Manchester and from there to the airport. She was heading off to Spain for a few months. Magaluf to be precise. She had never been overseas before and was looking forward to it. It would be quiet at the beginning of March but the weather would be warming up soon. After that, who knew where she would go? Because she definitely wasn't coming back to Stoke.

For the past few days, she'd been trying to decide on her new name. Her passport would say who she was but that wouldn't stop her once she was at the resort. The favourite choice so far was Arabella. She liked how posh it sounded, how different it was. As Arabella, she could be someone new. With money in her pocket, she wasn't going to waste the opportunity to make something of her life. For now, she was hoping to find work in a bar for the summer season. It sounded a good way to find some friends. Given what she'd had to do to make ends meet so far, she was looking forward to it. This was her chance to start again. Thieving the money was the last illegal thing she was ever going to do.

The train pulled into the platform and she walked towards the carriage. On board, she wriggled across a double seat to sit by the window. With a huge sigh, she sat back as the train pulled away, taking her out of Stoke-on-Trent forever.

Caleb heard the school bell go and sighed with relief. He still hated double maths with a passion but at least he was back at school with his friends. He'd been given a reprieve with Seth Forrester. He couldn't touch him now he was in prison.

Ever since Seth had been remanded, Caleb knew he would be rid of him for a long time. He would probably be a grown man capable of holding his own once Seth was out of prison. He never thought he would be a swot but after the lucky escape he'd had, he'd decided to study hard at school and make his mum proud. He was determined to make something of his life now; he didn't want to turn out like Seth.

After his visit in hospital from Forrester, he hadn't known what to do, nor how he would get out of the mess. When Seth had been arrested, he'd burst into tears and told his mum everything. She had listened, and not judged. She'd been shocked at his antics, glad that he had told her, but angry all the same.

Out of guilt, he'd shown her the money. She had taken it from him, counted it out and then given it back to him. She'd told him to put it towards a new pushbike to replace the one that had been wrecked in the hit and run; said he had to save the rest himself. She said what he'd done was wrong, but that she trusted him to learn a lesson from it. She was all right, his mum.

All he wished now was that he wouldn't get a call from Eddie or Leon Steele, hoping to take over where Seth had left off. It was so far, so good though. He wasn't sure they knew about him, as he was one of Seth's boys, but even so, he still worried about it.

'Are you coming out tonight, Caleb?' his friend Shaun asked him. 'We could go to The Hive.' The Hive was a leisure complex on the outskirts of Hanley, with a cinema and several restaurants. 'Hang around, see who we can spot.'

'You mean you want to see Sharon Parker?' He grinned, knowing his friend had a crush on one of the girls working in Pizza Express.

'Well . . .' Shaun laughed. 'That as well. Are you up for it? I can scrape enough together to buy a meal between us.'

'I think this one is on me.'

'Cool!'

Caleb grinned at his friend. This is what he should be doing when he was fourteen. Hanging out with his friends and chasing the girls. That was much more fun.

FIFTY-FIVE

Grace finished work that evening at six p.m. She was glad to be back to her usual working hours after the Harrison House incidents. She decided to call at the supermarket to get steak, salad and a bottle of something nice. Simon had been on a course in Birmingham that day and had called from the train to say he'd be home at seven. Some downtime, just the two of them, would be perfect.

They'd had Teagan to stay all weekend. Teagan had insisted on it, saying that she had missed her Grace time. It still astounded Grace how well they got on now. At one time, Teagan would barely look at her, let alone hold a conversation with her. Not that Grace would ever complain. She loved Teagan as much as if she were her own daughter.

She pulled up at traffic lights to turn right. Behind her she spotted a flash of light. Then she saw it again. Glancing through her rear-view mirror, she tried to focus. Someone was trying to get her attention.

She turned around and clocked it was a black Land Rover. The lights flashed once more. She sat upright so she could see the number plate better.

Eddie. He must have been waiting for her.

With a sigh, she moved forwards as the lights turned to green, knowing he would follow her.

She pulled into the car park at Tesco, driving around to the spillover area which was a bit further away from the store. She sat for a moment as Eddie parked up next to her. She was damned if she was going to get out and go to him. But then she realised she didn't want him in her car either. And as she didn't know what he wanted, she was best talking to him where she might not be seen. The car park was mostly full, the supermarket open twenty-four hours and to her mind never empty.

She got out, flicked the lock on her car and swapped one seat for another. Stepping up into the Land Rover, the luxury hit her immediately. The vehicle was top of the range and no detail had been spared.

Eddie put the interior light on, the tinted windows giving them no exposure. It was just the two of them.

'What do you want?' she broke the silence that followed.

'To see my half-sister. That's okay, isn't it?'

'No, it isn't.'

She heard him chuckle and tutted.

He held up his hands in mock surrender. 'Actually I have something for you.'

She turned to glance at him. Their resemblance was more uncanny close to. The eyes, the curve of the lips, the cock of the head. That was all she shared with the father who had made her – and his – life hell. Eddie reminded her of him so much, the younger George Steele who had made her terrified to make a noise or move a muscle for fear of what he might do.

Eddie handed a bag to her. It was a clear plastic carrier. Inside it was a white T-shirt, red liquid dotted over it.

Grace took it from him. Realising it could be blood, she left it in its wrapping.

'It belonged to Seth Forrester,' he said. 'If you have it tested, I believe you'll find the blood is Milo Benton's. I said Forrester had something to do with the assault in the car park of Harrison House.'

'We had no evidence, no witnesses and Benton wouldn't tell us anything at first.'

'Well, this implies he was at the crime scene.'

'Doesn't necessarily implicate him in the crime though.' Grace didn't want to say that Milo had finally told them it was Seth for fear of repercussions for the lad. 'He could have been helping Benton to get up after he found him beaten on the ground. It could have been transferred that way easily.'

'But Seth didn't tell you that, did he? He said he didn't know anything about the fight.'

Grace was about to speak again. How would he know that unless Seth had been boasting about hurting Milo?

'Is that what he told you?' she asked.

'It's possible.'

His answer was non-committal but it was good to have the T-shirt. Yet, even with that and the fact Seth had lied about his whereabouts, the crimes he was charged with afterwards were far more serious. Still, every case had to be solved.

'How did you get it?' she wanted to know. 'More to the point, why did you withhold it?'

'I only had it given to me last night.'

She rolled her eyes. 'You expect me to believe that?'

'Would I lie to you?'

'Yes.'

His laughter was loud, jovial, the sort you wanted to join in. But she knew there was more to this. She waited for him to enlighten her.

'Shelley Machin gave it to me. She came to see me last night, unsure what to do with it. After that she told me she was leaving the city.'

'You exploited her.'

'No, I didn't.'

'You used her to get information for you, just like you did with Clara Emery.'

'That's not exploitation.'

'Well, what would you call it?' She glared at him.

'If you must know I offered her a bit of money to tide her over.' He looked ahead for a moment. 'I think she'd been working for Leon too. You know what he's like. I saw what happened to those girls.'

'Are you saying he's up to his old tricks again?'

He shrugged, non-committedly. 'Now that Seth is no longer around, Leon would have her doing something unsavoury. You might want to keep an eye on him.'

'Meaning?'

'Let's just say that I wanted to get Shelley out of harm's way. Hopefully she's gone and won't come back.'

Grace said nothing. She looked out of the window. A woman was struggling to push a loaded trolley and hang on to her child's hand at the same time. The car across from them pulled away. Grace wanted to leave too. She placed a hand on the door.

'Think of me what you will but I did her a favour,' Eddie added. 'She's better off out of it.'

'Now that I do agree with.' Grace pointed to the bag. 'Thanks for this. I'll deal with it accordingly.' She wasn't sure what could be done about it now though. It couldn't be used as evidence as it had been taken by Shelley and not by the police with a search warrant. But it could be used to back up Milo Benton's statement that they had finally got out of him.

Outside in the cold night air, Grace stood and watched Eddie drive away. He hadn't needed to deliver that T-shirt to her. He'd wanted an excuse to see her. Was he still trying to get her on his payroll? Be an informant for the family? Well, she wasn't playing their game. Eddie and Leon could be in this together for all she knew.

Yet she couldn't just turn a blind eye when they used women to do their dirty work. Used anyone to do their dirty work, actually. It wasn't on.

She would find some way of stopping them eventually.

AUTHOR NOTE

To all my fellow Stokies, my apologies if you don't gel with any of the Stoke references that I've changed throughout the book. Obviously, writing about local things such as the *Sentinel* and Hanley Police Station would make it a little too close to home, and I wasn't comfortable leaving everything authentic. So, I took a leaf out of Arnold Bennett's 'book' and changed some things slightly. However, there were no oatcakes harmed in the process.

A LETTER FROM MEL

First of all, I want to say a huge thank you for choosing to read *Liar Liar*. I have thoroughly enjoyed writing about Grace and her team and I hope you enjoyed spending time with them as much as I did.

If you did enjoy *Liar Liar*, I would be forever grateful if you would leave a review on Amazon. I'd love to hear what you think, and it can also help other readers discover one of my books for the first time.

Many thanks to anyone who has emailed me, messaged me, chatted to me on Facebook or Twitter and told me how much they have enjoyed reading my books. I've been genuinely blown away with all kinds of niceness and support from you all.

You can sign up to my newsletter and join my readers group on my website www.MelSherratt.co.uk or you can keep in touch on Twitter @writermels and Facebook at MelSherrattauthor.

Thanks, Mel

ACKNOWLEDGEMENTS

I can hardly believe that *Liar Liar* is my fourteenth crime novel – it feels like it was only yesterday when I was tentatively publishing my first in 2011 and hoping that one or two people might like it.

Thanks must go first to my fabulous agent, Madeleine Milburn, and her ever growing team. Thank you for coffee, cake, Pimm's, pick-me-ups and everything else that looking after me as an author entails. Thanks to Team Avon – editor extraordinaire Helen Huthwaite, Oli, Sabah, Anna, Hannah, Dom and Ellie.

Particular thanks must also go to the close trio of friends I am very lucky to have – Alison Niebiezczanski, Caroline Mitchell and Talli Roland. I'd also like to thank Martin Tideswell, Editor of the *Sentinel* and SOTLive, for his cheerleading, friendship and support.

I want to say a huge thank you to anyone who has read my books, sent me emails, messages, engaged with me on social media or come to see me at various events over the country. Without you behind me, this wouldn't be half as much fun. I love what I do and hope you continue to enjoy my books.

Likewise, my thanks go out to all the wonderful book bloggers and enthusiasts who have read my stories and taken the time out of their busy lives to write such amazing reviews. I am grateful to all of you.

And then, my Chris. Without your support, I know I wouldn't have got this far. Love you to bits, fella.

Loved *Liar Liar*? Then why not get back to where it all started with book one of the DS Grace Allendale series . . .

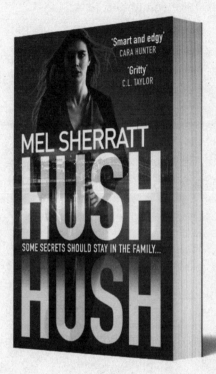

A gripping crime thriller from the million copy bestseller.

Available in all good bookshops now.

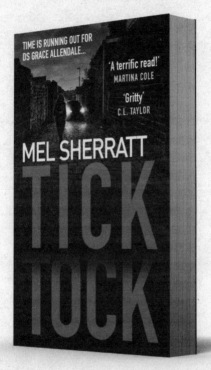